WHEN IT ALL
GOES DARK

ALSO BY
D. ALEXANDER WARD

Nightjar
Pound of Flesh
Beneath Ash and Bone
Blood Savages

WHEN IT ALL GOES DARK

COLLECTED STORIES

D. ALEXANDER WARD

When It All Goes Dark: Collected Stories
Copyright © 2024 by D. Alexander Ward

First Edition

All Rights Reserved

ISBN: 979-8218552565
Cover Art & Title Design © 2024 by Greg Chapman
Interior Design & Formatting © 2024 by Todd Keisling

Page 251 constitutes an extension of this copyright page.

This is a work of fiction. Names, characters, businesses, places, events, and incidents are either the products of the authors' imaginations or used in a fictitious manner. Any resemblance to actual persons, living or dead, or actual events is purely coincidental.

No part of this publication may be reproduced, stored in a retrieval system, or transmitted in any form or by any means, without the prior permission in writing of the publisher, nor be otherwise circulated in any form of binding or cover than that in which it is published and without a similar condition including this condition being imposed on the subsequent purchaser.

Bleeding Edge Books
www.bleedingedgepub.com

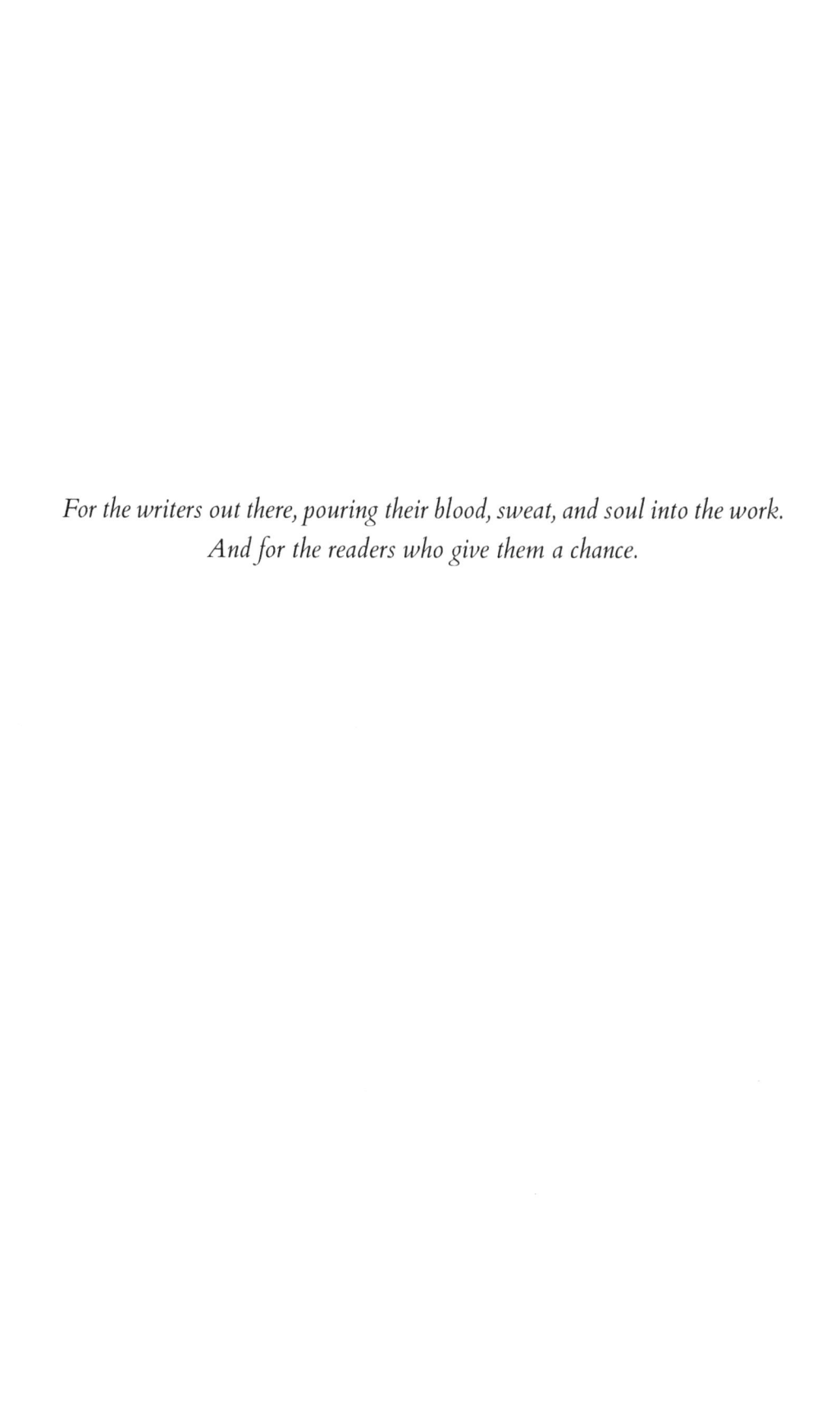

*For the writers out there, pouring their blood, sweat, and soul into the work.
And for the readers who give them a chance.*

TABLE OF CONTENTS

Author's Note	9
The Red Delicious	11
Notches	15
Broken Things	31
After the Fire	51
Adrift on the Sea of Trees	103
The Blackest Rite	107
Night of the Nanobeasts!	125
Cruel Moon	141
Dark Rosaleen	161
The Dying Place	187
Static	201
Acknowledgments	247
About the author	249
Copyright Acknowledgments	251

AUTHOR'S NOTE

I used to write more short fiction than I do now. For whatever reason, some time ago, for good or ill, I felt myself gravitating more to the longer forms of novellas and novels. I suppose it's no surprise given that a common problem of mine was producing a short story that came in below the maximum word count for a submission.

But…shit happens in publishing. Especially when it comes to independent, small press publishing. Most of the stories in this book previously appeared both online and in the pages of anthologies from certain presses, and even an earlier collection of them—all now out of print after some of the presses shuttered their doors. And when the press goes, their books go. And as the books go, so go the stories.

The stories were still there, though, haunting my thoughts.

I feel these stories still have some life in them—something left to offer. While by no means a collection of every short story, I tried to pick the ones that have stuck with me through the years. There are also a couple in here fairly new to the world.

In all cases, I popped the hood and went in, gave them a tune-up and an update. With some, I tried not to change too much of the unique (and often inexperienced) voice of them. With others, the revisions went deeper and significantly added things I felt were missing. They are far from perfect but they each represent the writer I was as the time—and that's all part of the journey. So, I present to you a selection of them, warts and all.

The yarns in here will take you on a tour of this writer's journey. While firmly rooted in the back roads, mountains, and the Capital city of my home state of Virginia, you will also venture out to the green fields of medieval France, the densely forested slopes of Mount Fuji, the vast and open waters of the sea, and an imaginary, eldritch university in New England. You'll run into serial killers, witches, shapeshifters, common criminals, undead pigs, mad scientists, ghosts, otherworldly demons, revenants, and creatures straight from the cutting room floor of those old, cheesy sci-fi B-movies.

You'll experience variations in tone from gory fun to dark and revelatory, from creepy to whimsical.

I hope you enjoy the places these stories take you. I hope you get something out of them.

-D.A. Ward
Hanover, Virginia
2024

THE RED DELICIOUS

Benjamin Thicke was a man plagued by should-haves. Especially now. Like how he should have sold his operation to that smarmy sonofabitch that came down here from Agri-Corp with a carpetbagger's smile and a briefcase of polished gator skin. Leather checkbook and fancy pens.

"That one's a dandy!" the man had beamed, handing one to Ben. "Writes upside down. You can keep it if you like."

As a counteroffer, Ben had proposed sticking it up the man's ass and writing the word "NO" on his goddamned colon.

The man had laughed it off but continued to press him on selling his family farm. Though he did so with a wary eye on that space-age pen in the farmer's grip.

After Ben had further told him to go fuck himself, the man flashed a smile and threw up his hands in a gesture of surrender. He seemed oddly pleased, and the farmer's victory too easily won.

It had been him, Ben now knew, that brought all this on. Mr. Alligator Briefcase had poisoned their pet sow, Miss Maple, on his way out. Slipped her an apple from his pocket, which Ben thought nothing of at the time. Now, though, he figured that Red Delicious fruit was tainted with something awful. Something evil.

Disease.

It had been no more than a week ago by his reckoning, but that apple had been the beginning of the end.

He should have never let Lottie talk him into keeping that sow. That was another regret. A hog farmer knows better. Or at least he ought to.

"You don't want to be getting attached," he'd warned her. "After all, good meat don't grow on trees. It's harvested by slaughter."

But his wife was bull-headed and had plenty of charm to pour on when she had a mind to do so.

Last Wednesday, Miss Maple came up ill. A hog farmer all his life and he'd never seen anything like it. Looked like greasy pig sickness at first, what with the lesions and the moist discharge through the skin, but then she quit eating and started wasting away something fierce. Before he could finish scratching his head over it or get a vet out to the farm, Miss Maple gave up the ghost.

Seeing as how she was their pet hog, Lottie insisted they give the sow a dignified burial. He protested—up and down he protested. But Lottie had a way with him that usually got her whatever she wanted.

The burial of Miss Maple would have to wait, however, seeing as how he was obligated to haul the youngest of his hogs to the market in Fayetteville come the morning.

The autumn weather was cool, so Ben put the pig on ice and stored her in the barn.

When Ben returned from Fayetteville on Sunday morning, it was as if the four horsemen of the apocalypse had ridden out to his farm. More than half his stock lay still in the pens, gutted and opened, not by some wayward predator but by the other hogs.

All of them bore the same ill look that Miss Maple had. Lean and sallow and hungry. Their snouts were caked and smeared with the blood of their brood.

They ambled aimlessly, but when Ben rolled down the window as he drove in, they looked up and made their way toward him. A drift of hogs pressed so hard against the fence that the bottom two rails snapped and out they poured. He throttled the truck toward the house, fetching the shotgun from the rack behind him as he opened the door.

He entered the house, calling for his wife.

"Lottie?" he called over and over again, searching room by room. When he didn't find her inside, he set his sights on the barn.

The two big barn doors had a man door to the right, usually left open except for the screen door, so as to give the building some airflow when he wasn't working in it. As he stepped through and heard the screen door smack closed behind him, it looked buttoned up just as he'd left it, but when he stepped farther inside, he could see that wasn't the case at all.

Lottie didn't like dogs but was fond of cats. When he found the first one eaten, he was sure there would be more. Miss Maple had woken from whatever deathlike state the sickness had put her in and she'd woken of a mind to have a snack.

Then he turned the corner and saw that it was even worse.

Lottie lay unmoving on the floor. Close by stood Miss Maple, head down and gobbling away at his wife like she was slop in a trough. Ben pulled one of the Remington's triggers. The blast was loud enough to scare off the hog, who glanced at the farmer with death-white eyes and wandered off. He knelt beside his wife and cried into his hands. She'd been eaten in half, her legs and hips nothing more than a gnarled mass of sinewy meat and bone, and Miss Maple had been feasting on the red coils of intestines from her belly.

Ben wept so loud that he didn't hear the spare sniff as his dead wife caught his scent, and by the time he felt the grip of her cold fingers on his leg, it was too late. Her teeth dug in and rent. He kicked free and sprawled on the floor. Behind him, she gorged on the chunk from his leg.

He scrambled away, grasped the weapon to his chest. There wasn't but one way for this to end and he knew it. But it would never end, not really. The sick hogs were roaming free now. Someone's pet or someone's child would become their next meal and outward the sickness would bloom from this backwater burg in the Carolina piedmont until it swallowed the entire world.

If they ever got around to naming the thing, he supposed it would be some long, Latin gobbledygook. But he wished he could name it. *The Red Delicious*, he would call it. After the plagued fruit that the devil with the gator skin briefcase had fed his sow and after the awful smile he'd seen on his wife's face as she supped on his leg, a blood grin from ear to ear.

Ben lay there on the concrete with the barrel of the shotgun under his chin and listened to the last sounds he would ever hear. Just feet away, his darling Lottie crawled hungrily toward him across the floor, legless and gored, painting crimson as she came. In the darkness somewhere, the sow snuffled. There was one shell left. Maybe he should've used it on Lottie, blasted her skull to bits. For her own sake. Or maybe he should've put down the hog.

Should-haves were a bitch.

But it was too late now, for both Lottie and the hog. Hell, it was too late for all the world, even though they didn't know it yet. Ben shut his eyes tight against the gathering dark, pulled the trigger, and knew regret no longer.

NOTCHES

"I heard all things in the heaven and in the earth. I heard many things in hell. How, then, am I mad? Hearken! and observe how healthily—how calmly I can tell you the whole story."
    —Edgar Allan Poe, "The Tell-Tale Heart"

I come awake with my jeans bunched around my ankles, slouching on the toilet in a gas station bathroom. I'm halfway through a cigarette that smoldered out a while ago but still dangles from my bottom lip and I'm apparently more than halfway through answering nature's call, so I decide to finish up both.

Lighting and dragging on my smoke, my head's clearing a little. I wonder how long I've been here like this. Hell of a bender last night, I guess. Or was it the night before? Either way, I don't reckon it's important.

I finish up, toss the smoke into the bowl, flush, and stand on shaky legs. I reckon I ought to be awarded a medal or something by the owner of the gas station, just for having the courtesy to actually use the toilet. Judging from the stank and stains that decorate the floor and walls, this particular porcelain throne don't get to see all that much use.

"Fuck the medal," I say, buttoning my jeans and cinching my belt. "Maybe a free fill-up, though."

Just then, I get to wondering about my ride. And since every memory in my brain more recent than a few minutes ago is dark and murky, there's a lot to wonder about. I go to wash up, roll up the sleeves of my flannel jacket, and reach for the handle on the spigot.

There's a nickel-plated 9mm Colt pistol in the sink. Walnut grip with half a dozen rough notches scratched into one side. Some were there when the gun came to me, some I've added since.

Not that I'm a killer, but it pays to look the part.

I check the clip and find a few rounds missing. Odd, but then again, maybe not so odd for the kind of day I'm having. I start washing up, looking down as I soap my hands, then something drops into the sink with a crisp little *plink* as it hits the porcelain. But the water's running and there ain't no stopper, so I only get a quick look before it goes slipping down the drain, a ribbon of blood trailing behind it.

A tooth.

Mine also, just like the gun. Except the tooth didn't look much like mine, which are crooked and yellow, some of them half-rotted. Mountain Dew mouth, it's called in the hill country of western Virginia, though I reckon you can find it everywhere there's poor folks. Naw, that sucker that just went for a swim had a nice shape, white and shiny. Looked more like one of my buddy Hector's teeth. Everyone calls Hector "Pearly" on account of his perfect teeth, see. He made it through three years in Powhatan Correctional—a gladiator camp, they call it—and came out not only alive but with his mouthful of pearly whites intact. A thing unheard of.

Me and Pearly have been tight ever since we were just kids growing up in Saluda, which is just a blip on the map among other blip towns that barely deserve the distinction. Like many of those towns, it was—and still is—nestled among family farms and so many creeks and rivers leading out to the Chesapeake Bay it'd make your head spin to count them all. His unpainted cinderblock house was right next to our weathered old Colonial with the leaning porch and sinking foundation. We spent the summers together on that porch, reading comics we'd lifted from the corner store, fighting over who could get the rabbit ears on the TV just right so we could watch *Miami Vice* and *Dallas* and *Hill Street Blues.* Always dreaming and scheming how we could have better lives than the hardscrabble one we'd been born into. Better lives, like the ones we saw on that TV screen.

But it was just a dream. Pearly's folks were migrant workers from Mexico or El Salvador or some place. From day one, they toiled in those fields and barns, picking tomatoes, corn, and soybeans for damn near slave wages. My old man had been a waterman all his life until long after the cost of fuel to run the boat was more than what he could catch and sell. Back then, whenever he got deep into a bottle of cheap whiskey, he'd rant about how the big companies were overfishing the bay and how the pollution was killing everything off.

But just ranting about an evil thing ain't never once fixed the thing. So, when Daddy sold the boat, quit the water, and went to work in the fields, me and Ma went with him—just trying to keep the lights on, you know—and Pearly was there, too.

Hell, me and Pearly have always been friends.

Anyway, I push all the memory lane shit to the side and look into the mirror and open wide. Sure enough, I'm missing one of those flat little numbers just to the right of my two front choppers. Red droplets ooze from the crater it left behind. I spit, rinse my hands, dry them on my jeans, and head for the door.

It's nighttime, the sky clouded and starless. Feels late, but I don't know. The sodium light burning high up on the outside wall of the building stings my eyes and my head so badly that I consider a retreat back into the shitter. But there's my ride parked over yonder in the lot. A red 1977 Lincoln Continental. A real boat of a car. Rough and faded on the outside, sure, but I keep the interior clean, and she runs just fine.

It's colder than a well-digger's ass, so I shove my hands into my jacket pockets and cross the lot, cursing the wintertime as I climb in behind the wheel. First thing I notice is the smell. It's earthy and sour. Could be piss, but I ain't sure. Second thing I notice is Brenda in the backseat, leaning against the door, eyes closed, mouth open.

I flick on the overhead light.

Brenda's a gal me and Pearly met a few years back. She runs with us every now and then, parties with us, fucks one of us every now and then. Nothing exclusive, though. Brenda runs around with whoever she wants *whenever* she wants. She's mean as a snake on a good day, but she gets real nasty sometimes when she's been in her cups or is good and high on uppers. Gets all riled and wants to fight. Used to be a trauma nurse at Norfolk General, until they caught her lifting pills from the hospital cookie jar—pills to support the habit she got because of that very same job. Pills to stay awake during her sixteen-hour shifts, then pills to fall asleep. And round and round it went. Same old story, no surprises. When she's not high, Brenda's sharp, quick, and usually more than a little twisted—just the kind of woman who'd run around with a couple low-rent motherfuckers like us.

She's not dressed for the cold, though. Acid wash jeans yellowed from the nightly fog of smoke-filled beer joints, a dingy black halter top that looks like it's choking her, and sandy yellow hair teased up to the stars with hairspray. Brenda always looks like she got lost on the way to a Whitesnake concert back in 1987 and somehow ended up here instead. She's trash, but so am I. She just wears it better.

I start the car and slide the heater to full-blast, rubbing my hands together in front of the vents on the dash. "Brenda!" I holler, adjusting the rear-view mirror to see her. "I swear to fuck, if you've OD'ed in my car, y—"

I stop not because I decide she has OD'ed—in fact, I can now see her breath fogging the cold glass of the window—but because I catch sight of myself in the mirror. My…my face. My eye. For a second I stop breathing because…shit, can that really be me looking back from that mirror?

A jagged scar, open but not bleeding, like split raw chicken skin, slashes a diagonal from my left temple to my bottom lip. The eye that it crosses over is grayed out, a white film over the iris. I press at it through the lid and find it soft and terribly fragile.

"Like a glob of Jell-O," I whisper.

"There's always roo-oom," Brenda says in a sing-song voice from the back, but for the moment I ignore her and keep staring at my poor damaged mug.

I was just in the shitter, checked my mouth when the tooth fell out, and I didn't look this. Unless I was too fucked-up to see it.

Or unless I'm just plain fucked-up and that's why I'm seeing it.

I turn around and look Brenda in the face. "What the hell'd you say?"

But she doesn't reply; just kind of lolls her head about. Eyes distant, like she's following trails, like she's tripping balls. And that makes some sense, don't it?

"Shit," I spit out, turning back around. "What the hell'd we get into?"

I try to remember but can't. Can't put shit together. The past couple days are a puzzle and all I've got are the corner pieces. Did me and Pearly pull a job? Our usual gig is a pharmacy. B&E smash-and-grab-type shit. Whatever we can get our hands on—from Oxy and Vicodin to Valium and Adderall—and get the hell out in less than five minutes. Then we unload the pills in Richmond, or sometimes sell to the River Lords, a local motorcycle club that buys in bulk.

I glance over at the empty passenger seat. "And where the fuck is Pearly?"

From the back, Brenda giggles like a devil. "Pearly's fishing," she says. "Pearly's gone fishing."

Damn, this girl is high, but maybe not useless. Pearly has a place on a backwater creek off the Pamunkey River. It'd be a stretch to call it a house—more like a shotgun shack. Picked it up at a county auction for next to nothing, which is about what it's worth. We spend time there, lay low there sometimes after a job. Maybe that's what she means.

I slam the shifter into drive and ease out of the parking lot.

Whatever's going on with me—bad drugs, bad booze, or just losing my marbles—I have to put it out of my mind.

Pearly will clear all this up. I just have to find him.

On the divided highway, I open it up and the engine growls as the Lincoln feasts on the empty roads of night, winding eastward, deeper into the river country.

An hour later, I pull up to Pearly's clapboard shack crouched at the edge of a tidal bog thick with reeds and cattails. It doesn't look like anyone's home. The place is a dark spot set against an already inky black vista, broken only by the brilliant lights of the paper mill across the river in West Point.

The mill, with its towering steel contours and skeletal crane arms blazing with light, looms in the distance like a stark and deadly temple of industry. The smoke rolling out of the stacks is elegant and pure white—fair weather clouds that belong to a blue sky, rising into the night instead and stinking of chemical rot. Breathing around here without retching is a learned skill.

Pearly's place don't have electricity or anything like that, but it has a genny which, if he was here, would be running and powering the dozens of naked bulbs strung up everywhere. Pearly ain't fond of the dark, so he won't even sleep with the lights off. I reckon that's on account of the times he spent in the hole back at the pen, but he don't like to talk about it much, so I never ask too many questions. It should look like Christmas around this place, but it doesn't.

I check the rear-view and find Brenda still sacked out in the back, still sleeping off her high. My face, lit from the glow of the dashboard, is still a mess. Even worse than before. My skin has gone fish-belly white and it's slick with a sheen of sweat.

Except I'm not actually sweating; I'm freezing even with the heater running on high.

It occurs to me all of this might be more than a bad trip from some bad dope. Might be something worse. Am I having some kind of stroke? Maybe it's brain cancer or some shit? I haven't exactly lived at the foot of the cross, as they say, so anything's possible.

All the same, it does me no good to keep wondering about it.

I glance out the window at the expanse of night around me. I know I'm gonna get out and check the place over, but I don't feel like leaving the warmth of the Lincoln. From my jeans pocket, I fish out a small key that opens the glovebox. In the box, I sift through random junk—a near-empty pack of smokes, an old burner cell phone, deck of cards, a Buck knife, book of matches—until I find the key to the Lincoln's trunk, where I'm pretty sure I've got a flashlight stashed.

Pulling on the door latch, I pause because, weirdly, there's something tumbling around in my mouth, and with it is the burnt, metallic taste of blood. I know what it is before I even spit it into my hand.

And there it is. The pointy tooth next to the one I lost earlier. It's covered in a pinkish slime of blood and saliva, but it still don't look like mine. Not with its perfect cone shape and the smooth, even brightness of it. I flick it to the floor, glance in the mirror just to confirm that, somehow, I'm still tripping, and sure enough there's now a gaping space along my top row of teeth. Also, still there? My mangled features.

"Jesus," I groan, then look away.

I decide to leave the engine running because I don't intend to linger here long. I don't even bother with locking the glovebox. The frigid dark slaps me across the face when I step out, and I find myself cursing the chill again. I go around back of the car, slip the key into the lock and raise the trunk lid.

The spare tire sits right in the middle of the deep well of the trunk. My tool bag's on top of it, a hammer and the wooden grip of a handsaw poking out. There are two nice, new duffle bags on either side, too, and like so much else today, I don't recognize them or remember how they got here.

I go to satisfy the next natural question and unzip one, then step back, rake a clawed hand through my hair, and blow out a long breath of smoke.

Brown Sugar heroin. A lot of it. More than I've ever seen, and certainly more than me and Pearly have ever sold. Must be about twenty bricks in this duffle, so I check the other and find the same.

Has to be a hundred thousand bucks of the stuff right before my eyes.

"Holy fuck. Where'd we get this shit?" I whisper to the night.

I zip them back up, grab the flashlight from the tool bag, and shut the lid, making sure it's good and locked. Leaning against the car a moment, I shove the trunk key into my jeans pocket and take a couple drags off my smoke. I wonder where the hell we'd ever come across that kind of haul. I could ask Brenda, but she's still in the back seat passed out hard. Anyway, who's to say she'd remember any more than I can.

Still, the question gnaws at me. Everyone we messed around with was small-time, and transactions were usually no more than a few thousand dollars at most. Who had the kind of capital and the juice for something like this?

And then, like a thought whispered into my ear, it comes to me.

The River Lords MC.

Mules, I think. *We were muling for the bikers. Picking up, then dropping off.*

That was it. I can't say the memory was clear as a bell. Everything, even things I damn well ought to know, still feels like a dream only half-remembered. Me and Pearly aren't gangsters. We're small potatoes—expendable nobodies. Using us, the River Lords don't risk getting caught with it if shit goes sideways. And if all goes well, we deliver it to them, and they give us our transportation fee.

But us dumbfucks decided to keep it, so we could sell it ourselves.

Talk about bad ideas. Christ, what were we thinking?

Could have been nice and easy. Should have been.

But I reckon there's nothing like a hundred grand worth of

smack in the trunk of the car to give a couple small-time crooks delusions of grandeur. I try to remember, for a moment, if it was Pearly's idea or mine...or someone else's. I try to recall, but my head is still swimmy and aches with every stretch of thought.

The cigarette pinched between my lips, I click the flashlight on and start toward the house. The front porch overhang is eaten up with rot and tilted like a smirk. A couple weathered wicker chairs flank the doorway and over to the right sits the generator, silent. My light flashes over a can of Steel Reserve beer on the railing. My preferred brand. I push open the screen door into the house.

It's grave-cold in here. Just as dark and quiet, too. The two rooms of the shack are nothing special. A couch and a couple of chairs we pulled out of dumpsters. An old TV set with rabbit ears and lots of empty bottles and cans piled up in the corner of the first room. No Pearly snoring on the couch, though, and nothing out of place.

I walk deeper into the house, and the second room—the bedroom, we call it—changes things.

There's a kerosene heater in the corner that's turned over, the fuel having soaked into the thin rug and the floorboards beneath. The sheets of the mattress shoved against the wall are mussed, which ain't nothing unusual. But there are pools and swaths of something dark, now frozen to the fabric in the chill air. It's all over the sheets. I don't have to guess what it is. Along the floor, heading out the back door, more droplets and splashes. The back window is missing a couple glass panes, and the edge of the door has a round hole burrowed into it that's cracked the wood in every direction. I slide my fingers over it as I approach and know it's from a bullet. I reach under my jacket to the small of my back, draw the Colt pistol, and think for a moment of the missing rounds.

Cautious now but also eager to see where this trail is leading me, I step through the door with the gun up. There's not much to the back of the house. Just a landing and some rickety steps that lead down to the dock stretching out over the creek. I take the steps with care. There ain't many sounds this time of year, just the lap of the water as the tide ebbs out into the bay, and the cold breeze rustling the reeds. But with the adrenaline surging through me right now, those gentle sounds are loud as firecrackers.

Out in the dark, down by the water, there is a memory—a truth that's calling to me.

I walk to the end of the dock, casting about with the flashlight. I don't see anything. It's too damn cold even for the croaker and spot and other fish that might occasionally breach the surface of these waters. I creep closer to the edge, shining the light down into the murk. And that's when I see it.

The faded red and white bobber dancing in the current, and with it the corner of a familiar blue bandana caught around the frayed rope all but invisible beneath the dark water.

It's Pearly's bandana—the one he always wears to cover the stringy hair of his balding pate.

I bend down, set the gun on the dock, take the rope knotted to the pylon in my fist, and pull. I pull and pull, but whatever's down there is heavy or maybe stuck on something at the bottom of the creek. It ain't coming up without a fight. So, I drop the flashlight, and it rolls across the boards into a position not at all helpful to the task. But it allows me to use both hands.

Part of me—maybe a big part—doesn't want to know what's at the other end of this rope. It's telling me to drop the whole damn thing and get the hell out of there. The other part of me is louder, like ants crawling in my brain, and demands to know.

I've never been one to debate the devil on my shoulder.

Squatting at the edge of the dock, I yank upward with the strength of both arms, but the other end of the rope still won't budge. I'm frantic now, so I keep tugging and jerking and pulling. Then I feel the release as the suction of the mud along the creek bottom is broken, and I go down onto my ass. Now, with legs kicked out like opened scissors, I keep on pulling, hand over hand. The rope that passes through my fingers is not only cold but wet, and stinks of brackish water mixed with the chemical waste from the paper mill.

It's a stench I now recognize:
It's what the Lincoln smelled like back at the gas station.
Most definitely not piss, I think.

Another heave with muscles burning from the effort and it breaks the surface of the water, flying out of it, and comes up over the edge with a metallic clatter. I go all catawampus from the sudden lack of resistance and the hand I shoot out to steady myself smacks the wide lens of the flashlight and sets it spinning. The object from the water comes to rest between my splayed legs, practically landing in my lap, and as my searching fingers catch in the web of chicken-wire, I am relieved to finally know what it is.

Just a crab pot.

A nervous laugh rattles out of me. I lean back a bit, gazing up at the cold stars and letting go a breath of relief.

Just a crab pot, nothing more.

So, I sit up to get a good look, and the chuckle at my own stupidity dies in my throat and spirals down into a low, keening sound I reckon I've not made since I was a boy. The flashlight has stopped its spinning and the beam of light shines upon the wire mesh of the pot.

Pearly's head is jammed tight into the bait basket of the pot.

And in his corpsy face, I see something of my own.

The gash that cuts a line from his temple to his chin. The same couple of teeth missing from his dead, opened mouth, frozen lips dribbling water onto the boards. The lifeless, white pallor of his skin soaked and slick from the river.

There's a scurry of tiny, young crabs picking at that pale left eye. As I gawk, a beefy adult blue crab—I can't tell if it's a jimmy or a sook—climbs over the others and pierces that eyeball with the sword of its pincers, plucks it free of the socket, drags it away.

And just like that, my left eye goes dark.

I'm half-blind now, but I see.

I see.

Pearly's been haunting me all along. My wounds are his wounds.

My ruined face isn't a bad trip, but an echo. A mask fashioned after his final likeness.

I'm scrambling, trying to make some sense of it, even if there's none to be made. Every sound is still loud as a freight train and the warble escaping my lips has joined with the banging of my heartbeat, all of it filling my ears.

That's why I don't hear what's coming.

In fact, I don't hear a thing until the point of a familiar Buck knife slips out of the shadows and presses against my throat—along with the impossibly even and sober lilt of Brenda's voice.

"You remembered anything yet, cowboy?"

I'm frozen still because it wouldn't help to move or try anything. All that time she spent as a trauma nurse; she knows just where to stick that blade. I'd be shitting my pants in seconds and done bleeding out a few minutes later.

"You still don't, do you?"

I reckon that I hoped it would all come back to me in a flashback, like on TV. Like the one on *Dallas* when, glued to the fuzzy images coming over the airwaves on that porch, Pearly and me finally found out who shot J.R. Ewing.

But I still don't remember shit.

Doesn't mean I'm not putting it all together pretty fast, though. And as I hear the low rumble of motorcycle pipes pulling up to Pearly's shack, it all clicks into place.

"Nope," I say. "But I ain't stupid either."

"Well." She leans over to snatch up the Colt pistol from the dock. "That's debatable."

Pearly and me agreed to mule the heroin for the MC. It's coming clearer now. It was our first time. Easy money. Until *someone* got us thinking how we could keep it all for ourselves. One big score to get us the fuck out of this backwater town forever. Brenda got us daydreaming about sunny Mexican beaches and endless cervezas. A devil on our shoulders whispering into our ears the whole time.

Me and Pearly just ain't that ambitious. Not on our own.

We ain't that clever.

"You weren't even high, were you?" I ask. "Back at the gas station."

She shifts her weight and saunters around from behind me. She drops the hand with the knife to her side, hooking her thumb in the pocket of her jeans next to the bulge of the burner phone from the glovebox, and brings the gun up, smirking.

"Oh, Lord knows I've had enough experience to fake it." She puffs out her cheeks and blows. "Didn't expect the little cocktail I mixed up for you and Pearly to work so well, though. Or have such…" She searches for the words. "Savage effects."

She's circling around me now, like a lioness at play. I hear other footfalls too. Heavier ones. Motorcycle boots coming down the dock toward us. There's a smell in the air of motor oil and gasoline and smoke. Flames crackle and dance behind me as the shotgun shack goes up like a torch.

"I thought you were takin' care of this," a man says, his voice sharp like snapping bones.

"I am, Baby!" she replies. "Just taking my time is all."

He snorts and spits.

The two of them get to making out. Lips and tongues smacking, all of it sloppy. Like teenagers. Like new lovers, or maybe—it now occurs to me—like old ones. Like I said, she would fuck me and Pearly now and then, but she never kissed us quite like that.

The man slaps her ass and trudges back up the dock toward the blazing shack. "Let me know when you're ready to burn him," he calls over his shoulder.

"Long as I get their fee, darlin'."

She blows him a kiss. A sweet gesture, so alien in this lethal moment.

I notice now that Brenda's bare shoulders are covered by a worn black leather jacket so big it practically swallows her. I have to admit, it's a good move for her: getting in tight with the River Lords. It's as much about status and power as it is money. But eventually, she'll be looking over that next hill. That's for damned sure.

"That biker man you were kissing on better watch his back." I snort, then my gaze drifts down to Pearly's severed head in the crab pot. She nudges it with her boot.

"You did that, you know," she grins.

I shake my head like I'm trying to get a buzzing mayfly out of my ears.

"No," I groan.

"Went plum crazy, like some animal. Some beast. All that smack sitting in the house and the two of y'all cranked up and paranoid. It was soooo damn easy."

Tears fill my eyes and the whole world goes blurry until I blink them away.

"Pearly was my *friend*," I blurt out.

The anguish drips from my lips like Spanish moss. I want to call her a liar, but because I am haunted by Pearly's face—because my murderous deed has been catching up to me all along—I know it must be true.

A memory comes; not something imagined. My eyes are as black and empty as the creek at night. I'm high on something, high on everything, probably. Pearly is face-down on the dock, the night and the water stretch out in front of us, and he is screaming. My knee digs into his back, and with the first stroke, the handsaw chews into the flesh just above his shoulder. I hold it an angle, just like Brenda tells me.

"Oh, God, what'd I do?"

It comes out like a question full of spit and tears, but I know the answer already.

"Sorry, darlin'." She shrugs. "I went overboard on the amphetamine, I guess."

Brenda kicks the crab pot over the edge. It splashes into the creek and sinks from view along with all that's left of Pearly. Watching it disappear into the frigid water sends a chill through me that bites deep, like I'm going into that cold darkness with him.

"Probably too heavy on the Propofol, too." She sighs. "It was one hell of a night. I wish you remembered more of it."

She presses the muzzle of the pistol to my head, just behind the ear. "You and Pearly…I had y'all so afraid one of you was gonna fuck the other over." Brenda leans down now and whispers, her lips so close it might be mistaken for a kiss. "Y'all couldn't see that I was fuckin' you both."

I bow my head as if in prayer.

I'm scared here at the end, trembling, squeezing my eyes shut. Just instinct, I guess. Bracing for the crack of the pistol and the fraction of a second of terror before it all goes black. I don't even notice she's slit my throat open until the warm rush comes spilling down my chest, and I fall over onto my side.

She leans down, plunges her hand into the pocket of my jeans, and retrieves the key to the Lincoln's trunk. With passing interest, Brenda watches gouts of my blood spurt onto the weathered boards. She holds my Colt by the barrel and drags the reddened blade of the Buck knife across the walnut grip, scratching another notch into it.

A notch for me.

A notch all her own, earned the old way.

They'll soak me down with gasoline soon and put me to the flame. Maybe I'll be long-gone by then. Maybe not.

I cough and try to breathe, but all I can manage is a gurgle. I'd hoped death would be quick, but I reckon it's never quick enough.

Sometimes it's not the gun pointed at you, but the knife you didn't see.

That's what gets you.

Sometimes—every damn time.

BROKEN THINGS

1

The boy was well-mannered; he had to give him that. In spite of the circumstances of his upbringing. Although, if the truth be told, Gibb couldn't claim to know a whole lot about such things. Even though he was their closest neighbor, it was still a good mile and half from his front door to the front steps of the failing cinderblock hovel where Mick Hagan and his family lived. Like most folks who worked straight jobs around town, he liked to keep contact with the Hagans and the sort of folks they ran with at a minimum. They had never bothered him, though. So, for his part, to speak ill of them would be downright un-Christian.

Sitting at the breakfast table, Gibb's eyes scanned the sports page of the local paper but the information there—the wins and the losses and the injuries and the trades and the drafts—only skimmed the surface of his mind before hurtling off elsewhere, ultimately unabsorbed. His thoughts continually returned to the boy sitting across from him, picking at a bowl of Cheerios with his nose stuck in some comic book. He was quiet, too, that boy. Of course, if Gibb had seen what the boy had seen, he reckoned he might not be much for conversation either.

"Mister Buxton?"

Gibb lowered the top edge of his newspaper and looked over the reading glasses perched at the edge of his nose. Clancy wore a worried expression on his face.

"What is it?" the man asked. "Cereal gone soggy? I'll fetch you some more."

Gibb started to get up from his seat.

"No, sir. It's just that…" the boy seemed to be struggling with a question he wanted to ask.

"Yes?"

"Was my Daddy a coward?"

The man laid the paper on the table and breathed in deep.

"Now, why would you ask that?"

Clancy shrugged and his eyes went to the floor.

"I heard one of the policemen say it."

"When?"

"When they was carrying Daddy out of the house this morning. All covered up in that long, black bag."

Gibb felt a knot rise in his throat. Jesus, the things this child must have seen.

The prevailing thought all over the county was that Mick Hagan had gotten what was coming to him. After all, Mick and his young wife, Faye, were known to be involved in the local drug trade. Gibb was never sure if they were buying or selling or what, and it seemed the police could never quite put it together either because although Mick had often been hauled into the sheriff's office for questioning—including the occasional overnight stay—there just wasn't anything to pin on the man. So, a couple of nights ago, when the police arrived at the Hagan family home and found Mick shot to death, they came to the reasonable conclusion that it had been a nefarious transaction of some kind that had gone bad.

He didn't know Mick from Adam, but the young man had always been neighborly and could be counted upon to help out in a pinch. Not the sort of thing you would expect from some dealer or hophead. Hell, last winter Gibb had gone across the way to ask about borrowing a hack saw blade in an effort to mend a pipe that had frozen and burst. Mick had furnished not only the saw but had also come back with the older man in the middle of a January night when it was colder than a witch's tit outside, crawled under Gibb's house, and replaced the dang split pipe while Gibb stood by and handed him tools. Gibb had offered twice to pay the man for his help and was refused. On the third try, with Gibb feeling damned near insulted, Mick agreed to take a little something for his trouble, although what he had paid him—seventy-five bucks and three Mason jars of canned okra—was a pittance compared to what his help had been worth to the older man. No, Mick Hagan had never done any harm to him, no matter what was said about the family around town. And sure as shootin', no boy ought to ever be made to think that his father a coward.

"Clancy, you listen to me real good, all right?"

The boy nodded.

"By all accounts I've heard, your daddy was shot defending your momma. And that ain't what a coward does. You hear me?"

He nodded again, silently, though Gibb could see tears creeping to the edge of the boy's eyes.

"Don't ever let nobody tell you different."

The boy was in a world of hurt. Gibb had never had children of his own and his wife had passed away some years back, so he didn't have much practice at meeting the emotional needs of others these days. But the poor, broken child was in need of reassurance and human contact, and for some inexplicable reason, he actually seemed to cotton to the old man.

"Come 'round here, son," Gibb said.

Like a shot, the boy was out of his seat. The old man closed his arms around the boy awkwardly, fumbling for a meaningful embrace. Clancy laid his head against the old man's chest and wept into the fabric of his flannel shirt.

"It's gonna be all right, Clancy. This too shall pass."

When the boy had stopped bawling, he caught his breath and turned his face toward the light spilling in through the kitchen windows.

"Mister Buxton, where's Momma?"

The old man inhaled a rough breath, his heart suddenly in his throat. The sorrow of this ten-year-old boy was catching like a bad cold, and he had to shut his eyes tight to fight back sympathetic tears.

"Nobody knows," he whispered to the boy. "I'm sorry, son, but nobody knows."

The old man followed the boy's gaze, peering out the window at the cold day beyond the glass. The sky was white with a blanket of cloud cover. The trees were sticks of gray and brown, the yard a mixture of drab green and a tan that matched the tall grass growing at the edge of the woods. Deeper into the hills and hollows, it was more of the same, Gibb knew. The world was awash in a cold dormancy that whispered of loss and seemed an echo of the boy's sorrow. What he wouldn't have given for a stray bit of color splashed onto the landscape just then; for a single bluebird, perhaps, to alight somewhere in the gloom.

2

Sheriff Varney and Gibb were hunting buddies or had been at one time. Gibb didn't have the bones or stamina for it anymore—to sit up in a deer stand at four o'clock in the morning, freezing his nuts off and hoping for a buck to pass by close enough that he could bag it. These days, his joints caught fire just getting out of bed.

That night, after the boy had gone to sleep, he dialed Varney's home phone to have a word with him about what had happened at the Hagan place. He had some matters of curiosity that were eating away at him, and he was not above exploiting their personal relationship to get satisfaction. After exchanging some cordial greetings with Varney's wife, Brenda, she asked Gibb to hold while she got her husband on the line.

"What's doing, Gibb? The Hagan boy okay?"

Gibb scoffed into the phone. "As okay as could be expected after such a thing, I reckon."

"Mm-hmm. It was good of you to take him in for now. Until we can get things sorted out."

"What happened over there, Varn?"

"Drug business is a tough business, Gibb. When things go wrong, they tend to go *real wrong*."

"Yeah," he said, nodding. "Y'all find any drugs in the house?"

"Oh yeah. Plenty of pot and some prescription meds."

"Hmmm," Gibb commented.

"What is it?"

"Just always figured they would be selling heavier stuff than that."

There was a sigh from the other end of the line.

"You trying to complicate this for me, buddy? I don't need no more complications."

"Sorry. No, just…trying to understand."

"It's a hell of a thing, I know."

"That it is."

Gibb conversed with the sheriff a while longer and mentioned that one of Varney's deputies had been shooting off his mouth about Mick Hagan being a coward within earshot of the boy.

"I apologize about that," Sheriff Varney said. "Understandable, sure, but still…there ain't no call for that."

After a little more of Gibb's prodding, his old hunting buddy was forthcoming with a few more details. According to what they had pieced together from the scene and from the boy's statement, there had been a late-night knock at the door and Faye had woken Clancy, then hidden her son in a bedroom closet. Sitting there in the dark, the boy had heard the scuffle from down the hallway. The hollering and screaming at first, and then the gunshots. Six in all. Three of them were hits and the other three were misses. The boy had waited until it was quiet in the house before he emerged. Once he did, what he found was his father dead on the floor in a pool of blood and his mother nowhere to be found.

Mick Hagan had been shot three times by a large caliber pistol at close range. One shot had taken off the first two fingers on his right hand. There was another such wound to his torso, but not his heart, and a third that had taken out a sizable chunk of his head above his right temple. Near his hand, the police had found a hunting knife whose blade was smeared with blood that belonged to someone else—presumably his wife or the perpetrator.

"This is all we know from the scene," Sheriff Varney said. "We'll see what the medical examiner in Richmond has to say."

Gibb nodded. He had heard about the knife from his niece, who worked dispatch at the Sheriff's Office. He listened on as Varney continued.

According to Clancy's statement, that's when the boy had gone running over the hill in the dark and the cold, in pajamas with no shoes or socks on his feet. Moments later, he was knocking frantically on Gibb's front door. At which point Gibb had called the police.

"Any word on the mother?" Gibb asked.

"Not yet, no. Could be that with her husband dead and the drugs in the house, she got scared and hit the road and she's in the wind. Or could be that she was part of it all. Maybe some kind of double-cross."

"Double-cross?" Gibb balked. "You done watched one too many cop shows on TV, my friend."

"That right? What makes you say that, Sherlock?"

"Look, Varn, this kid…he's pretty healthy. Well-fed, educated, respectful. Hell, he's got better manners than the Queen of England. So, the boy's had some proper upbringing. I just don't see how a mother who raises a boy like this just up and runs out on him."

"Mmm-hmm. That is interesting," the sheriff replied, but Gibb could tell he was being patronized.

"Damn, Varn. You even got anyone *looking* for Faye Hagan?"

There was a moment of silence from the other end of the line.

"I don't think I care for your insinuation," Sheriff Varney said, his tone terse and whip-like.

That was answer enough for Gibb. The police had Clancy's mother figured as on-the-run and not worth the effort it would take to find her.

"Jesus, Sheriff," Gibb said, his voice dripping with disappointment.

"Now, listen here, buddy—"

But the old man was done listening. He hung the phone back on the receiver and stood there a moment, shaking his head and feeling sick inside. He pulled a bottle of Cutty Sark off the pantry shelf and poured a few fingers into a glass. He sat at the table and sipped it. So, Mick Hagan had been a drug dealer. Pills and pot. So what? Times were tough and they had been for a long while. And maybe someone had come for a buy but had decided they'd rather have it all at no charge. Maybe there had been a tussle and then a gun was pulled, and it didn't turn out well for the young man. Gibb could buy all of that. It was plausible.

But if someone had come for the drugs, why leave any of it behind?

And he couldn't see that the boy had been neglected by either parent. Especially not the mother. The boy had been *cared for*, so it made no sense that he would be left behind. Not all-alone, given to the whims of fate.

The old man finished his drink and poured another. Just for good measure.

3

Gibb was going through the house, locking doors and turning off lights for the evening. It was his usual ritual before bed, but he had to remind himself that he wasn't in the home alone now. He had a guest, so he turned the light on in the hall bathroom and cracked the door in case the boy needed to use it during the night. He had set him up in the spare room that hadn't been used in a coon's age—certainly not since his wife had passed. As he walked toward the room, he slowed and leaned his head close to the door.

If the boy was sleeping, he didn't want to wake him by opening the door, but if he was upset, perhaps he should go to the child. He dearly hoped that Clancy was sleeping.

From within the room, he heard the sound of the boy's voice. Muffled as it was, resonating through the closed bedroom door, he couldn't make out the words, but it had the cadence of a conversation. A single side of one anyway. He wondered if the boy might have a stuffed animal that he confided in. A dopey looking zebra or lion or bear who bore witness to Clancy's innermost thoughts and fears. But in the few things that they were able to bring from the crime scene of the Hagans' house, he hadn't noticed a stuffed animal among them.

Better check, he decided.

He opened the door wide enough to slip his head in. The boy lay on his bed. A night light plugged into the wall in the corner cast a starburst against it that dissipated through the room. The only other illumination was the blade of dim light from the cracked door that fell across the boy where he lay in bed under the covers.

"Clancy? You all right?"

"Yes, sir."

"Need anything?"

"No, thank you, Mister Buxton."

Gibb sighed.

"Can't you sleep?"

"Don't know. I ain't tried yet," the boy answered, his voice small in the darkness of the room.

"Ah, okay. It's just…I heard you talking, and I thought maybe you couldn't sleep."

"It's okay. I was just talking to…" the boy trailed off.

"What's that?"

The boy whispered something so low that Gibb's old ears had no hope of catching it, but he got the sense that it wasn't meant for him.

"What'd you say, Clancy?"

"I was talking to Daddy, Mister Buxton."

The boy sounded unsure about revealing this to him, but Gibb closed his eyes and nodded.

"You know, that's okay, Clancy," he assured him. "My wife, Henrietta passed on years ago. And even though she's up in Heaven, I still talk to her all the time."

"Oh, I ain't talking to Daddy up in Heaven, Mister Buxton."

"You're not?"

"No, sir," the boy said, whispering as if someone who was not meant to might hear.

"Daddy's right here. Under the bed."

4

Clancy lay there in the dark, speaking with his father until his eyes grew tired, and he began to yawn. He didn't want to stop talking because the boy was afraid that if he let himself drift off to sleep, something would change, and he would wake up in the morning and be all alone again. Right now, he wasn't alone. Daddy was there.

And Daddy was telling him things.

There was a bad man who came to the house that night. His Daddy told him that they had done some things to make ends meet, he and his Momma. Some things that maybe weren't always right but had kept food on the table and clothes on their backs and a roof over their heads.

But someone they had business with had taken a nasty shine to his mother, and that night, the bad man had come for one thing but taken another.

Daddy had tried to stop him, but the bad man had taken Momma, and Clancy's father didn't know what the man had a mind to do with her. Worse than that, there wasn't any time to do things the right way and tell the police. She might not last that long and if the bad man caught a whiff of them coming, they would be too late to help her anyhow. And as much as Daddy wanted to help her himself, he couldn't anymore. He was of no more use to her or his son than a gust of wind, he had explained.

It had to be Clancy. He was the only one who could get to her in time. The only one who could save her.

"Like a superhero?" the boy asked.

Yes, Daddy had said. *Like a superhero.*

He was scared but Daddy told him that he would be with him the whole time. That he would help him along the way and things would be just fine as long as Clancy did as he was told. They would need to get going early in the morning, though. While it was still dark out, well before the rooster crowed.

"I'm scared, Daddy," he said, lying there on the bed, staring up at Mr. Buxton's ceiling.

A voice comforted him in the darkness, though only Clancy could hear it.

"Hold my hand so I can sleep?" the boy asked, turning on his side.

He reached over the edge of the mattress, letting his arm slide downward along the edges, over the rails of the four-post, tester bed. Until his fingers grazed flesh. His father's hand enveloped the boy's, but Clancy could feel something was different. The wedding band on Daddy's hand was cold to the touch but not as cold as his father's skin. On that same hand, Daddy was missing two fingers. The digits had been ripped away, leaving only rough nubs of meat and bone.

It soured his stomach to feel it, but he said nothing. At least he was not alone now. He wove his own fingers in with those remaining on his father's hand. There was comfort in it and, exhausted, the boy slept.

5

He woke in the morning to Daddy's voice in his head. It was time. Clancy dressed in the clothes that they had brought over from the house but saved the shoes until he was outside. He didn't want to be clomping about the house in his duck boots and risk waking the old man. In the kitchen, the boy found a small flashlight in a drawer, tested it, and slipped it into the pocket of his ski coat. Then, stealing silently out the back door, he sat on the steps and laced on his boots. He wished he had thought to bring gloves, for the dark of early morning was bitterly cold. He shoved his balled-up fists into his coat pockets, set off across Mister Buxton's yard and entered the wood at the far edge. He had to stop by his house. Daddy had told him there were some things there that were needed. He could get some gloves then, too.

Clancy used the flashlight occasionally when he became unnerved in the blackness. But he had spent a great deal of time in the backcountry with his Daddy and mostly he knew there was nothing to fear. This early in the morning, in winter, not much of anything was up and moving in the woods and certainly nothing he need be concerned about. It wasn't long before he emerged onto his own gravel driveway.

The house had been locked but Clancy knew where the hide-a-key was. The yellow tape the policemen had sealed the door with gave way when he twisted the knob and opened the door. He stepped inside and flicked a light on. The boy made for his room and tried not to glance down at the stain on the floor like a half gallon of spilled red paint where his father had died.

In his room, he pulled gloves from his dresser drawer and glanced at himself in the mirror. Daddy was with him. He couldn't see him right now, but he felt him nearby. Doubt crept in as he regarded his wiry, prepubescent frame.

Could he do this?

"Just like a superhero, remember?" he said, hoping to bolster his spirit.

On the way out, he spotted something of his on the floor near where his father had fallen. It was an old Halloween mask that Momma had been teasing him with a few nights before. A plastic face of the puppet-turned-real boy, Pinocchio, it was half broken just beneath the elongated nose. Its rounded, rosy cheeks framed by an exaggerated chin and dark eyebrows were covered in dots and drops and thin lines of dried blood. But the elastic string was intact.

Every superhero needs a mask, he thought.

He reached down and picked it up, then stepped out of the house and made his way toward the shed out back.

Moments later, Clancy had gathered everything he was told he would need. An orange flare gun that looked like a six-round revolver, extra flare cartridges, and a pair of bolt cutters. Now he was on his ATV, roaring through the darkness toward the old, abandoned dog kennel on Pinetop Knob. That's where Daddy said the bad man lived and where his mother would be. He would take the four-wheeler only as far as the narrow dirt road that began to snake up the hillside from the bottom of the mountain. Pinetop was a runt, though, as far as mountains went and he would have no trouble walking up it in a matter of minutes. At the top, he would listen carefully—no matter what, he had promised—to the instructions given him by his father and sneak in, find Momma, cut her loose and then slip back down the mountain free and clear. That was the plan.

Just like Batman or maybe Daredevil. As he trod up the road, he wondered at what his superhero name might be. After all, he had no powers. Just a broken mask. Walking on, Daddy's voice came to him again and told him about what he would find there on Pinetop and how they would carry out the plan.

There was a saying that he had heard once, though. The boy couldn't remember exactly how it went but it was something about the best laid plans of mice and men.

6

The old kennel building lay in disrepair on Pinetop Knob, its aluminum sides rusted and dingy. A single exterior flood lamp bathed the front entrance in light. There was another door several paces off from it, but it looked forgotten and unused.

He would probably find her in the part where the dogs were kept, Daddy had told him.

Where the dogs were kept. It sickened him to think of his mother in a cage like some captive animal.

The unused door led to where the cages were, but it would be locked from the inside. When Clancy had asked his father how he knew so much about this place, Daddy had explained that he had done business with the bad man out here on occasion. He had done business with him, but he had never liked him.

The front door it was, then. Hopefully the bad man was still asleep. His father had said it was likely. He said the bad man had a habit of smoking something called "crank" which kept him up late into the night and made him sleep for hours into the day. He hoped that the door wouldn't be locked. The man was a careless sort—up here on Pinetop all alone, fearing nothing. But if it was locked, things were liable to get a bit more complicated.

Clancy approached the door and snuck to the window next to it, peeked over the corner to see inside and make sure no one was there. It was dark inside and quiet. He went to the door, reached out a trembling hand and wrapped it around the cold metal knob. He turned and it clicked, the door pulling open.

The boy breathed a sigh of relief.

When it had been a kennel, this had been the main entrance. There was a tall counter and two small, adjacent offices where desks still sat, unused and now piled with stacks of boxes and papers. The beam of his flashlight fell over the dusty surfaces and walls, then landed on a set of steps that ascended a few feet and turned, continuing upward into the darkness. They led to an apartment upstairs where the bad man lived. To Clancy's right stood a metal door that pushed open easily. Before he crossed the threshold, though, his father's voice came to him and cautioned him to turn off the flashlight. There were windows in the apartment above that looked out over the kennel cages and the flashlight must not be seen.

"I thought you said he was asleep."

I said he should be. Can't be too careful, son.

The boy nodded and switched off the light, stepped all the way into the kennel and quietly pulled the door closed behind him. He stood there for a moment, his eyes adjusting to the darkness. The unused door that he had seen from the outside lay at the end of an aisle that bisected a dozen or more cages and above it an exit sign still shone with a dim red light that proved to be decent enough to see by.

The place smelled like a mixture of gasoline and animal urine. It was foul and Clancy held his arm against his nose as he walked down the aisle. Most of the cages were filled with junk—spent metal barrels of oil and other high-smelling chemicals, and every sort of metal scrap that could be imagined. The debris flowed out of the cages and lined both sides of the aisle, sometimes encroaching into the middle of the walkway. Collecting scrap metal and selling it was how the bad man made a living and from the look of this place, he would be set for a good long while.

About midway down the aisle, there was a break in the cages and an open entrance into some other room. But the faint red light did not reach into its dark confines, so Clancy was not of a mind to have a further look. Just then, he noticed that down at the far end, near the exit sign and the door to the outside, there was a cage that did not appear stuffed with scrap. He hurried toward it and had to restrain his elation when he saw his mother there, lying on a dirty mattress inside of the cage. But his happiness was soon dampened, for she was face down and unmoving. Not knowing if she was even alive, he resolved to get the cage open quickly. A padlock and a chain wrapped around the post kept the door closed and Clancy approached it, holding the bolt cutters up toward the chain.

Then something moved in the darkness. Something that was not his mother.

He froze and listened, slowly lowering the bolt cutters to the floor. Looking behind him, he saw nothing at first. Then a whispering sound as something moved toward him. Out of the corner of his eye, he saw a dark shape scurry across the floor, and he gasped and stepped backward but lost his balance. As he tumbled toward the floor, he saw that the dark shape had been nothing more than a plump, disgusting rat who then continued on his trek, paying him no mind. On his way down, he slammed against something and something else wobbled and then fell; a piece of metal clanged to the ground and shattered the silence of the cavernous space.

The darkness was soon to follow. High in the wall behind him, the row of windows that had been black before now glowed as a light was turned on in the room above. Clancy glanced up to see the silhouette of a man painted against the light. The bad man was looking out over the kennel floor. Clancy didn't know if he could see him or not, but he shook violently there in the cold dark, stifling a whimper that threatened to escape him.

"Hello?" sounded the broken, frightened voice of his mother. "Is there someone there?"

Clancy wanted to call out to her, but he dared not.

After a moment, the room upstairs went dark again but then there came a sound that rang into the space of the kennel. It was music. Old music. A man's voice, smooth as silk, crooned into the dark.

Clancy had never heard the song before, but the singer crooned on about deepening shadows gathering splendor and fingers of night and twilight time—none of which Clancy understood. It sounded like a love song, though. Like one of the songs his Momma and Daddy used to dance to in the living room in the late evening after dinner when they thought he was asleep. Only here in the kennels with his mother trapped like an animal, it didn't feel like a love song at all.

In the cage beyond, his mother began to sob. The bad man—the Twilight Man, Clancy decided to call him—must have played this song whenever he came to hurt her. Would he come to hurt her again now, Clancy wondered?

The boy cursed his own clumsiness and the clanging metal that had given him away.

No time for that, son. The Twilight Man knows a fox has crept into the henhouse.

Clancy's senses burned with the sudden knowledge that he had just become prey. He needed a place to hide, and his eyes went immediately to the break in the cages and the black room that lay beyond the entrance.

Like the rat that had startled him, he scurried across the aisle and into the darkness. He clicked his flashlight on, cupping his hand over the lens to subdue the beam. The room had once been used to bathe and groom the animals but now was just another space filled with junk. A bathing stall on the far wall stood empty, a plastic curtain still hanging by a few rings on the rod across it. He could pull the curtain closed and hide there, he thought.

Too obvious, came Daddy's voice. *Could be a useful distraction, though.*

Clancy leapt to his feet and went to the stall, pulled the curtain across the opening and then turned and saw an upended steel box on casters across the way. It was meant to hold tools and was too small for a man but not for a child. Clancy crawled into it, killed the flashlight and tucked it in his coat pocket. His fingers grazed against the flare gun and so he gripped it. He sat there, terrified. He tried to calm himself, to build confidence where there was suddenly nothing but timidity and fear. He had to be brave for Momma. He had come this far, and he would not fail. Just like a superhero.

Clancy pulled the half-broken Pinocchio mask down over his face and waited.

7

With the music playing as loud as it was, he never heard the Twilight Man coming but he could see the steady light of a camping lantern swinging as he entered the room, throwing jagged, enormous shadows from the scrap over the walls. Dark, ethereal shapes that danced as the Twilight Man moved through the room, stalking him like a tiger.

"Don't know what you come for, whoever you are," came the man's voice, thin but somehow menacing. "Walkin' into my lair just as pretty as you please."

The Twilight Man chuckled darkly.

"But you'll be leaving in pieces."

Clancy's heart was pounding in his chest, and he found himself once again having to stifle a whining sound that wanted to come squeaking from his throat.

Daddy's voice came to him then, assuring him that he would be all right but that they had to work together now. His father was going to summon all the power that he could manage to help him out but when the moment came, Clancy had to be ready to use that flare gun and make it count. No fear. His Momma needed him to be strong.

The boy nodded even as tears began to towel up in his eyes behind the mask.

A moment later, the Twilight Man was standing in front of him. He was not as tall as his shadow in the window had suggested but was no less frightening. The camp lantern was grasped in one hand as he held it aloft and looked about the room. In the other, the man grasped the handle of a double-headed hand axe.

The Twilight Man seemed to notice the closed curtain on the bathing stall then. Though he could see none of the villain's face, Clancy could feel him smile in the dark as he stepped toward it.

"Mighty considerate of you. Sure will make the clean-up easier."

The Twilight Man reached out and swiped the curtain aside with the axe.

Clancy could see the man's shoulders slump as he beheld the empty stall.

Just then, the camp lantern went off. The boy had thought it an intentional act but in the blackness that followed, he heard the Twilight Man cussing the thing and rapping on it as if trying to knock something back into place and get it going again. The lantern began to flicker on and off.

The boy also wondered if something else had changed, if a door had been opened. A deep cold had settled into the room.

"Jap-made piece of shit," the Twilight Man spat as he tapped the lantern again and it roared brightly back to life.

But they were not alone in the room, the boy and the Twilight Man.

As the man looked up from the lantern in his grip, his eyes widened, and the axe slipped from his grasp.

Standing before the Twilight Man was the ruined form of Mick Hagan, his deathly pallor even whiter in the lantern light and the deep red of the missing chunk of his head glistening as if it were fresh. The ghost's mouth was frozen wide-open in a silent scream of rage and a broken hand with missing fingers reached out, desperately clawing at the killer.

The lantern dropped as the Twilight Man's legs went from under him, stumbling backwards into the bathing stall. His boot caught on the curtain and ripped it down where it cascaded to rest atop him like a blanket. His eyes were still wide with fright and now his own mouth was opened in a wail of terror.

Now was the time.

Clancy, the masked hero, crawled from the box and stepped in front of the Twilight Man who was clinging to the walls of the stall and screaming. Without hesitation, he brought the pistol up and shoved the barrel into the open maw of the monster. There was a loud pop as he pulled the trigger and filled the head of the Twilight Man with fire and smoke.

Firebringer, Clancy thought. That was his name. That was his power.

He stepped back and watched the man writhe as the flesh of his head and neck cooked from the inside. Burning light spilled down the villain's throat and melted tissue, fissures of light opening his skin and pink flames erupting from his eyes.

"Who's there?" his mother called out.

He turned but no longer saw the awful vision of his father standing nearby and the deep cold that had seized the room had abated.

"Momma!" he hollered, then ran out of the room and down the aisle.

She was on her knees, fingers clinging to the chain-link of the cage. When she saw him, she blinked and then backed away, looking at him strangely.

He realized then that he still wore the mask.

The boy reached down and took the bolt cutters in hand, brought them up and snapped them down on the chain that held the cage door closed. The chain fell to the floor and as it did, Clancy removed the hood of his coat and slid the mask up on top of his head.

His mother looked at him sideways, not believing what she saw. "Clancy? Son?"

He held his hand out to her.

"Come on, Momma. Daddy says we need to go."

She scrambled to her feet and went to him, taking her son in her arms.

In the grooming room, the sparks from the flare had found a puddle of solvent that sat around a slowly leaking barrel of it. It had begun to catch, and the flames danced in the room. There were too many half-empty barrels of such things in this place. It would go up like a tinderbox and they would go with it if they didn't get out soon.

"Hurry, Momma!" he cried and pulled her along with him as he ran for the unused door.

Both he and his mother fumbled with the deadbolt and the lock that had become rigid with disuse and the cold. Finally, the locks clicked back, and they threw the door open. Outside, the sky was brightening gradually as the sun began to rise somewhere below the horizon, forming a swath of deep blue that would soon overtake the darkness of night.

Faye Hagan stumbled and went to the ground. Clancy stopped to help his mother up. As he bent down to grab her, he saw a dark shape standing in the open door to the kennel. Orange flames roared behind it. His mother saw it, too, and she cried out in fear.

It wasn't the Twilight Man, though. It was a shape familiar to the both of them—Clancy's father.

"Come on, Momma," the boy said and urged her back to her feet.

Just then, the boy heard a voice in his mind and the door to the kennel was slammed shut.

I love you, son. I knew you could do it.

The voice didn't say goodbye, but Clancy knew that's what it meant. He felt a lump of sorrow growing in his throat and tears came to his eyes.

"Who was that, Clancy?" his mother shrieked.

"Daddy. It was Daddy."

"Daddy? Son, your Daddy's gone," she said, her voice breaking as she did so.

Clancy nodded and tugged her along toward the road that would be their salvation.

"Yes, Momma. I know it."

The boy fought the urge to collapse in a heaving, weeping pile of exhaustion and despair. He wouldn't see his father again, he knew, but he had his mother back and that gave him heart. The strength to push on came from something else, though—a brave fire that had grown within him that morning which did not belong to boyhood but was a portent of the man he would one day become.

Like his father. Better than his father, even.

After all, he wasn't alone anymore.

Clancy and his mother made their way down the hill, together at last at twilight time.

AFTER THE FIRE

1

It had been three days since the last recurrence of the dream, and so it had been three days now that he'd gone without sleep. Not that he hadn't nodded off now and then, eyes wide, saliva collecting beneath his open jaw as his primeval brain snatched what rest it could. But this brought him no refreshment and no renewal and always he woke with a start and a panic.

Hypnogogic myoclonic twitch.

That's what Dr. Cyrus had explained it to be—that occurrence of being jarred awake after suffocating in freefall. Hypnic jerk was another term for it. "Sorry about that," the doctor said, returning to his seat from a phone call.

"Everything all right?"

Dr. Cyrus waved it off.

"Yes, fine. Just a billing issue."

Frank could only imagine the kind of phone call that would pull a shrink out of a session that had only just begun. Billing issues had to be pretty far down the list. Whatever poor bastard was on the call probably had a gun in his mouth. Frank found this oddly amusing until he realized that, with the way things were going, it could easily be him on the other end of that line within a week. Maybe less.

The doctor relaxed in his chair, crossing one leg over the other's knee, leaving his notepad perched there along his pen.

"So, you were saying you haven't slept. Been three days?"

Frank nodded.

"And this is because of the dream?"

Frank grimaced. Here they were wading into murky waters. He would try his best to clear it up. The nightmare had visited him occasionally all throughout his adult life. He explained to the doctor that while it was a thing experienced while asleep, it was also a memory. One from long ago—a thing he'd always hoped to be rid of years ago.

Frank eyed the psychiatrist warily, wringing his hands as he shifted in his seat.

"You a local boy, Doc? Lived here in Richmond for a while?"

The doctor nodded.

"I grew up across the river in Manchester."

"You ever heard of the Ginter Park Witch?"

He smiled and let go a breathy chuckle.

"Sure. Everyone knows that yarn."

"Yeah," Frank said, his mouth going dry. He rubbed a hand across the three-day-old stubble on his face. "Well, here's what you don't know about it. I was there that day."

Doctor Cyrus leaned in; his interest piqued. Leaned in like a young boy sitting by a campfire as ghost stories got passed around, hanging on the edge of every word, eager to hear the next one. And here Frank was, just telling it.

It was August of 1957. One of those rare days deep into a Virginia summer when there was actually a breeze to provide some relief from the oppressive heat of the day, though young boys seldom noticed such things. Four such boys were busy with a game of baseball by the gurgling waters of the creek that ran through Bryan Park. A couple of days ago, it had rained, and the ground was soft and green beneath their feet as they tramped about, hooting and hollering their way through another day of their summer vacation.

Frankie Neely stepped up to bat, hovering over home plate.

Back then, home plate and all of the bases were marked by a pile of soda bottle caps left by every kid who had played ball and had ground the bottle caps into the dirt at the park. Rather than withering over time, the bases endured, every bottle cap from every kid slowly gathering red clay and dirt around them until they formed a mound just like the real ballplayers stood on.

Today, Frankie was awake in his aspirations. He was a boy without doubt as he swung that baseball bat through the air.

He spat into the dirt just like he'd seen Hank Aaron do on the television. He wiped his sweaty hands on his trousers and choked up on the bat as he took his stance, his eyes keenly fixed on the pitcher.

"Don't you let this one by you now, Francis," the pitcher taunted.

He spat again and swung the bat through the air, admiring the whooshing sound.

"Go screw, Hitler," he grumbled back to his best friend, Lane Histersen.

Lane and his family were Jewish, so – in the way that children do - the boys at school had taken to calling him Hitler whenever they wanted to get under his skin. Which usually worked quite well.

The boy grimaced and pulled back. He let go a fastball that might have rocketed past him and the umpire both, only to end up on the other side of the creek. But on this day Frankie was just quick enough. He smiled as the bat cracked against the ball and sent it flying far, far over the heads of the other boys. As he began his run around the bases to what he was sure would be a homer, he grinned wildly.

"That's bull!" Lane said.

Frankie gave Lane a big smile as he walked across home plate.

"You putz!"

Frankie and Lane, the respective and self-appointed Captains of their teams, had begun arguing about who had won the game just as soon as it had ended. Neither boy was very good at keeping score and so the results of any game they played were always a source of much debate. As they trudged up the road toward Ginter Park where they lived, they saw a fine, blood-red Chevy convertible drive by, loaded with members of the fairer sex, cackling as the radio played. The high school girls were all decked out in bright, crisp summer clothes with tops that showed their bare, tanned shoulders. They wore wide, dark sunglasses. and their long hair rippled and tossed in the wind as they drove by. These daughters of the Ginter Park wealthy were as close to Hollywood starlets as anything the boys had seen. Since Frankie and Lane had both recently began to notice the charming nuances of the womanly form, they stopped and practically broke their necks to have a look.

"Well," Lane sighed, "they sure are something."

"Yeah."

"We're gonna get us a car like that someday, you know?"

Frankie scoffed.

"That a fact?"

"Uh-huh, my Poppa said he's gonna get me one when I turn sixteen."

Lane's family came from old money. It had something to do with trade and shipping things on boats well before the Civil War and then shipping different things on boats after the war was over. Frankie never really understood what it was all about.

"No kidding?"

"No kidding."

"Well," Frankie thought about it. "That'll be cherry, won't it?"

"Damned cherry."

They crossed over Hermitage Road into the streets of Ginter and Frankie wiped at a thick layer of sweat collecting on his brow.

"What're we gonna do this afternoon?" he asked.

"Well, I do have an idea," Lane said, cocking his head and regarding Frankie skeptically. "But it ain't for no wuss. It's a no-wussies-allowed kind of thing, you see."

Frankie rolled his eyes. At the ripe old age of twelve years, Lane was more concerned with acting manly than any boy Frankie knew.

"What's the idea?"

"You sure you ain't a wussy, Neely?"

Frankie registered his response by reaching out with his fist and landing a jab on Lane's shoulder.

"So here it is," Lane said. "We go to the witch house."

Frankie stopped and looked at Lane, his eyes narrow and his mouth crooked with doubt.

"Ain't no trick to that, Lane. We walk by it all the time."

"No, see, we're gonna go in. Let's see what's really in that witch house."

It was the house on the corner of Wilmington and Lamont. Every kid in the neighborhood called it the "witch house," and while none of them could know the full history of the place, over the years, they had all listened as their parents spoke of it at dinner parties and in hushed conversations when they assumed the kids weren't nearby, much less listening to every word. From that, the kids had cobbled together a history of their own to tell and tell again while sneaking a smoke of their parents' cigarettes by the creek and in other dark, secret places.

The House at 702 Wilmington Avenue belonged to a young widow well known in the city as Madame Beatrice LaFontaine. Many years before, Henry LaFontaine, lawyer and legislator in the state government, married a scandalously young girl named Beatrice Moore who hailed from the boonies somewhere south of the river, a place well beyond Manchester. Once married, she joined him in the city and Senator LaFontaine had a new home built for them in Ginter Park.

There they lived, alone but for two or three colored servants. It was a home that Henry and Beatrice LaFontaine had intended to fill with children. Most say he chose Beatrice to be his wife for her youth more than anything else. She was happy to oblige. Her desire for a large family was well known among their friends and neighbors. The chance for such happiness would not come, though. It was whispered that Beatrice turned out to be barren and unable to bear a child past a few weeks into a pregnancy. Nevertheless, her husband sought to encourage her, telling her that the Lord worked miracles every day. This he did despite her growing tendency toward melancholy and aloofness. All hope vanished, however, one crisp night during the Christmas season when her husband was found in his study dead from an apparent heart attack. She had passed him by all afternoon, it was said, even planting a kiss on his cold lips as she had his tea service removed from the room.

She thought he was sleeping.

After the Senator's death, his wife became a ghost among their many social circles. Galas and parties and fundraisers came and went, the last drop of French Champagne drained from every glass at every soiree, and Madame LaFontaine was nowhere to be found.

They whispered of her grief and her retreat from the world. They wondered about her money. Then, one evening, the whispers ceased. She had become forgotten.

Perhaps that's what she wanted.

After all, her self-imposed seclusion worsened as time went on.

At the house on Wilmington Avenue, her needs were catered to by an increasing number of servants who seemed to come and go so often that it was impossible for the neighborhood gossipers to keep track of them. Despite whatever needs they served in the household, minimal attention was paid to the outside of the home. While it could not be described as having fallen into total disrepair, it was not esteemed by onlookers as much as the other Ginter Park estates whose lawns and gardens were tended to often and always appeared immaculate. It was the home's dreadful façade, patchwork repairs, and the Madame's own hermitic ways that led Ginter Park's aristocrats to speak of the house with disdain.

Rumor and the allure of the mysterious had given rise to naming her a witch. An old, gnarled thing who dwelled inside, turning her servants into all manner of detestable creatures whenever they displeased her or raised her ire. Maybe we only halfway believed it back then, but even half-belief can turn the world on a dime when you're twelve years old.

"You want to break into the witch house?" Frankie shook his head. "You gotta be screwing with me."

"Heck no, I'm serious," Lane insisted. "My Mom said the old hag is away visiting family somewhere."

From where they stood, they could see the house blocks away, shrouded in trees and tangles of ivy that grew up its sides and on every single thing around the house. Its narrow castle-like shape stood against the failing afternoon light. Replete with sharp, high angles and weathered copper spires that rose from the tips of the rounded towers on both sides, the house gave the onlooker the impression of an imposing, ancient fortress. Even in the heat of the summer day it looked dark, cold and foreboding.

"How're we gonna get in?"

Lane picked up his step and crossed the street.

Frankie followed after him.

"I happen to know that she keeps a window on the first floor out back unlocked. It's a servant's room without a toilet," Lane declared proudly. "Way I hear it, the old coot that stays in there is a little touched in the head and can't work the window latch to slop out the pot. So, it's always left unlocked."

"Shut up, Lane," Frankie dismissed. "You don't know any such thing. Besides, nobody even uses chamber pots anymore."

"The witch does," he replied.

"Anyway," Lane waved it off, started walking again, "those ones she didn't turn into toads and whatnot, she took with her – so the house is empty. There's a bench somewhere out back we can use to climb up to the window. Unless you're a wuss."

Frankie eyed the house which loomed ahead and crept closer

with every step he took. He feared it and its ill reputation, but then getting inside would be quite a story to tell back at school when summer was over. He imagined the lauding they would receive from the other boys and the curious and admiring looks they might get from the girls.

"No," he relented. "I ain't a wuss."

2

They'd had no trouble at all scrambling over the high stone wall that surrounded the garden behind the house, the ivy and kudzu so thick it gave their young bodies no bother to climb it. Once in the garden, they stalked carefully toward the house until they were standing on the weatherworn bricks of the patio. Decaying remnants of old iron furniture were scattered about, unused, with weeds and vines tangled around them.

"Look," Frankie whispered, staring down at a large, discolored area of the patio.

There was a spot where the red bricks were darker, almost wet looking. It was one of the many legends of the witch; that she had once become so angry with a young servant that she chased the boy all about the house, finally ending up on the widow's walk that looked out over the garden. While the boy pleaded with Madame LaFontaine for forgiveness, the witch took the young boy by his hand and whirled him around and over the railing where he fell to his death on the patio below. It was said that she left the servant child there for many days and let the carrion birds slowly pick at him. This she did as a warning to the other servants against such disobedience. She eventually had the boy buried somewhere in the garden, but it was said among the kids that the stain could still be seen on the patio bricks where he died.

"Damnation," Lane remarked, then pointed over to a bench near the back walls of the house. "That's our ticket."

Together the boys picked up on the old iron bench and moved it under the window. After getting it into place, they paused a moment and wiped their sweating faces. They exchanged a familiar look, each boy aware of the significance of the moment. This was the point of no return—last chance to back out. Neither was willing to do so.

"You spot me," Lane said as he climbed up onto the seat of the bench. "I might need a leg up or something."

"All right," Frankie nodded and joined his friend on the seat of the bench.

As Lane scrambled up the back of it, he gripped the windowsill and pushed against the lower part of the glass. Sensing his difficulty, Frankie grabbed the boy by the ankles and steadied himself as he lifted him up a bit. Now able to reach farther up the glass, Lane pressed upward and in. Frankie thought for certain that Lane would crack the glass pane, leaning into it so, but after a moment they both heard the scraping sound of the window as it rose up and opened a way into the house. A draft of cooler air came pouring through it.

Lane looked back at his friend with a mischievous grin on his face.

"Last one in's a rotten egg," he remarked, and clambered up the side of the house, over the sill and flopped like a fish onto the hard, wooden floor inside.

Frankie got a foothold on the back of the bench and followed likewise and before he knew it they were both standing inside the house, feeling like grand adventurers who had just broken into an Egyptian tomb.

The curtains were drawn, and the room was dark even for such a bright summer day. As his eyes adjusted, Frankie thought it didn't look much like any servant's room. It was full of fine things, ornate chairs with plush, velvet seats, and paintings on the wall. There being no bed in the room and a low Victorian table in the middle, it seemed more like a parlor to him.

"You sure nobody's here?" he whispered to his friend.

"You hear anybody except for us?" Lane replied.

Frankie supposed not, for the house was as quiet as a graveyard.

The parlor opened into the kitchen where slants of the afternoon light spilled in through a few small windows, though there was nothing of interest to be seen. They made their way through it and down the main hallway. Each room they came to was dark and cool, the curtains tightly drawn. It made it difficult to see what was about and a few times Frankie bumped into things he was sure would be expensive or impossible to replace should they fall and shatter on the floor.

"Dang, Lane," Frankie scowled. "All your daring me crap and you didn't think about a flashlight?"

"Well, I didn't know I was gonna be breaking in with the klutziest guy in Ginter," Lane muttered to him.

From a nearby table with a candelabra, Lane plucked two candlesticks. Lighting the wicks from a box of matches that lay beside them, the soft orange glow illuminated their surroundings as they walked through the house and gazed at all the adornments on the walls and knickknacks on the tables. The Madame certainly had a love for the finer things.

They ascended the stairs to the second floor and found much more of the same. For the home of a reviled witch, Frankie thought, the place seemed disappointingly unremarkable.

As they crossed the hall toward another room, Frankie stopped. Beneath a window at the hallway's end was a table whereupon sat framed photographs, some that looked to be from the time of the Civil War—some even earlier. Setting his candlestick down on the table, he held the pictures up and studied them. They were photographs of many different people from many different times. Lane came and peered over his shoulder.

"Everybody in these pictures is sleeping," he remarked.

"No. They're dead."

Lane looked closer.

"What the hell?"

The small frames, a dozen or so of them, depicted people young and old in various poses that seemed strange and unnatural considering that all of the subjects had passed away. Some were propped up in chairs, surrounded by possessions that had been important to them in life, and looked only as if they'd dozed off on a hot summer afternoon while waiting for some unknown moment to arrive. Others were lying on beds or in coffins festooned with ruffled fabric and lace, hands crossed at their chest or stomach with personal effects laid around them. Most of the pictures were of adults or the elderly but a handful were of children no older than him and Frankie and in some of them the expired persons were photographed with their eyes open.

Seeing these, a coldness spread over Frankie's skin, raising his flesh and screwing up his face in disgust.

"Ew!" Lane clapped Frankie on the shoulder and gestured toward the pictures, "Look at this one!"

Frankie leaned closer and in the dark of the house and the dancing candlelight, they beheld a terrible image of an elderly man, dressed in his finest suit for his journey onward, laid out on a Victorian lounge sofa. His head was lolling unnaturally to the side, his thin and drooping face turned toward the camera and his eyes pale with the whiteness of death, staring emptily out of the photograph. Underneath, written in elegant script, it read *Brendan M. Moore, 1873.*

It gave Frankie the creeps, though he tried to slough it off.

"I've seen these kinds of pictures before. My grandma has an album of them on a bookshelf in her house."

"Yeah?" Lane whispered. "Is your grandma a witch?"

Frankie gave his friend a shove and Lane shoved back, and the two boys wrestled for a moment before both of them tumbled into the table, sending picture frames and a candlestick scattering across the hallway floor.

"Spaz!" Lane hollered as he fought off Frankie's slaps and punches.

"Yeah, well you're a–"

Both boys stopped their fooling around and listened, for they had both heard it. As they stood silent and motionless, they heard it again. A voice, weak and quiet, almost inaudible.

"Helluh…helmph meh…"

They could barely tell from where the sound had come but both their heads turned to see a door just down the hallway that stood slightly ajar. Frightened but overwhelmingly curious, both boys eased closer to the door and slowly pushed it wide open, the hinges creaking. A flight of stairs led upward to the attic. They shared a questioning look and then they nodded in agreement.

They crept up the staircase with Lane lighting the way. Then they were at the top, staring into the darkness of the cavernous old attic. They could sense movement and hear breathing. There was a terrible smell about the place that was much worse than the normal attic odors of old papers and moth-eaten clothes, more vile than must and dust collecting on rafters and mildew in the corners. It was something else entirely. Frankie saw there was a portal window that looked out the front of the house, but its curtains were drawn. He stepped over and pulled them back, flooding the attic with afternoon sunlight.

It took their eyes a moment to adjust to the brightness but after a moment they saw very well what Madame LaFontaine kept in the dark confines of her attic.

Frankie looked about, wide-eyed and aghast, unable to move or to even breathe.

He could hear Lane standing beside him, frozen to the floor as well and there was a new sound that penetrated the room. It took Frankie a moment to sort past what he was seeing, to understand what he was hearing. It was screaming. Lane was standing beside him, his face gone completely white, his mouth open wide, and he was screaming.

Lane was screaming.

That was the dream, the nightmare, the memory. By the time Frank had finished telling the tale, Dr. Cyrus was properly appalled, and the hour-long session was at an end. He took a moment to explain to Frank that such traumatic experiences, though they may be decades old, were still capable of marring the psyche of an otherwise well-adjusted person. As he wrote out a prescription for zolpidem to help him sleep, he recommended that Frank schedule another session so they could continue to work through the issue.

"Getting well takes time," the doctor said as he handed over the slip of paper.

Frank nodded, though he had no intention of returning to spill yet more of his darkness for the doctor to analyze. He'd wanted nothing more than the prescription, and now that he had it in hand, he didn't plan to see Dr. Cyrus ever again. All he needed was sleep. With a few days of rest uninterrupted by the nightmare, it would eventually pass, and he would be fine as frog's hair. Just like every time before.

For Frank, the nightmares were nothing more than a passing storm to be weathered, and now he had the means to do so.

In the days following his appointment, he experienced a reprieve from the relentless dream that haunted him. At first, it was not wholly eliminated but instead came in short, troubling flashes that would wake him. However, under the calming influence of the zolpidem, he was able to fall back asleep almost immediately. After a few days, he was able to sleep uninterrupted through the night but continued to take the medication as a measure of precaution.

Once again, his days and nights became ordinary.

The previous year, after he'd been let go from the *Times-Dispatch* newspaper, he began doing some freelance work for *The Weekly Beat*. It was a free paper that, true to its title, endeavored to present a weekly accounting of the city's events and nightlife with a great portion of it focused on restaurants, bars and music venues. It was the sort of fluff journalism that he had abhorred during his time with the *Times-Dispatch*. Frank was not now in need of money and never really had been, even as a reporter. He was more or less set for life due to his late father's very successful printing business. However, his

"Painting the Town" column in *The Beat* provided an activity into which he could pour his attention. And, after all, it was journalism of a sort. He reckoned that it was better than nothing.

Once the nightmares had faded from view and his ability to focus on other things returned, he resumed his attendance of local clubs and bars in the evenings. He'd sit there on those nights, drinking club soda or Coke and watching bands of every variety, and then he would render his opinion on the show, the venue, and the food. And he'd do it in a thousand words or less. After a week of nightlife, he usually had enough material for a month's worth of writing for *The Beat*.

Frank had not been much of a night-owl for some time now and this gig certainly didn't come naturally to his constitution, but now it actually felt good. He was glad to be back in the saddle and going through the motions of everyday life. He woke in the mornings, prepared himself a sensible breakfast, went to the mailbox, and sat alone at his kitchen table, reading through the paper and enjoying the work of those reporters and columnists that he knew well. Always, he finished up by glancing through the real estate circulars, marveling at how large the city and surrounding areas had grown and chuckling with disdain at the half-cocked names given to these new subdivisions and housing developments with cookie-cutter mansions and private pools. These gated communities as inauthentic as any he could imagine, peopled by yuppies with their imported vehicles and their South American maids and nannies. It was all so much bad theater to him, but it was becoming the new standard of living for the affluent.

The days that week in late August had been among the hottest on record and Frank felt every humid degree of it as he made his way back to his car from *The Weekly Beat's* headquarters on Cary Street. As his usual poor luck would have it, the air conditioning in the building had been out and he'd had to wait around longer than normal to drop off his copy to the editor, who summarily thanked him and congratulated Frank on his getting over the summer flu bug so quickly. Not having felt inclined to share his nightmare troubles with this editor who was no more than a casual acquaintance, he had told the man that he was down with the flu. It was a white lie and one that wouldn't lead to someone questioning his mental state. He had nodded his thanks and left the building.

Several blocks away, he climbed into the driver's seat of his 1969 Plymouth Valiant. Glancing in the rear-view mirror, he wiped beads of sweat from his brow and opened the collar of his shirt. He started the car and slid the AC control as far to COOL as it could go. In its day, the Valiant had come off the line without climate control but when he had it restored the year after his father passed, he'd had the system added. Such modifications took away from the value of the car as a classic, but then it was Frank's first and only car. Though it was a far cry from the '57 Chevy that Lane had assured him they'd be riding in at a much younger and thunderous age, Frank never intended to rid himself of the Valiant no matter how many upgrades or transmissions or rebuilt motors it took to keep it in good working order.

He pulled out of the parking space and headed east toward the Boulevard that would take him home to Ginter Park. Halfway there, he remembered noticing the orange medicine bottle this morning with a solitary pill of zolpidem inside. So, he steered the Valiant toward the Old Dominion Pharmacy on the outskirts of his neighborhood to remedy the issue.

"I'm sorry, sir, but there are no refills for this prescription in our records."

He looked up at the elderly woman behind the counter, a bit dumbfounded.

"Well," he said, "it's a new prescription, so maybe there's been a mix-up or—"

"No, sir. It says real clear right here that any refills must come from your psychiatrist."

His psychiatrist. Frank shook his head at the thought. He was inclined to argue with the woman further but thought better of it.

"Look, is Randall around?" he asked, glancing at his watch to see if it was lunchtime. It was not.

"Yes, sir, but he's gonna tell you the same as—"

"I'd like to speak with Randall if you wouldn't mind ma'am."

She narrowed her eyes, nodded grudgingly and walked away to find the pharmacist that had been filling all of Frank's prescriptions since he was a teenager.

Standing there in line, a score of sick people at his heels bristling at the delay, he glanced up at the parabolic security mirror and watched as they coughed and snorted and shuffled their feet with impatience. He shook his head in an attempt to communicate his frustration to them and then his heart went cold as he saw a familiar face appear from the corner of one aisle and linger in the walkway, then disappear into the next aisle.

He blinked his eyes hard as if to shake off the sight and convince his brain that it was a mistake; a trick of the mind and nothing more. His stare lingered on the end cap of toothbrushes that the figure had vanished behind, though, and the only thing that snapped him back was the voice of the pharmacist.

"Frank, you all right?"

He turned to see Randall, the pharmacist whose store name tag was as old and faded as the man himself. Still, he couldn't summon the will to respond.

"Frank?"

"Yeah," he finally acknowledged, only halfway recovered from his moment of confusion.

"Frank, you okay?"

"Sure."

The pharmacist nodded; his head skewed with skepticism. "You sure? Look like you've seen a ghost."

Frank caught a glimpse of his distorted self in the mirror just then to find that his complexion had gone sallow. He endeavored to focus on the task at hand, though, and turned his full attention to the pharmacist.

"No, Randall, I'm not okay," he found himself blurting out. "I've been having trouble sleeping. And the doctor gave me these pills… zora…zola…"

"Zolpidem."

Frank snapped his fingers.

"That's it," he said, gathering his wits about him once again. "So, I should have a refill, right?"

"Sorry, Frank. It looks like this was a one-time scrip. If you need more, you'll have to call the doctor."

Frank was listening, nodding, but his attention was drawn to the mirror and that aisle.

With no response from Frank, the pharmacist attempted to smooth things out a bit.

"I'm sure it's just a misunderstanding. Let the office know and I'm sure they'll call in a refill for you."

"Uh-huh," Frank responded, his gaze still trained on the mirror even as he backed out of the line of patrons. "Yeah, thanks," he muttered absently as he broke from the line entirely and headed toward the end cap with the toothbrushes.

"Frank?" he heard the pharmacist call to him, though he paid him no mind.

As he rounded the end cap he brushed the contents of the display aside as if it were a curtain, resulting in an unintended display of awkwardness and noise. Frank stepped into the center of the aisle and looked for the figure. His adrenaline was up, and he had all the swagger of a gunslinger from an old Western, except that his mouth had gone dry, and his limbs trembled like the green branches of a sapling in a cold and powerful wind.

Down the aisle there was nothing like what he had seen. No one at all, in fact. Only a mother and her child bending to view the array of cold medicines on a shelf. They looked up at him warily, the woman's face screwed up with concern and she reached a hand down to the shoulder of her child, and it was then that he realized that he was making a spectacle of himself there in the pharmacy. The woman looked downright frightened. As a means of ensuring them that he meant no harm, he managed a half-smile and a nod in their direction, then made a beeline toward the door.

The short drive to his home on Confederate Avenue was the longest ride of his life. He endeavored to rationalize what he had seen. A brief failure of the senses. A mind overwrought from the recent spate of the nightmares. These explanations were entirely plausible.

Sitting there alone, though, with the summer evening slowly diminishing the afternoon sun, such explanations lost their power. The figure he had seen in the pharmacy was Lane. Not a shuffling, floating apparition, nor a chain-dragging haunt like the ones from the ghost stories of his youth. Not an illusion or hallucination brought on by the pills or anything else.

It had been Lane. More than anything, he recognized the figure not by its death-white pallor, but by its freakishly opened jaws locked in an eternal scream that did not resonate in the physical world but invaded the mind of Frank Neely, who knew it well from the darkest of his dreams and memories.

As night overtook the twilight, Frank sought out the last of the zolpidem and swallowed it down with a gulp of water from the tap. He felt better knowing that it would eventually work its magic but still it was not the sort of pill that would take the edge off or calm the nerves right away. For that, he looked elsewhere and quickly found himself in a staring contest with the liquor cabinet.

He had given up the sauce shortly after being let go from the paper. No one had said that his drinking had been a factor—they were far too polite and courteous to drag his personal demons into the light—but Frank had known. There had been a time when

Frank Neely was the kind of reporter who got his copy in before his deadlines and delivered them as crisp, white sheets unmarred by barely legible notes in the margins, crumple marks, and splashes of spilled bourbon. At one time, he had been the kind of employee who didn't over-drink at office parties and retch the contents of his stomach out into the *Times-Dispatch's* toilets. It was a consideration that he was younger then and lacked discretion. Good judgment and maturity might have caught up with him eventually, but then his adult bout with the nightmares began and the booze and partying did nicely at filling the haunted nights of fractured sleep.

So, it had continued. It had worked so well, in fact, that when Frank had decided to hop onto the proverbial wagon, in that moment of clarity he couldn't even remember the last time he'd had the nightmares. Surely, it must have been years. While Frank had been stumbling through his life in a bourbon fog, the nightmares that had once stalked him had receded into the dark somewhere, but he had failed to notice.

That afternoon, though, after the pharmacy, with the sight of Lane wandering by in the mirror still fresh in Frank's mind, he wanted a glass of bourbon more than anything. Just two fingers. Just enough to calm his nerves. The liquor cabinet in the dining room was empty, of course, and his battle with it was more a battle with himself, but in the end, he decided to indulge in an old vice. Just not *that* old vice.

After a quick search, he found a stale pack of Merits in the coat pocket of his tuxedo, which had only ever seen action at black-tie events that he'd attended professionally. He had said goodbye to the nicotine even before he'd sworn off booze, but since he seemed to be digging up old friends lately, why not? Certainly, it was the lesser of the two evils.

He spent the rest of the afternoon in the shade of the back porch, under the boughs of the towering elms and birches that his mother had planted so many years ago. They had grown to enormous size and provided an ideal canopy of shade and coolness to the backyard and garden on hot summer days. Sitting in the creaky, metallic porch rocker that he'd inherited along with everything else, he sat and smoked and sipped on cold soda. After a while, with the last cigarette smoked, he went inside, turned on the television and sat in front of it, intentionally letting his mind go blank but for the images and sounds playing across the screen.

When he awoke in the chair Friday morning, the television still on and flashing the local news, he was pleasantly surprised to find that he'd slept through the night without incident, without nightmare. As he poured his juice and stepped into his slippers to go out for the paper, he caught a glimpse of the empty orange pill bottle on the counter. In that moment the previous night's uneventful sleep was little more than cold comfort.

3

Frank spent the day in a state of worried anticipation about the night to come. He busied himself with correcting and massaging copy for the next column that he had written for *The Beat*. The work was completed in short order, and when he was done the day was moving into the lunch hour. He made himself a sandwich and washed it down with soda, gnawed on some potato chips and then filled the rest of the afternoon watching re-runs on TV and perusing old books plucked here and there from his bookshelves. When the late summer darkness finally settled on the world, he was lying in his bed, the reading lamp on and a stack of books a dozen or more high cluttering his nightstand. With an old book held aloft in his hands, he struggled to retain his focus as he thumbed through the pages of Truman Capote's *A Tree of Night*. His legs rubbed together restlessly beneath the cool sheets, and he turned this way and that, seeking but not finding a suitable position. His eyes were heavy and despite his nervous energy, the urge for sleep got the better of him at last and he drifted off into the darkness.

What came was not the nightmare that he had always known. He dreamt, instead, of waking in the middle of the night and walking downstairs to his kitchen with the aim of having a cold beer from the fridge. As he stepped down off the last stair, he sank into water that nearly came up to his hips. Undaunted, he sloshed through the cold, down the hallway to the kitchen. The swinging kitchen door, closed though it was, was wreathed by a brilliant glow that emanated from within. Had he left the kitchen light on? Apparently so. He pushed the door open and stepped in to find it bathed in a hot, white light. So bright was it that he drew his arm up over his eyes to shield them, and only then did the room come fully into view.

Lane stood in the center of the kitchen, the water lapping at his waist, his eyes white and staring down. It struck Frank that, just as he had seen this phantom in the pharmacy, his childhood friend did not appear blackened and burned as he might expect, but rather he seemed more like a drowned thing. His cold lips moved to form silent words, and as he watched, Frank was overcome with the feeling that he should be hearing, should be listening, should be learning something from this. As he followed Lane's gaze down to the water, he saw dark shapes floating there that he could not name. Looking longer, he saw that they were bodies, dark-skinned and mauled in innumerable ways.

When he looked back to Lane, he saw that every surface of the kitchen was aflame and the roar from the hungry fire suddenly filled his ears. He wanted to turn and flee but something had grazed his leg, and he looked down to find one of the cold dead things grasping at his leg. With a sharp breath, he drew back but lost his balance and felt himself falling. The fiery room blistered and disintegrated above and around him, but he fell backward all the same—to the water below and to what lay in wait there.

With a choking gasp, Frank woke in his bed to find a tangle of sheets wrapped around his legs and a sheen of cold sweat on his skin. Awake enough to remember the dream for the moment but powerless against the pull of sleep that tugged at him, he plunged back into the murky depths of his unconscious.

4

On Saturday morning he awoke from a shallow, fitful sleep. Flinging his legs over the bed to stand, he felt the restlessness and fatigue dry and hollow in his bones. His first steps toward the bathroom to relieve himself were weak and uncoordinated. The nightmare, although not the same, had returned with a vengeance, as if it knew he was trying to rid himself of it. Frank leaned forward over the toilet and his spent mind wondered how he would make it through another night. He wondered if he even could.

Frank showered and dressed, then went downstairs. His steps down the hallway toward the kitchen were slow and reluctant. Opening the door, he found his kitchen as it should be and pulled a tall glass of water from the tap. He crushed ice into the glass and sat out back on the porch, swallowing it in impatient gulps. He was so damned thirsty. He went back for a second glass and then another and another. Once his thirst had been slaked, he cast a glance over to the empty pack of cigarettes from the night before and found himself wishing there were more to smoke. He wondered what he should do with the rest of his day. It was a brief respite from the turmoil that surely awaited him with the onset of nighttime. He wondered, but he already had an idea forming in his head.

Time to visit old friends, he thought with dark amusement. *Time for a trip down the rabbit hole. Down memory lane.*

5

After he'd had a little something to eat, Frank fired up the Valiant and took a drive. The places he intended to visit were merely blocks away and certainly within walking distance, but there was something about being in the car that offered a comfortable separation—a safe space. In case he changed his mind. In case it became too much to bear. As he drove up Chatham Road and took a right, he saw the side of Lane's old house come into view. Making the turn, he found Palmyra Avenue surprisingly vacant of cars for a

Saturday morning. It was a beautiful day, though, with an unusual lack of humidity and many people had no doubt taken to the city's parks and avenues, thrilled to be outside.

He pulled the Valiant to a halt, cut the engine and stepped out. The old Histersen house seemed strangely untouched by the years that had passed. The English Tudor style home was well-maintained and the landscaping along the front was much the same as it had been decades ago, full of carefully placed azaleas and rhododendrons and hydrangeas bordered by monkey grass and a rainbow of perennial flowers. Mrs. Histersen would have been proud of the current owners had she been around to appreciate it, but she had passed away a few years ago in a nursing home, many years later than Lane's father.

Sheepishly, Frank walked toward the house with the good and proper intention of asking the owners if it would be alright if he visited the garden in the back. Admittedly, he hadn't put a great deal of forethought into this idea, and as he imagined trying to explain the circumstances of his request, he cringed at how very odd it sounded in his head. As he neared the steps that led to the porch and the dark-stained double doors of the front entrance, he spied white slivers of envelopes hanging from the mailbox. Below them lay a pile of mail that was wound tight in a rubber band. From this, Frank deduced that the owners, whoever they may be, were away and had forgotten to put a hold on their mail delivery.

Since there was no one to prevent him from visiting the garden, Frank wandered around the side of the house. Though the garden and patio had changed much, the edges were still rimmed by hollies and the droppings of oaks from neighboring yards. He'd been there the day that the Histersen family buried their dog, a gray colored and notoriously horny dachshund named Lothario. After they had buried him, Frank had joined Lane in the upstairs playroom and together they had wept for the loss of the animal in the way that young boys do, sitting apart from each other, never touching, but exchanging awkward, knowing looks and speaking of everything else in the world but the poor, departed Lo.

With the passing of the family dog, Lane's father had gifted his son a grave marker for Lothario that was inscribed by a professional. It was rock-solid, his father had assured him, and would last forever and would still be there when, one day, Lane took the house for his own. It was put in place at the edge of the garden where Lo was buried.

A day or so after the witch house had burned and Lane along with it, Frank had overheard his parents one night discussing that there was little left of anyone, including Lane, to be found among the wreckage and while the Histersens had salvaged some remains to bury, there was no way to be certain that they belonged to their son. "Ashes to ashes, dust to dust," Frank remembered his father offering as final, ironic comment.

Lane's funeral had been a very private, very religious affair and neither Frank nor his parents had been invited to attend. Unable to pay his last respects, one evening Frank slipped out of his window and stole off to the blackened lot where the witch house had stood. He had scooped a handful of ash from the rubble into a Royal Crown Cola bottle, then snuck into the back garden of Lane's house and dug with his bare hands into the dirt on the other side of Lothario's grave marker. He placed the bottle of ashes there and covered it with earth. He had done so without any final words—no eulogy of any kind—but with plenty of tears streaming down his face.

Today, Frank returned to offer the words he should have uttered twenty-eight years ago.

That morning, a plan had come together in Frank's mind. He had never been a superstitious man, not a believer in spirits or fortune tellers or curses. Even his adherence to his Christian upbringing had become more of a cultural characteristic than a spiritual devotion and manifested only in the few decorations he placed on the outside of his home during the month of December. That aside, he was so desperate to be rid of the nightmare that he'd reached the point where he was willing to consider the impossible as possible. Whether the nightmares and the vision in the pharmacy were the result of Lane's restless spirit visiting his old friend or were simply an involuntary unearthing of the unspoken things that weighed on Frank's heart and mind, it hardly seemed to matter. If he could make peace with Lane and with himself, perhaps this blight on his life would pass away for good.

Closure. That's what he sought.

Wouldn't Doctor Cyrus be proud, he thought to himself.

There were two parts to this undertaking, though. His words for Lane were the first. Contemplating the second part inspired within him far more dread.

In the shade of the old oaks and pines, Frank found the headstone just where it had been placed years before. Tangles of ivy sprawled across the ground in the area, mixed in with old leaves and sticks, but he approached the stone and knelt before it. The marker itself was covered in a green film and thick moss grew around the base but the inscription was still clear.

Lothario, Treasured Family Dog of Eleven Years.

Frank said a quiet greeting to Lo and then pulled a folded bit of paper from the pocket of his trousers. He moved around to the back of the marker and sat down in the brush, legs crossed, which proved to be more of an effort for his older self than he might have thought.

"I know I should have come by a long time ago," he said, looking around at the greenery and blooming flowers of the garden. "It's been…almost thirty years since…" he trailed off. "I never went to see where your folks buried you because I always figured it wasn't really you anyway. Far as I'm concerned, this spot right here is where you're buried. Even if your folks never knew it."

The song of a robin echoed in the trees somewhere and there was a bustle as a couple of squirrels went zipping by. It brought a smile to Frank's face and then he nodded his head, unfolded the paper in his hand and glanced down at it.

The piece of newspaper had yellowed with age, but its neatly shorn edges framed the article from the *Richmond Times-Dispatch* dated 1957. "This is an article from the paper. Came out the day after the fire. The day after you died."

A lump was forming in his throat and the muscles of his face began to tremble as he felt tears come to his eyes.

"There's a long first part to it about what happened, but we know all that, don't we? I just…for some reason, I thought it'd be right for me to read this here."

He cleared his throat and held the article out in front of him.

"In the end, thirty-seven lives were lost. This number included Lane Histersen, one of the two young boys local to Ginter Park, who observed the terrible things in the LaFontaine house. The deceased child had unintentionally caused the fire when, in the confusion of their discovery, a lit candle was knocked off a table near the drapes of a window. However, I am happy to report that his close friend, also from the neighborhood, managed to escape the blaze—amazingly enough—without a scratch."

Frank folded the clipping and slipped it back into his pocket, his own voice echoing the last few words over and over in his head.

Without a scratch.

Suddenly, Frank felt himself reach the breaking point and he burst into tears, his breaths shallow and mournful. He felt the pang of old guilt that had so long hollowed him, for the truth of that day, which he had never spoken, was one of lies and cowardice. Only Frank knew that he'd lied to the police that day in 1957. Only Frank knew that it had been his own candlestick and not Lane's that had fallen off the table, rolled across the floor and eventually set the curtains and the house ablaze. It had happened when they shoved each other as they wrestled around—just two boys being boys.

Is your grandma a witch?

Lane's joking words had set off the shoving match—just before they heard the muffled cries coming from the victims in the attic. Because of it, because of that singular moment, their world was forever changed. Moments later, in that musty hell of the attic, a deeply frightened Frankie turned to flee and left his best friend frozen to the attic floor in terror.

Left him to burn.

"I'm so sorry, Lane. So goddamned sorry," Frank lamented. "I should have told the truth. But we were so young, Lane, and I was afraid of what would happen if they knew."

He wiped his snotty nose with the length of his forearm.

"In that attic, I should have made sure you were with me. I should have, Lane. I just…I thought you were right behind me."

Frank hung his head, blubbering.

"Why didn't you follow me, Lane? Goddammit, why didn't you follow me?"

He wept for a while, speaking no more. Then, gathering himself and brushing the dirt from the seat and knees of his pants, he stood and walked away.

He stopped and turned back for a last look.

"I wish you were still here, Lane," he whispered. "Instead of haunting me."

Frank walked out of the cool shadows into the heat of the bright, midday sunlight. The vinyl seats of the Valiant were searing hot, having been baking in the sun in front of the Histersen house. Frank started the vehicle up, gave one final glance toward the home and breathed a sigh. It was a breath expelled from relief, from owning up. It was the breath of a man newly unburdened.

6

He had intended to steer the Valiant directly to his next destination, but as he wound slowly through the streets of Ginter Park, his sorrow drew him off the chosen path and toward another place that he'd not seen in quite some time.

The liquor bottles on display in the front window of the ABC store gleamed in the sunlight. Bottles upon bottles were stacked in display. Blue-tinted gin, earthy brown bourbons, green vessels full of Irish whiskey, and more. So much more. A rainbow of broken promises and hollow comfort shone with a truly magical aura.

He lingered there a moment, unsure, but deep down knowing exactly what he would do next.

He gripped the door handle and walked in.

Once inside, Frank was struck by the smell of the place—both sterile and chemically sweet. It was a strange mixture of aromas.

It had been three years since he had partaken. Three years of living a better life, a healthier life. But what had it brought him? Not an end to the nightmares, not a reprieve from the pain of guilt. Not the desire or ability to find and settle down with a woman. And not a single goddamn friend. Not one. At least back in his drinking days, the other barflies had passed for friends, if only in the shallowest sense. It had been a far less lonely existence, even if it had been something of a lie.

"Can I help you find something?" the lady behind the checkout counter asked.

"Bourbon," he croaked, his voice suddenly weak to the task. "I'd like a bottle of bourbon."

Now, sitting in the Valiant, Frank glanced at the brown paper bag that shrouded the bottle of aged Tennessee bourbon sitting on the seat next him and the pack of Merits he'd purchased from the cigarette machine. He wasn't sure if the drink he was about to take tonight was celebratory in honor of his cathartic moment at Lane's house or if it was borne of the uncertainty and the dread of what the night would bring. Perhaps it was both.

"One more stop to make," he said aloud, looking at the bottle in the seat. "Let's go for a ride."

7

The LaFontaine witch house had stood at the intersection of Wilmington Avenue and Brook Road across from Ginter Park Baptist Church. The church had been there since before the 1800s, a fact evidenced by its immaculate stonework and gothic architecture.

The LaFontaine house had been a fitting compliment, being of a similar style. Gray stone walls and rounded turrets had given it the look of a castle in the imaginations of the young and had no doubt contributed to the whisperings about the house among the children of the neighborhood.

Now it was nothing more than an empty lot. The remnants of its foundation stones might reveal themselves in the winter but were otherwise hidden—overgrown with tall grass and sticker bushes, dark-tinged milkweed and the occasional underdeveloped tree rife with kudzu vines. Even those trees had a gnarled look about them, though. As if the ground itself was poisoned and would not permit anything beautiful to grow there.

Since the idea had come to him that morning, Frank had done a great deal of thinking about the old house and about Beatrice LaFontaine. Since growing up, he had never regarded her as a witch—not in the sense of a cauldron-stirring, twisted thing of dark magic. He'd always seen her as inherently evil, certainly. However, in an effort to disabuse himself of that polarized view, he should try and sympathize with her. He should come to see her not as some faceless boogeyman but as a human being in her own right. If the gossip from back in those days was to be believed—and Frank had no reason to doubt it—then it was not so great a stretch to imagine how bent her mind might have become in the face of her inability to fulfill her heart's desire.

Women whose bodies prevented them from bearing children were outcasts in that time, and well known to sink into deep depression. Losing her husband so suddenly on top of all that...Frank could imagine how she might have been driven to very dark places in her mind. Then there was the possibility that a serious mental illness may have manifested as well, and once this was a consideration, he found it plausible that she could have gone utterly mad through no fault of her own. After all, only the deranged would do the things that she had done to her servants and their children.

Frank was not making an attempt to forgive her. He could never forgive her—for what she had done to those poor people. But then she had not been directly responsible for Lane's death either. That had been the blunder of two nosy boys who'd had no business prying into the dark corners of her life. And, certainly, Frank himself was more to blame for that than Madame LaFontaine. No, it was not forgiveness that Frank sought, but reconciliation.

Sitting there in front of the empty lot, he weighed the value of getting out and tromping around the grounds again. He realized then that even though the house was adjacent to a main road, all his life he had unconsciously taken any and every other way to get in and out of the neighborhood. As a grown man, he had not even so much as driven past the lot. Deciding that there was nothing to be gained from a closer visit, he was content to sit behind the wheel of the Valiant and observe it from afar. He envisioned in great detail the days and nights of loneliness she must have endured and could imagine better than most what it might have done to her. Was he so different? Now a forty-year-old spinster in his own right with the skeletons of guilt and failure and regret and addiction crowding his closet, he felt a bizarre kinship with this woman of distant memory. Through this new lens, understanding her came much more easily. The truth was that he now pitied her. He pitied her very much.

His regret was that he had not come to this way of thinking sooner. How much of his life had been consumed by the black feelings he had harbored for her? How much of his life might have been improved and more enjoyable if he had found the means to let go? In his years at the paper, he had rehashed the tragedy of 1957 in print no less than a dozen times. Some had been nothing more than references or mentions but others had been serious examinations of the event and the failure of the authorities to apprehend LaFontaine. His notebooks and scrapbooks full of every bit of information he had been able to gather about her seemed now to him as bars of a prison cell that he had erected to frame her as a villain. But in the end, Frank was the only prisoner, trapped in a cell of his own making.

He regretted that. And he also regretted not trying to discover more about her as a person, this woman called a witch who had very likely died lonesome, insane, and anonymous in some foreign country where she had fled prosecution for her crimes.

From within the weeds and brambles of the overgrown lot, a murder of crows took flight into the blue summer sky, headed elsewhere. Taking it as a cue, Frank did likewise and started the Valiant. He watched the empty lot fade from sight in his rear-view mirror.

8

At home that night, Frank prepared a chicken and vegetable casserole that was his mother's recipe and ate at the dining room table, the television blaring the local news in the next room. Paying little attention to it, his thoughts were instead trained on what he would do after dinner. Though he hoped for the best, in light of his new perspective on things, the nightmare had a foothold on his psyche that was decades deep and may not give up so easily. He feared the dreams to come, but for the first time in a long time, he knew that the sun would rise again and again. And one day, the nightmares would eventually pass. Nevertheless, after washing the dishes from supper, he twisted the cap open on the bottle of bourbon and poured a generous glass for himself as he prepared to take a very deliberate step off the wagon of sobriety.

The first and second glass he took outside along with a few cigarettes. He sat on the porch and occasionally roamed the garden, listening to the night sounds of crickets and locusts under the stars. His confidence and curiosity propelled by the alcohol, he took his third glass and more inside where he gathered together his scrapbooks and notebooks of material and placed them before him on the coffee table. He opened one of the first albums in the collection to its empty page, peeled back the plastic sheeting and slipped the folded piece of paper he had carried with him to Lane's house back into its place. Smoothing out the plastic film, he stared at the old newspaper article and the bold, black letters of the headline. He took another sip of the bourbon and felt it warm and mellow in his veins and decided to read the first bit of the clipping again, if only for posterity's sake, for the day would soon come when he would not visit these things again.

"LOCAL HORROR!" the headline read, followed by the reporter's name and the date from 1957. Below that was the substance of the article. Frank took another drink and skipped over the droll requisite introductory paragraph and onto the second. He knew its sensationalist prose so well that he could have recited it by heart like some bit of macabre poetry.

> "Upon entering the blaze of the topmost floor of the LaFontaine manor, the firemen were greeted with a sight equaled only by the utter disregard for humanity demonstrated hitherto by the Third Reich. An unspecified number of colored servants were caged, chained, and otherwise bound by various means and appeared to be the focus of several forms of inhuman torture and experimentation. Many were found to be expired upon discovery, though it was unclear if they had died from exposure to flame and smoke or from their ghastly injuries. A very few who clung to life were carried out by the firefighters and other heroic onlookers before the flames became too overpowering, though the conditions of these particular servants ran the gamut from unconscious to wild-eyed and babbling. Others were nearly catatonic. Within minutes, the inferno raged out of all control and the firemen had to abandon their search for the local boy and any remaining occupants. The depravity of what had been done to those rescued from the flames was immediately apparent. The mouths of many had been sewn shut. Other mutilations included such things as the removal of natural reproductive organs and their crude replacement with organs from the opposite sex. Some were found with their most private orifices sealed by stitching and

cauterization and subsequently left to die of starvation or to drown in their own waste. The jaws had been removed from some and the indispensable senses of the eyes and ears from others. One particular survivor, carried aloft by the firefighters and volunteers, had been carved free of all of his skin, leaving him raw and pink and appeared to one onlooker as 'more like a Christmas ham than a human being.'"

Frank took another drink of bourbon and tested himself. That last ghastly bit of the paragraph had always filled him with hatred and abhorrence for Madame LaFontaine and, though he found that it still struck him as horrifying, he felt his newfound understanding of her prevail.

He took another drink in celebration of that.

Frank continued through his scrapbooks, re-reading the old articles and his own pieces with a fresh perspective. And every triumphant read was rewarded with another sip or another finger or two of the bourbon.

Suddenly sleepy, his eyes beginning to close of their own accord, he slammed shut the scrapbook and leaned back against the soft cushions of the sofa. On the television, the title credits of the classic Technicolor film of Margaret Mitchell's "Gone with the Wind" began to play and he watched blankly as dramatized scenes of the Civil War, and the charm and intrigue of old, southern plantations filled the screen. Then, quicker than one might slap a tick, Frank was fast asleep.

*F*rank *is standing in the middle of a wide vein of cool water that moves swiftly around his knees on its way elsewhere. The moon is high and bright, and the sky is dark but for the gleaming of stars that number in the millions. Their light plays upon the rippled surface of the water, and he has a vague sense of tall trees close by. Staring directly ahead, he can make* out a dark patch that slowly forms a figure as if from the fabric of night itself and he finds himself moving toward it. As he edges ever closer, the moonlight illuminates the details of the figure and he sees that it is his old friend, Lane. He squints and then closes his eyes a few times, attempting to banish the illusion, for he knows it cannot be.

More than that, he wants it not to be.

The young boy is as he remembers him from so many years ago, his wiry stature unblemished by the toll of age. He is dressed in the very same clothes as the day he died, with a worn, leather baseball glove wrapped around his left hand.

Frank speaks to him as he approaches. He tells his friend that he'd just gone to see him. He asks the phantom if he heard anything that Frank said there in the backyard garden of his home. But the boy just smiles and raises his gloved hand, beckoning Frank to follow as he turns his back and strides up the waterway. As Frank pursues him through the water, he becomes suddenly aware of a fire on the horizon. It seems on a near shore and its source is difficult to understand, but it blazes in red and orange hues that fill the sky and overpower the serenity of the moonlight. Frank feels his foot misstep and catch on something, and he looks down at the dark water to see what he's sunken into. No shape is visible, though he senses something moving beneath. Beneath the water. When he looks up again, Lane is standing before him, suddenly close.

"Lane, I'm so sorry," Frank says, a desperate plea of desperation in his voice.

The boy smiles and nods but raises his hand again and points to the right, to a shore that is dark and close. A dead and twisted tree empty of foliage stands alone against the starry sky. It is alight with flames, and rogue embers from it drift away on the wind like fireflies. As Frank narrows his eyes, he sees that it is not only the tree that glows. Nearby, a larger thing that he cannot see is also burning.

Then he feels the touch of a cold hand on his arm. His eyes drift away from the flames and meet with those of his childhood friend. Within those deep pools of self, Frank senses many things. Forgiveness, yes. But he senses no rest, no peace.

Again, Frank begins to speak, feeling his lips creak open to utter more words of apology but the phantom turns his gaze toward the shore, pointing insistently toward the fiery glow.

He woke from the strange dream with the memory of it fresh in his mind. Sitting up on the sofa, he rubbed at the sleep crusting the corners of his eyes and wondered what time of night it was. His head was heavy and aching from the booze, so he stumbled into the kitchen and pulled a glass of water from the tap. He fumbled for the bottle of aspirin in the kitchen's medicine cabinet. After struggling for a moment with the cap, he plucked two of the white pills from the bottle and washed them down with a gulp of water as he glanced out of his kitchen window. To his surprise, the first rays of sunlight were setting the eastern sky aglow.

It was dawn and he'd slept through several hours of the evening without any memory of the usual nightmare, only the curious dream about Lane with his baseball glove, the water, and the fire. Still woozy and uncertain of the time, he glanced at the clock over the kitchen sink.

5:45. Frank smiled, a little sense of triumph mixing with his relief.

In the background, the television still blared, and he recognized it as the final moments of *Gone with the Wind*. Scarlett O'Hara was lying prostrate on the grand, red staircase lamenting the loss of Rhett Butler, who had just told her that, frankly, he didn't give a damn what became of her now that the war was at an end. In her moment of heartbroken despair, her mind was filled with the voices of her father, of Rhett, and of Ashley Wilkes. *"Land's the only thing that matters. It's the only thing that lasts. It's from this you get your strength; the red earth of Tara."*

Suddenly, something began scratching at the back of Frank's mind. Something about the film? No. Something about LaFontaine? Yes, that seemed right, but what connection was there between LaFontaine and the film? He could recall nothing.

The red earth of Tara.

Tara, Tara, rang the voices in Scarlett's mind, and they echoed in the mind of Frank Neely as well.

He knew the word not only from the novel and the film but also from history. It was the name of an ancient place—the hilltop fortress of the High Kings of Ireland. But that wasn't it either.

It scraped at his memory for a long while. Then one more word came to the fore and the connection was made. Not just Tara.

Tara Moore.

Had he been in a more sober state, he might have dismissed it as pure and meaningless coincidence. But the bourbon from the night before still raged with quiet fire in his veins and, as such, he found himself still indulgent of old obsessions.

Frank stole into the next room and sat on the sofa. He rifled through his scrapbook albums for some time, finding no mention of the name. Abandoning them, he turned to his spiral notebooks. There were four of them, each full of notes that encompassed all of his research into the fire of 1957 and his notes on Madame LaFontaine and her family along with disjointed personal thoughts and observations that certainly painted him as a man possessed. Surely, he had been that, and to see the old, drunken scrawls in the margins made him cringe. He slogged through them, though, wincing often and shifting in his seat uncomfortably. He continued his search until he found the entry he was looking for.

"As the search for her began," he read his note aloud, "Madame LaFontaine's only sibling, a sister named Tara, was interviewed by the authorities but cleared of any suspicion of involvement or knowledge of her sister's bizarre human experimentations. Reference: *Times-Dispatch* article from 1958 and mentioned again in a follow-up article from 1970."

Frank recalled the articles he'd cited and flipped through to find them. He found no article from 1958. He had read it, clearly, but the clipping had never made it into his scrapbooks. He chided himself for this blunder.

Opening another of the albums, he came upon the follow-up article from 1970. Written only one year prior to him being hired on at the *Times-Dispatch*, it was a small write-up done—predictably—as part of a Halloween section that included local spook stories and grotesque trivia. He skimmed the first few paragraphs covering other legends such as the haunted Capitol building and the iron dog of Hollywood Cemetery before he came to the Ginter Park Witch and read through the lines of print until he found it.

'The Madame Witch left behind a sister, Tara, wife of local hog farmer; the late Benjamin Statton. Currently, Mrs. Statton resides at her husband's old plantation home along the James, south of the city near Henricus. Authorities have confirmed that, unlike her sister, she is no witch.'

Even all these years later, Frank groaned at the reporter's pithy attempt at a punch line.

Though he had forgotten, further examination of his notes revealed that he had learned of Beatrice LaFontaine's sister, as his research had brought him across the police report of the interview from 1957 in which she had disavowed any knowledge of her sister's whereabouts. In fact, the report had mentioned they had been estranged from each other for quite some time and she'd had no contact with Beatrice for many years. Tara had fallen so far out of her sister's favor that she could not even be bothered to attend her wedding to Benjamin Statton several years before.

It was something that he had simply judged as immaterial before and because of that, Frank had never considered interviewing the sister. He had felt it was apparent from the police report at the time that she would have nothing of any substance to add to either the incident itself or the possible whereabouts of LaFontaine. It had made perfect sense back then and the reasoning was still sound even now, so why was this paltry bit of information now weighing on his mind? Besides, in all likelihood, the sister had passed away by now and she and her husband's farm along the James River had been usurped into some bloated neighborhood. He'd never find it even if he wanted to.

Then there came another spark of recollection that niggled at the back of his mind. Property had something to do with it. Something evocative of the fictitious plantation of Tara but something real. Real property. Real estate.

Frank walked back into the kitchen and sorted through the stack of mail until he came upon the colorful, twelve-page real estate circular. He'd flipped through it just the other day and had seen something—a thing to which his mind was now returning. Then, in full-color, pictorial glory, it was there on page nine; an advertisement for a new housing development.

'Tara's Bend.
Rural, old South charm and beauty just minutes from the city.
Come to the river. Come home.'

Below that, the advertisement promised expansive mansions and sidewalks, all secured within this new, gated community scheduled to be completed next summer. *Easy, riverfront living and opulence on eighty-five acres of untouched farmland along the James.*

The location of the development seemed to generally match the location of the family farm mentioned in the 1970 article and, he thought, the usage of the name Tara could not simply be coincidence. Perhaps the old plantation home was still standing after all and it had become the anchor for the development, as so many old farm homes were, now modernized and renovated to be included in the community as a club house. It was a possibility he felt inclined to investigate further.

That meant going there.

Frank poured himself another glass of water. He wondered what he could hope to find there and what his motivation was for wanting to look into it. After all, wasn't he moving toward putting all of this behind him now? Isn't that what he'd realized needed to happen? On the surface, this act of investigation seemed the opposite of that but as he pondered what drove this impulse, he recognized that it did fall in line with his new outlook. If there was anyone left who he could speak with, a niece or nephew maybe, someone with knowledge of the Stattons and LaFontaines, it might add to his viewing Beatrice Moore LaFontaine less as a monster who lived in his imagination and more as the deeply troubled soul she had actually been.

Even if nothing came of it, he reasoned, it would be nice to get out of the city for the afternoon and take a pleasant drive through unspoiled country.

9

Frank ambled along the roads in the Valiant, fields of tall grass bordering both sides of the wide gravel road. Up ahead, he saw the brightly lit and impressive sprawl of the development's model home sitting on a landscaped and manicured lot that was easily two acres and more. It seemed that getting the model built was of the utmost importance so that potential buyers could have something to visit and gawk at, walking through its furnished rooms and imagining their life as it might be inside of such a place. The vast amount of the development land itself was still wild with vegetation except for the gravel pathways and a few lots that were cleared to the bare earth in the early stages of site preparation. As he drove slowly, looking for the original plantation home, the late summer sky was darkening and dusk, with its subdued blue and amber coloring, was settling over the land. He rounded what he judged to be the farthest end of the development, preparing to continue on that path and back toward the main entrance but then brought the Valiant to a stop as he glimpsed a structure nestled behind a dense thicket of trees. From the road, it was nearly invisible.

It was a house. A very old, nondescript colonial style farmhouse that was a far cry from the grandeur that the word *plantation* brought to the minds of most who heard it.

Frank pulled the car off the road and into the grass, cutting the engine. Stepping out, he took a deep breath of the country air and detected the sweet smell of honeysuckle growing somewhere close by. He slammed the car door shut behind him and at the sound, a flurry of fireflies exploded into the air, taking flight and blending in against the first stars beginning to show through the haze of the early evening sky.

The house was as it had stood for many years, no doubt, and while it was not completely run-down, the years and the elements certainly had a grip on the place. The white paint on the siding peeled like detritus from a cancer that had long ago begun feasting on the house. A few of the windows, broken as they were, had been covered with plastic. Old copper gutters hung limp along the eaves, pulled away by kudzu and other vines that had grown unchecked, and the roof was covered in spots with thick moss and the crud of years of neglect.

Even so, lights burned sparsely inside. Frank tramped down the overgrown driveway toward the house. The steps that led up onto the front porch had been allowed to rot, so he took some care in ascending them. It was late in the evening to be calling on anyone unexpectedly, but he had come this far and there was no turning back. Standing before the faded, peeling green paint of the front door, he patted his pocket to make sure his pen and notepad were there and then he rapped on the door. He had decided that, in order to inspire as much cooperation as possible, he would flash his old press credentials and introduce himself as a reporter. A moment or two passed before the knock at the door was finally answered.

An old woman of smallish but sturdy stature opened the door and eyed him curiously.

"Can I help you?" she creaked, her voice lending an air of frailty to her.

"Yes, ma'am, I'm a reporter for the *Times-Dispatch* and I was hoping I could ask you some questions about the previous owner of this house."

She wrinkled her brow and tilted her head.

"Previous? Ain't no previous owner. You must have the wrong house."

He considered it for a moment as she began to close the door.

"Ma'am," he interrupted. "I was hoping to find someone who knew Missus Tara Statton."

"Miss," she replied.

"Come again?"

"*Miss Tara Statton*, son. That's my name. Haven't been a Missus for many years now."

It seemed incredible that LaFontaine's sister was still alive, still living out here in the boonies and doing so all on her own. Momentarily flabbergasted by this unexpected turn of good fortune, he held up his hands.

"Oh, ma'am, I apologize. I thought for sure you had moved away from here by now."

She snorted.

"Young man, old folks like me don't just up and move away."

He nodded his understanding.

"What'd you say your name was?" she asked, cocking her head and squinting her eyes at him.

"Frank Neely, ma'am, From the *Times-Dispatch*."

"And what's this about?"

"It's about your sister. It's about Ms. LaFontaine."

"Been manys a year since anyone come 'round asking about her."

He smiled and nodded but didn't back off. "Well, there's always interest in a good story."

She regarded him silently for a moment. Then, perhaps seeing he wouldn't be put off, she opened the door wide and shuffled aside.

"Might as well come on in then. I'll tell you whatever I can."

The inside of the home was in much better shape than the outside, even though patches of wallpaper peeled at the edges here and there and a modest coating of dust sat uniformly on most everything. The furniture looked to be old and of fine making. Pictures and other heirloom objects adorned the walls, tables, and shelves of every room.

She ushered him into the parlor where he took a seat on a wide armchair, removing his pen and notepad from his pocket. She sat down in a small, claw-footed chair across from him.

"So, what is it that you want to know that ain't already been told?"

He wrung his hands a little as he considered how to answer the question.

"Actually, it's mostly a historical piece. Every so often an editor at the paper gets a bee in his bonnet to drudge up a familiar story and puts it out again for the sake of public interest. Local interest, I suppose. But if there's anything more to learn, well, I wouldn't mind hearing that, too."

"All right," she nodded.

"Your home is lovely," he remarked. "It was built by your late husband's family?"

She nodded.

"Benjamin died back in sixty-five. Left it to me and I done the best I could with it but it's a lot for an old woman to keep up with."

"Is the home going to be part of the new housing development?"

"Nosir. The construction company offered me plenty of money. Wanted to buy me off and send me packing. I sold them the land, sure, and for a pretty penny, too. All of it but ten acres around my house here."

She glanced around, a sour look on her face.

"Don't suppose I know what to do with all that money, though. Can't really polish an old place like this."

Frank nodded and shifted in his seat.

"Still, it must be nice to have the development named after you?"

"Came up with that one on their own, I'm afraid. Tara's *Bend*? Reckon it's on account of the river curves quite a bit and gets narrow and shallow right behind the house here."

"Of course," Frank said and looked back down at his notepad. "Be alright if we discuss your sister now?"

"I suppose that'd be fine."

He leaned forward.

"Her home in Richmond burned in the summer of fifty-seven. That's when they discovered the victims."

"I remember it very well, Mr. Neely."

"Knowing what happened to the victims, Ms. Statton, did you ever see anything in your sister…any indication that she would have been capable of such things?"

"Nosir," she replied, "Beatrice was always a gentle, demure sort. I was what you might call a tom-boy. Beatrice? She was all lace and curtsies."

"Lace and curtsies," he repeated, and scribbled notes on his pad.

"So, you were surprised to find out about the things she'd done?"

"Surprised is one way to put it. Shocked me to the core, that news did. Didn't believe it at first. I never imagined it was possible."

As he watched her speak, he could tell the interview was upsetting her. She looked down at the floor often and her fingers sought each other out, fidgeting.

"Of course," he replied, scribbling. "I can only imagine."

She splayed her hands out over her knees and let go a sigh.

"You care a drink, Mister Neely?"

"Yes," he said, looking up from his notes. "That'd be great."

She stood and went over to a set of glasses and a decanter, removed two from the tray and busied herself with pouring as Frank leaned over his notepad.

She set Frank's glass on the table and returned to her chair. She turned hers up and drained it, refilled it, and then brought the other glass to him. He nodded his thanks and took a polite sip. Old, oaky, brilliant flavor.

"Were you and your sister very close growing up?"

"Not especially." She shook her head. "Being so at odds and all, we tended to run in different circles. Never had a great deal in common."

He nodded, scribbled.

"Forgive my bluntness on this next question, Ms. Statton," he offered, "but your sister was a barren woman, is that correct? Unable to have children?"

"That is…" she sighed, drifting off a moment. "That is correct, yes."

"Any history of mental illness in your family?"

Tara Statton set her glass down on the table and leaned toward him. "Just what are you suggesting, boy?"

Frank had to back-pedal a little. He hoped he could salvage the moment and that this would not be the end of their chat.

"Well, I always wondered if she might not have suffered some kind of a psychosis that was made worse by the heartbreak of being barren. And later by losing her husband so prematurely."

"Husbands die, Mr. Neely."

He nodded.

"I understand. It's just that I was hoping to be able to paint her in a more sympathetic light. Instead of…well, you know…"

"The Ginter Park Witch?"

Frank nodded.

"Well, I can't tell you much about the why of it all. Far as I know, the person she became couldn't have been more different than the young girl I once knew."

Frank snapped his notepad closed and leaned in.

"What do you think it was, Ms. Statton? What do you think it was that drove her mad?"

The old woman considered the question, staring off into a corner of the room, off into nothing.

"Mad?" she whispered. "Was she mad?"

It was as if a stray, reflective thought had slipped her mind and crossed her lips unintended.

Frank was digging a little deeper than she was comfortable with, he could tell, and he felt sorry for her. But still he had the need to know as much as she could divulge.

"Pardon?" he replied.

She turned to look at him and for the first time during his visit, she managed a warm smile.

"Would you care for some tea, Mr. Neely?" she said as she stood and moved toward the hallway.

The old woman's whiskey must have been some powerful stuff. After just that sip, he felt a bit woozy. Tea sounded good.

"Thank you. Yes, that'd be nice."

She shuffled off down the hall to the kitchen. Frank scrawled a few more notes in his pad and closed it.

He sat back and took another sip of the whiskey. He could hear her busying herself with the teapot in the kitchen, and so he rose to wander the parlor and inspect the many furnishings and decorations.

Frank feared that the interview would not last much longer. It must be difficult for her to dredge up such old memories of her sibling. After they took tea, he figured he had maybe another ten minutes of her time. He wandered the parlor. Adorning the walls were paintings and finely crafted sculptures set upon shelves. Pictures of Tara and her sister posed together though even the old photos seemed to let on that there was little warmth between the two of them. He also noted that they seemed remarkably similar to each other in appearance.

"You certainly favored each other," he remarked. "Were you and Beatrice twins?"

"That we were," she called from the kitchen.

As he glanced over some of the other photographs, he considered how different Tara seemed to be from her sister. Two sides of the same coin. One rough, the other smooth.

"It's sad that you never heard from her again. I imagine she lived a very lonely life after the fire...when she ran away from it all."

It was a shameless attempt to probe further into her life and elicit a response, he knew. For a moment, as he heard her in the kitchen, cabinets opening and closing and the clinking of ceramic cups, he wondered if it would draw a response of any kind.

"Loneliness is for folks uncomfortable in their own skin, Mister Neely," she offered in reply. "Sisters are funny things, you know. You despise so much about them, but before you know it, you wake up one day and find that you've become the other. My sister? It's just as well she's dead and gone. I didn't have much use for her anyhow."

Frank nodded, though it was sad to hear and seemed an unduly caustic remark. Being an only child, though, he'd never known much about sibling rivalry. And with no wife and no close family, there would be no one to mourn him when he passed. So, he understood little about such things.

As he surveyed the room, something caught his attention. It was a photograph of an old man reclined on an antique chair, eyes whitened and absent of life. A picture that he had seen many years before, though it was faded and the details hard to discern. The last time he had looked upon it, he had been in the dark hallway of Madame LaFontaine's upstairs. It unnerved him to see it now, but that was not what stole his breath. The photograph had been slipped into a frame slightly larger than was necessary, and upon closer inspection, the contours of it revealed more. Edges thin and jagged, wilted and blackened as if having been chewed by heat and flames.

He blinked and shook his head, scarcely able to believe what he was seeing. It was not a copy but the very same photograph. If they had been so estranged, why would Tara have bothered to retrieve anything at all from the rubble of the burned LaFontaine home, especially when they had harbored such ill will for each other?

The teapot in the kitchen whistled with a slow boil.

It came to him in a flood; the truth that had eluded both the police and journalists for nearly thirty years.

He glanced around the parlor at all the fine antique furniture and then strode into the next room, the family room, and found it decorated just as ornately. It bore not the touch of a woman who was hardscrabble, but rather one with an appreciation for the finer things. Someone who was *all lace and curtsies.*

Then he recalled something else that she had said just a moment ago about her sister.

"Just as well she's dead and gone."

It had been assumed by all—especially Frank—that Beatrice was long in the grave by now.

His eyes narrowed and he looked toward the kitchen.

"Ms. Statton?" he called out for her, though there came no reply.

Of the two twin sisters, one was indeed dead and gone, but it was not Beatrice.

The teapot continued to scream.

10

Frank strode down the hallway into the kitchen and out the screen door at the back of the house. The old, rusted spring attached to the door was still strong, and as he stepped through, the wooden frame cracked as it slammed shut. It was full dark now and the moon was bright in the sky. Its pale glow splintered into a thousand shards of light as it fell onto the rippling surface of the river lapping at the edge of the yard.

She stood with her back to him, staring out at the water. He wondered for a moment if he could be mistaken, if his obsession had finally gotten the better of him, but then he noticed the smell.

It was the smell of death, rot and decay. Of chemical preservatives like formaldehyde.

He glanced around the backyard to see animal cages stacked three and four high all along the outer wall of the house. Some were made of chicken wire and others of wood, many with the flayed and decomposing remains of vivisected creatures lying inside. Possums, dogs, cats, squirrels, raccoons, and others too mutilated to tell. Forced to accept animals as her subjects, it seemed that the Madame had continued her dark, strange work after coming to this place. Seeing this macabre menagerie removed any doubt from Frank's mind.

"You lied to me," he called to her.

It was a moment before she responded.

"I ain't the only one's been lying," she said.

"Reporter," she scoffed. "You ain't been a reporter for many years now."

He was genuinely surprised that she knew this about him, that she knew of him at all.

She turned to face him.

"See, you ain't the only one who does their research. I used to read all your articles, boy. 1957. Two little snot-nosed boys went poking 'round where they had no business and one of them got hisself killed; burned to death. Him and a gaggle of worthless darkies."

Frank couldn't move, couldn't summon the words to form a reply.

"Couldn't let go of it, though, could you? Couldn't move on or let me move on either. And what's it gotten you, Frankie? Nightmares, maybe? Got you fired, that's certain. They tired of your fixation, didn't they?"

He shifted, her words needling under his skin, stinging with truth.

"They tired of it because it's the past and *nobody* wants to dig up the past," she snorted. "Nobody except you."

His mind reeled. All these years, all those nightmares, and here she was. A slight thing shriveled by age and yet still the monster.

"Oh, I suppose I always knew this day would come." She continued, stepping toward him. "You must be mighty proud of yourself, to be so smart. To finally know the end to your newspaper story."

Her dark eyes were trained on him as she circled him slowly. It was then that he noticed her careful and deliberate steps. She was not as old and feeble as she had appeared. That had been another ruse. Every move, every breath of her life was a calculated deception. Under her gaze, Frank felt shrunken and small, like a child.

"That what you come here for? Little Frankie, his hour come 'round at last, come to write the end of his scary little story?"

He glanced about, nervous, his eyes falling over the yard and the shadows of the evening. Next to a small stand of dogwoods, he noticed a stone that stood upright out of the earth. Benjamin Statton's headstone.

"You came here, didn't you?" he managed. "After they found you out. After the fire."

She nodded.

"And she let you stay, your sister?"

A devil's grin crept across her sharp, weathered face.

"Tara never *let* me anything," she spat. "I wanted something from her, I took it. Always been that way. Ever since we was kids."

He looked long at the gravestone, the revelation settling over him. One stone, two burials.

"So, you took her identity," he remarked. "You became the other. You became the person you despised."

She sneered, quite pleased with the notion.

"Did you kill them both?" he asked. "Or did you let her live?"

"Like I said, Frankie, I never had much use for her anyhow and certainly not for her no-count farmer husband."

He shook his head.

"She lived for a while, though. She did. I allowed it so that I could take my time and break her down."

She glanced over to a work bench and Frank's eyes followed. Atop the bench sat an array of metal tools, sharp and bladed and wicked, whose purpose was appallingly clear.

When their eyes met again, he noticed that she carried something in her right hand but in the shadows, he couldn't make it out. As she brought it up, he first saw the polished wood of the stock and then the black length of the barrel as she wrapped her claws around the shotgun.

She trained it on him.

"What to do, what to do, little Frankie?" she taunted, circling him.

Frank imagined his last moment. Madame LaFontaine behind him, pulling the trigger and blowing his back out. His spine would snap, and his shredded entrails would cover the ground before him.

The red earth of Tara.

"It's too bad, Frankie. You had one more newspaper article in you. Would have wrapped it up nice and neat."

In trying to do right, trying to be the better man, Frank realized that he had been so very wrong. He'd been wrong to pity her, to see her as an unwell human being; to see her in shades of gray when all that she was and all that she had ever been was black and cold and absolutely evil. It was ruinous to pity such monsters.

Then she crossed back into view and stopped before him. Her grip on the weapon tightened and he saw her slide her left leg out behind her to steady herself against the kickback. Knowing it was coming, Frank did not feel terror, only numbness and sadness for the life that she had denied him and that he had, through his obsession, denied himself.

"Gonna make an awful mess of you, boy," she said and racked a shell into the chamber.

His lips formed a bitter, skewed smile.

"You did that a long time ago."

Click, he heard.

Click. Click.

When she looked up from the jammed shotgun, Frank saw something in her eyes that she was not practiced at feeling. It looked like worry. It looked like fear.

Click, click.

Frank didn't wait for another attempt. He stepped forward, grabbed the barrel of the weapon and ripped it from her grasp. At this, she stiffened with pride and resolve even in the face of her failure.

Beatrice looked down at the shotgun in his hand, cursed it and cut her eyes at him.

"Just dumb luck, that's all. Reckon now you'll get to write that ending to your newspaper story, Frankie."

She spread her hands wide over her head and looked up as if reading something grand that was written in the stars.

"Little Frankie Captures the Big, Bad Witch."

It would make a tidy bookend to this horror which had run like a river of fear through his life. There was no denying that. It would mean public vindication for him and perhaps a brand-new start. Frank glanced at the dead things in the cages all around him, stacked among the containers of formaldehyde and ether and an assortment of other chemicals.

He pumped the shotgun, ejecting the shells and then tossed it aside.

"Not the ending that I have in mind," he said, his hands balling into fists at his sides. "Not for you."

The cool river water was splashing around his legs before he'd even had time to formulate a plan. His right arm was locked around Beatrice LaFontaine and he was dragging her from the yard through the brambles and cattails along the bank and out into the shallows of the river. She struggled against him, though she was no match. She screamed into the night, cried out in distress, but there wasn't a soul to hear or help her. She had sought out the isolation of this place, murdered and stolen the life of her only sister. That she was utterly alone in this moment was a thing of her own making.

Frank stopped when he could feel the water at his waist.

The witch continued to flail in his grasp. Frank stumbled and for a moment it seemed that she might break free. He redirected his momentum, though, and heaved her upward. She slipped his hold and went flying backward. The witch crashed against a large rock that protruded from the riverbed, the brittle bones of her spine splintering under her skin and musculature.

As the nerves were severed, she could no longer feel her extremities. Not the chill nor the wetness of the water.

But she could feel the sinking.

For a brief moment, she was a prisoner in her own body, unable to cry out, unable to move. Her mouth skewed and agape, she began sliding down the surface of the rock slowly. Frank sloshed through the river toward her, watching as she gasped for breath. After a moment, her head slipped below the surface. He brought his leg up and leaned into it as he pressed his foot against her chest. And down she went. Down, down into the darkness waiting.

Bubbles rose and burst on the water's surface. Frank stood there for a minute or two, her pale and ghostly form suspended against the black mud of the riverbed, all warmth having been washed from her pallor.

She was silent and unmoving beneath him.

As a torrent of emotions from revulsion to elation washed over him, Frank began to weep, though his tears were not for the old witch now dispatched to what he could only hope would be an eternity of endless torment. No, he wept for the loss of his boyhood friend and for the lives of all those who had been swallowed by LaFontaine's malevolence.

Tearing his eyes away from the dead woman, he looked up at the starry sky through eyes filled with bitter tears.

The moon above was beautiful, shattering on the river and casting a pale glow over the land. Perched on the bank near the house, he saw an old, decrepit tree. It had long been dead and naked of the green life that was so abundant all around him in the thickness of the Southern night. He recognized the scene, though. Knew it all from a dream and knew what must come next. He reached down into the water and gripped the soggy length of the witch's hair. Dragging her limp form behind him, he made his way toward the shore, toward the house.

Frank unceremoniously dropped her body in the center of the foyer. One by one, he fetched the containers of chemicals from out back of the house. He emptied the entirety of one over her body. The rest he splashed about the house, under curtains and onto the furniture and all of her fine things that would soon be nothing more than ash. He saved the last of it for the skeletal old tree that leaned longingly toward the river. Once the tree was alight and roaring in the darkness, he set flame to the parlor and watched for a moment as it slipped through the house like a serpent of fire.

Stepping off the front porch, he felt a rebirth well up from within, as if some lost part of his soul had returned to him at the very moment of her last, watery breath.

Pulling away in the Valiant, Frankie almost smiled.

He left the old witch behind to be consumed in the flames, just as he had been consumed on a youthful summer's day so long ago.

ADRIFT ON THE SEA OF TREES

Snow melt filled the streams and creeks that crisscrossed the mountainside. So loud was the sound of moving water that it very nearly muted everything else, even the screaming.

He hurried through the Aoikigahara forest, frantic and without any clear sense of direction—and he was feeling it with every wayward step. He was a city boy. *From Baltimore for Chrissakes.* He had no business traversing the slopes of Mount Fuji in the middle of the night, half a world away from everything familiar.

To his right, he could make out a gentle glow and wafting through the air was the smell of smoldering embers. He sloshed through a swiftly running brook and found himself right back at their campsite.

Her screams seemed even more distant now.

"Hoshi!" he called out. "Where are you?"

His voice echoed through the cavernous forest, then the screaming stopped. The woods went silent. He drew a labored breath, quick and whistling through his teeth. He shouldn't have done that—shouldn't have screamed for her. In that fleeting moment of quiet, he sensed something in the dark woods raising its head, taking notice of him.

Then she began again, her shrill cries ringing off the thousands upon thousands of tall trees and thick canopy that blacked out the moon and stars above. He ducked into the tent and rifled through their belongings. He found the small flashlight in Hoshi's pack, clicked it on. The blue walls of the tent fluttered in the night breeze. Before him lay their sleeping bag, cold and empty. The scent of her still upon it.

They'd come to Motosu, where his wife had been born and lived for a time before coming to the States. She had wanted him to see the beauty of her home for himself. The miracles of springtime that the country had to offer. In the morning, they would travel back down the slope to a park where they would take in the scenery—fields and lakeshore transformed into cotton candy by the Shibazakura, or pink moss, that flourished this time of year. This they would do after a night together in the silent woods, drinking wine—well, he would anyway—and nuzzling by the fire until their heavy eyes ushered them inside the tent where they would slumber together inside the one sleeping bag they had brought with them.

But the forest, dark and looming thing that it was, had other plans.

Hoshi had gotten up in the middle of the night—to answer nature's call, he imagined—and never returned. Her screams had woken him, though, and a few frantic moments later, he had found her charm bracelet there in the dirt not far from the tent, the chain snapped at its weakest link.

He tore his eyes from the sight of the empty sleeping bag and, with his reverie now broken, he was off again, charging into the night, desperate to find her.

The thin beam of light bounced around as he ran, illuminating stark, green foliage among the towering black trees. He crashed through a patch of bamboo and found himself teetering on the edge of a deep gorge that yawned below him.

But Hoshi's screams had stopped. He couldn't say when exactly, for he had been adrift in the forest for what seemed an eternity, his hammering heart and racing thoughts the only sounds now filling his ears. A wind rose up and whispered through the trees; a hushed sound like the voices of those who called this forest by a different name. *The Suicide Woods.* A place many stepped into and never returned. Shamed by some failed endeavor or another and bound by a fanatical code of honor, over the ages, many Japanese had come here to meet with an honorable death by their own hand.

For him, the forest's striking beauty was made hollow by these deaths. The earth was damp with loss, with tears of the unrequited. And now he was one of them. He collapsed at the edge of the gorge and wept.

Something snapped close by. A twig or a reed bent to the breaking point. Then another and another until it became a barrage of sound. Something was moving through the stand of bamboo toward him. He shined the light ahead and waited.

When Hoshi's face appeared between the reeds, he swooned. She came forward, a tender and loving look in her eyes. Eyes bulging and tinged with red, broken blood vessels. Dressed in the Ravens jersey she'd worn to bed, her skin was as pale as ash in the moonlight. About her neck dangled a dark shape that hung limp between her breasts. A rope, old and moss-covered, the looped end tight around her throat. It slipped around her hip and the other end of it stretched back through the reeds.

"No," he sobbed. "No, Hoshi."

She lifted a cold finger and stroked his cheek. Had she brought him out to the Sea of Trees to say goodbye and take her own life? But they'd had plans for the next day. *Plans for the next twenty years.* He shook his head. No, she wouldn't do that, *couldn't do that.* There was too much to live for. Even through the drape of the jersey that she wore, he could see the modest bulge at her belly.

"Come, husband," she entreated, squatting next to him.

She plucked the noose from her neck and slipped it over his head. "You're not—" he sobbed through hot tears, "You're not Hoshi." She smiled. *It smiled.*

"No," the dead thing said in its native tongue. "But you will join her all the same."

Behind it, in the bamboo, he glimpsed others standing witness. Empty eyes stared out at him, all of them long dead from their wounds. Opened flesh, broken necks, gunshot craters, needle marks. They were the lost ones who had come to the forest to die and had never been found, swallowed up by time and the trees.

The flashlight cast slim shadows over pale, necrotic faces.

The dead thing took up the rope's slack and yanked it taut. It took his hand and brought him to his feet, standing with his back to the gorge. It planted a kiss upon his lips and shoved. As he fell backward into the chasm of eternal night, he understood.

Some entered the Sea of Trees to die with honor. *Seppuku*, it was called. But how many—like Hoshi and himself—how many had met their ends at the hands of Aokigahara's unquiet dead?

Stars wheeled overhead. He closed his eyes.

This forest was a place of sorrow, and they should never have come here.

There was a crack as the rope pulled tight. Somewhere in the lonely gorge, a chorus of owls wailed a death song to the abiding mountain.

THE BLACKEST RITE

1
The Catacombs

The old, dark walls of the catacombs beneath Machecoul had been the lone witness to the shrill and desperate screams of the young maid. When Gilles de Rais slid the bar from the door into the ritual chamber, he was dismayed to find that the young girl had chewed through her gag sometime during the night. Following behind him, his eager servant Henriet began to stammer his apologies, fearing that the wrath of Lord Rais was sure to come, but Gilles held up his hand to silence the man. His gaze was fixed on the girl. Glaring at her, he strode into the room and drew back his hand. Instead of recoiling, the determined little thing screwed her face up in defiance and let go a cry that was filled with not only terror but anger and rage at her captor. It ceased, however, as he put his hand across her pretty face and she went sprawling on the floor, the chains that bound her hands and feet rattling against the damp stone.

He smiled at her.

"You will make a fine offering, indeed," he said. "With such spirit as you have, your body will make a glorious vessel for her return."

Gilles set about securing a tougher gag of leather across the young woman's mouth. As she writhed on the floor, her peasant's dress slipped high above her knee, and he felt the red lust rise within him again. A pity she was a maid, he thought, and not one of the young men he had enjoyed so many times before. Callow, tender lads of fair hair and willowy flesh whose screams he had found more intoxicating than the best of wine in France.

"What shall I do?" Henriet asked, breaking Gilles from his fond reminiscence.

"You've done well, Henriet," he replied. "She is nearly as stirring to the eye as the Maid of Lorraine herself. Watch over her. I go to fetch the sorcerer."

The servant bowed his head, glad in the knowledge that he had pleased his lord.

Gilles' gaze drifted to the south wall of the chamber, where lay his greatest possession. There was a high altar that was hewn from solid oak and draped in fine, black silk. At the center sat a pile of ash and charred wood, a few blackened pieces of bone, and a smoke-darkened skull. They were all that remained of Joan d'Arc, the Maid of Lorraine, his greatest commander, and the savior of France. Gilles had risked his own life to take them from the smoldering pile years ago when the bishop had burned her alive. With the help of a few trusted soldiers, he had gotten to the remains before the hounds of England could toss what was left of her into the waters of the Seine.

At the time, his loyalty and love for her had driven him, though it would not have been for nothing. With the sorcerer's help, he would see her returned to her countrymen, given a new life as a thing of unimaginable power that would be bound to his will. Together, they would lay waste to the royal fools who had long denied Gilles the power and riches he deserved and France the majesty of its destiny. A destiny that only Joan had understood, having seen it in the visions granted her by angels.

He glanced for a moment at the many shelves of brass and copper urns which held the fruits of his exploits over the past few years;

hundreds of them, each one filled with the blood of those he had defiled and slaughtered, keeping only the blood and their most beautiful assets. A hand, a foot, a neck, a head, an ear. He could scarcely remember, for they had all been such beautiful lambs. A wolfish smile crept across his face, and the dark-haired nobleman swept out of the chamber and down the long passageway that led to the surface.

Sliding the slab aside, Gilles emerged into the crumbled remains of a stable and into the cool and fragrant evening. He nudged the stone back into place and walked through the wood toward the nearby road. In the faint moonlight, he could see his coach sitting idly, the horses snorting and scraping at the earth in their boredom.

"Poitou!" he hissed into the darkness, and the sleeping coachman startled awake.

"Oui, my Lord?"

"Let us go to the inn."

His servant took up the reins as Lord Rais climbed into the cabin. "For the night, sir?"

"No, I go to retrieve the sorcerer, Francois. He waits for me. There is much to be done, so hurry those beasts!"

The reins snapped and the whip cracked and in a flurry of dust and thundering hooves, the coach went tearing through the countryside in the dark, racing the moon.

2
The Sorcerer

Gilles de Rais was a hunted man, and this knowledge weighed upon him like a satchel of stones hanging about his neck. The duke's men had seized his castle in Tiffauges, from which Gilles had fled none too soon. Sitting outside the inn, he waited for Poitou to return with the sorcerer and sought to rid himself for those few moments of the melancholy that had come over him, thinking instead of grander times when he had served with honor both his beloved country and his commander, The Maid of Lorraine. These days, he was named a foul thing, a demon, a devil. It saddened him, for as much as any nobleman, he had loved and been loyal to the church for many years, despite the hungers and perversions that stirred within him.

Without use as a soldier and commander of men, he was thrust into a life of quasi-nobility and boredom. After Joan d'Arc's execution and despite his appointment as Marshal of France, he quickly tired of the court and its political intrigue. Taking leave of such things, he began to indulge his basest lusts and desires, for which no price was too great. It was not long before he had found himself unable to honor his debts and a mere stone's throw away from being penniless. In an effort to gain back his fortune, he had put a great deal of trust and hope and coin into the promises of a conjurer and alchemist, who proved to be nothing more than an inept disappointment. Having been taken for what little money he had left, Gilles sent the man away and began his search anew. That was when he met Francois.

He watched from the plush confines of the coach as the sorcerer scurried out of the inn and climbed into the cab. In a moment, Poitou was back in his seat and had roused the horses to go clomping away and down the narrow streets of the village.

"Much wine tonight?" he asked the long-faced magician, who leaned back into the thick cushion of the seat and smiled a wordless, glassy-eyed reply.

Gilles reached out and snatched the half empty bottle from the sorcerer's grasp and took a heroic pull from it.

"Well, sober yourself, man. We've much to do. It is time. Henriet has brought us the most splendid offering of a maid you can imagine."

"Is that so?"

Gilles nodded his head. "Such purity, you can smell it on her."

Settling back, Lord Rais took a few more sips from the bottle and watched the night roll by.

"And what spirit this one has!"

There had been those who warned Gilles against taking Francois into his confidence. They called him a charlatan, a fakir, but he knew better than those fools. Francois had instructed Gilles in the ways of high magic and the black arts. He had witnessed the calling forth of demons from the netherworld and had tasted of the power and prosperity they could grant a willing supplicant.

Then there was, of course, *the book.*

On a rainy winter night, Francois had rapped upon the door at Tiffauges and, with much excitement, had unveiled the book for Gilles. It had been a find rarer and more prized than anything the nobleman could have ever hoped for. *Les Livre Rouge de la Ruine— The Red Book of Ruin.* It had come to be called this by men, for the book itself bore no actual title. It was a tome so old and vile that not even Francois himself could guess its origin. Within its pages, the sorcerer explained, were summonings and appeals to denizens and fiends far older than even the Church had ever known. Dark things from an ancient time with names so strange as to be nearly unutterable by the human tongue, save for those learned enough. Francois was just such an adept.

The remainder of the journey was made in silence, each man lost in his own thoughts. As they rounded a bend in the road, the dark and sprawling shape of Machecoul castle could be seen in the distance.

"I understand that your brother has taken your childhood home for himself," Francois remarked.

Gilles nodded.

"You are fast becoming a man without a country, no?"

"René is a fool," Gilles replied. "He is content to lick the boots of his masters so long as they feed him scraps from the royal table."

"Then, if I may ask, why do we go there now?"

Just then, the coach turned sharply off the main road onto a path leading into the thick of the wood.

"We do not. I would not dare encroach upon my brother's newfound fortune," he replied with a bitter smirk, "We go to the catacombs. To the secret bowels of Machecoul."

Moments later, having hidden the horses and coach in the wood far from the road, the three men silently moved beneath the towering trees of the forest.

"My grandfather, Jean de Craon—a great man, as you know," Gilles began.

"Of course, my Lord," Francois nodded.

"Those were the troubled days, when nobles sought to control other nobles. Before the Maid united the country. Treacherous times, those were. And Pépère was never one to be caught unawares."

"How do you mean, Lord Rais?"

Gilles went on to explain to the magician that in the days of his grandfather, there had been many enemies, not the least of which were the marauding Burgundians who sought control of the province of Brittany, where Machecoul stood. Jeanne de Craon constructed a web of catacombs in the caverns beneath his home as well as a passage that led away from them and emerged below the floor of a modest coachman's stable at the edge of a far pasture. This had provided his grandfather with a place to hide as well as a means of escape should his castle ever be overrun. Within Machecoul the entrance to the catacombs lay hidden in plain sight in the front hall of the castle itself, well-disguised, but was now a long-forgotten secret.

"Not even my cunning brother knows of its existence. I am the one and the last."

Just then, they saw the shape of the dilapidated stable. As they entered, Gilles directed Poitou to pull the stone slab aside. Narrow stairs descended into the darkness beneath the earth, a single torch hanging on the wall. Francois seemed reluctant.

"All is prepared?" the magician asked.

"Oui. I have prepared the room just as you instructed."

"And the book?"

"Soaking in blood. As you instructed."

Francois nodded in approval and cast a long, lingering glance at the moon reigning high in the starry sky. The rite that would be performed was dangerous, and part of him wondered if it might not be the last time he would ever look upon it.

If they succeeded, though…oh, the glory!

They descended the stairs and made their way down the passage and through the tunnels to the ritual chamber. Once there, Gilles proceeded to show Francois how he had worked to make sure all the arrangements were perfect. The sorcerer walked the chamber, his hands clasped behind his back, and inspected things. The nobleman had done well, Francois judged, having made certain that there were plenty of supplies needed for such a rite as this. Salt, ash, paints of every color. Incenses and other implements of high magic were arranged on a long table set against the rough-hewn walls of the chamber. *The Red Book* lay soaking in a stoup that Gilles had stolen from a church in Nantes. Normally, such vessels at the church entrance were filled with blessed holy water, but—in a very personal and obscene gesture to the pompous clerics of the Church—Gilles had filled the stoup with blood.

Early on, Francois had explained to Gilles the nature of the frightful tome. Unless it was soaked for several hours in the lifeblood of a person, the book, written long ago at the feet of demons and dark gods from a world beyond, was unreadable. Its many incantations and descriptions of rites had been written in an obscure language that some sages believed to be the tongue of the fallen angel, Lucifer and his minions. Soaked in blood, the writings within the book became clearer, revealing the entirety of the book's content.

Francois glanced over to the young maid that was lying on the floor, bound in chains and gagged with a leather strap. There on the cold stone, she flopped about like a fish caught from a river, her cries muffled and amusing.

"Such fight in that one," he commented.

Lord Rais nodded. "Worthy of Joan herself."

Francois smiled as he ran his fingers along the smooth, thick wood of the altar that Gilles had constructed, upon which sat the remains of the great heroine.

"All seems to be in order," he said. "My compliments, Lord Rais."

The nobleman bowed his head in acceptance. "When would you like to begin?"

Gilles stared at the offering, writhing and groaning on the floor. He smiled.

"Now."

3
Laurent

Riding hard from the north, a contingent of soldiers loyal to the Duke of Brittany tore through winding woodland paths and across the supple, green fields of the countryside toward Machecoul. Among them was a cleric of the Church, an old man named Jean Pelan.

Whipping his mount to speed, he pulled alongside of the soldiers' leader.

"Must we ride with such haste?" he shouted over the rapid thrusting of hooves.

Captain Marcel Laurent glanced over at the cleric as he tightened his legs around his horse. The old man was nothing more than an annoyance to him. His riding skills were poor and his grumblings numerous.

"We ride with haste as the duke himself has commanded us—to apprehend the villain, Gilles de Rais. I believe the bishop's instructions to you were the same, no?"

The cleric struggled to keep his mount steady within the formation of men.

"Certainly, Captain Laurent. But I am old and not suited for this frenetic cavalry charge."

Laurent rolled his eyes and cast a final, disdainful glance at the holy man.

"We ride as soldiers ride. Keep the pace or do not; whatever is your pleasure."

With a spurring to his mount and a loud cry, Captain Laurent sped away from the cleric and farther toward the front of the formation. The old man did the best he could to keep up with them as they burned a path forward, the white face of the moon bathing the hills and fields in an otherworldly glow.

4

Ritual

"Bring the bitch to me," Francois ordered with the chilling callousness of a chef.

Poitou and Henriet stirred but looked to Rais for permission.

"Whatever the sorcerer asks, you must do it," he instructed them, nodding to Francois. "And I shall do the same."

The servants thrust the girl to the ground before him. She growled and spat through the binding tight across her mouth. He looked down at her with eyes that almost seemed to convey tenderness.

"Lord Rais, if you would, please shed a bit of her blood."

Gilles unsheathed his braquemard, the short, double-edged blade with which he had taken the lives of so many of the young when he had tired of the pleasures of their flesh. With great eagerness, he grasped the maid by her wrist and dragged her closer to him. In her fright, desperate for something to which she might cling, her fingers grasped at empty air. Gilles took a liking to those fingers, and he swung his blade, ripping her hand open at the top of her palm, severing the flesh and bone, a pair of her fingers falling cold to the floor as her blood poured forth. Her muffled scream brought him joy and he smiled as he held her wrist over the book and tightened his grasp, squeezing her shaking appendage and milking it like he might crush a strawberry.

As the tome was awakened from its dormancy, it made itself known. Each man felt a presence, enormous and looming, in the chamber that was not there before. It was dire and unsettling and fantastic. It fed off the blood, the pain, the screams of anguish and rage.

The sorcerer took the book in his arms and opened it. He began reading from it. The strange, demonic words vibrated against the walls as his voice slowly grew from a dismal drone to a powerful crescendo. The panicked heartbeat of the young girl drummed in the ears of all those present and there was no mistaking the palpable nature of the force that was growing in power as weird words called it forth.

"Take her to the altar!" Francois cried out maniacally to Gilles, "Spill it all! Take the wench's life!"

Gilles was happy to oblige. He dragged the red-soaked maid to the altar and pressed her up against it. He reached to his other side and grasped the hilt of the sword that hung there. Drawing it from the scabbard, he was lost for a moment in appreciation of its simple beauty; a plainness that cleverly concealed its power.

It was known as the Sword of Fierbois; the blade to which Joan had been led by the voice of Almighty God. Hidden in St. Catherine's church at Fierbois, Joan had found it wreathed in a Heavenly flame, and by God's direction she had taken it as her own. With it, she had spilled the blood of many a traitor and invader and had served the glory of France.

He sneered as he thrust it into the young girl's tender, white belly and felt it find purchase in the wooden altar behind her. She flailed for a moment, pinned and gushing her lifeblood into every fiber of the oak, the warm crimson pooling around the ashes and remains of Joan d'Arc.

Lord Rais found it enthralling to watch.

"Back to the safety of your circle, my Lord!" the sorcerer called to him, pausing in his reading of the incantation.

Gilles turned and started toward the refuge of his magical barrier but, looking again upon the dying form of the girl, he could not resist one final cruelty. Drawing his braquemard, he slid it across her throat and the blade bit in deep. He watched as her head tilted backward and a wellspring of blood came spilling over her breasts and down her broken form. His nostrils were filled with the stench of her peasant shit as she soiled her rags in the throes of death. It was a hideous delight, and he relished it as he returned to his circle drawn in salt on the floor.

The sorcerer Francois continued the summoning, mouthing the inhuman syllables, and the men watched as a pale mist formed above the altar and reached dark, smoky fingers down to the ashes and skull set atop it. Another length of it snaked out of the darkening cloud forming above them and plunged itself into the open mouth of the sacrifice. The gag about her face disintegrated and fell to the floor. Though her mouth was agape, no scream could be heard. Her eyes went suddenly white and cold as the last of her lifeforce was drained, replaced by that of another.

It seemed the walls of the chamber and the very bones of the men trembled as this dark thing came to pass. Then, with a bewildering abruptness, there was a silence and calm in the air. They looked on as the form of the sacrifice became still, the bloodied wounds beginning to heal before their eyes. Moments later, she stirred, then stood erect, and the blade that had pinned her against the altar clanged to the floor. She rose as might a wraith, her movements fluid but for an occasional spasmodic twitch that had no place in the natural world. She looked around the chamber, confused.

"What have you done?" she cried, nearly weeping, to the sorcerer.

Francois was stunned, his mouth agape. This…the blackest rite he had *ever* performed…had actually worked. Faced with the undeniably genuine voice of Joan herself, the sorcerer could not manage a reply.

Gilles knelt and stared with adoration. "My lady, we have brought you from on high, back to the world," Gilles offered, his lip quivering with joy at finding himself in her regal presence once again. "Back to France."

She whipped her head around to see who it was that spoke to her with such familiarity. As her eyes fell upon him, he could feel a blackness gathering in the air. She was growing angry, he judged, and the breathable air itself seemed to flee from the chamber. The Joan-thing moved between Gilles and the sorcerer slowly, back and forth, taking their measure.

"Commander Rais," she croaked.

A smile lit his face.

"You do remember me, then?"

She cocked her head to the side.

"A soldier you were. But never a hero. One among many you were. I do remember you, and even now I can hear your vile and petulant thoughts, Gilles de Rais."

His joy at seeing her washed away in the flood of her caustic words; there was anger welling up in his throat. Did she not understand? He had done this for *her*. For her and for the glory of France! Surely, she must know that. And yet this is how she would speak to him?

She chuckled.

"For the glory of France, indeed!" she cried out, then swiftly flew through the air toward him, halting just outside of his protective barrier. "I can see the hollow chambers of your black heart, Gilles de Rais, so I know that it is for your own glory and power that you have done this thing…and I know what joy you took in doing it."

She stretched out an arm and motioned to the hundreds of blood-filled pots that lined the walls of the ritual chamber.

Now terrified and unable to speak, Lord Rais looked to Francois, hoping the magician would assert some control over this summoned thing, for by the laws of magic it was bound to do his bidding.

"Joan d'Arc," Francois stammered, "Lord Rais and I have summoned you here to serve as a revenant and you *will do as we command*."

She approached him, smiling in a strange and menacing fashion. While her wounds were beginning to heal, the body of the peasant maid still bore the scars and bruises from the beatings she had received from Gilles as a matter of sport. Her ragged clothes were awash in her own blood and worse, the long locks of her hair twisted and matted into a wild mess that crowned her head. Her smile revealed a mouth of jagged, broken and missing teeth that had been knocked out and had not yet begun to return. She was, Francois thought, an altogether ghastly thing to behold.

"And what, pray tell, is it you would bid me do?" she asked.

"Kill," Gilles called out to her, his anger now a growl in his throat, "Kill the treacherous rat, King Charles, that I may take his place and bring about your vision—a new age for France."

The thing snickered bitterly.

"Kill the Dauphin? To supplant one tyrant with another far worse? I think not."

"You will do as we command!" the sorcerer Francois spat at her.

"Will I? Why do I not simply kill you now where you stand, sorcerer?"

"I command you and am protected from you, summoned bitch!"

"Oh," she said, her eyes cast downward as she played at remorse. Then a hungry grin spread across her battered face.

Francois's gaze followed her own, down to his feet and behind him where he could see that the thickly poured salt of his circle had been scattered away by the struggling wench when they had carried her to slaughter. He opened his mouth to curse her, but the words never came.

The revenant held out her hand and the Sword of Fierbois rose into the air and came sailing toward her. Her thin, weathered fingers closed around the hilt. Deftly, she raised it and swung. The head of Francois Prelati came to rest on the ground. His knees buckled and his arms jerked with spasms as down came the rest of him in a heap of meat and blood on the chamber floor. *The Red Book* fell with him and slammed closed.

It was the last sound Gilles heard before the screams of terror. He turned away from the fallen sorcerer to see Henriet and Poitou crying out in fear as they fled from the chamber and down the passage toward the secret entrance into Machecoul above. Drawing his blade, he considered following after them, but the Maid was before him, stalking around his circle of protection and leering at her prey.

5
Wrath

Captain Laurent and his men were gathered in the front hall of Machecoul, leveling bitter accusations of treason at René de Rais when a sudden, plodding noise rose from inside the walls. There was a dull thud and then a crack as an ornately framed section of the wall tumbled outward and crashed to the floor in pieces. Stumbling out of this hidden passage came two men.

At this, Laurent and his men drew their blades.

René recognized them as his brother's servants.

"Henriet? Poitou?"

The servants were white-faced and covered in a nervous sweat.

"Explain!" René demanded. "From where have you come?"

The two men did not respond, catching their breath.

The captain's ire was raised, though, and so he took Poitou by the neck and pressed him against the wall, demanding an answer. When the slight little man found his voice, he jabbered through an explanation of the fantastic events that had transpired in the catacombs below.

Laurent seriously doubted the truth of the servant's ramblings, but he felt certain that the fugitive Gilles was present and was up to something most unsavory.

"He is down there?" Laurent snarled at the servant.

Poitou nodded, then crumpled to the floor as the captain waved his men forward down into the passageway, the Cleric following closely behind and clutching at his rosary, whispering Latin prayers as they descended into the darkness below.

Gilles spat at the revenant and brandished his blood-darkened blade as she circled him, her white eyes watching him closely.

"I have given to you life! This is how you repay me?" he growled.

She sneered. "Life is not yours to give, swine."

"Is it yours to take?" he retorted, his voice quaking with fear.

She said nothing, only flashed him a grisly smile.

"And how long can you wait, coveting me like a peasant dog, hungry for a meal it cannot taste?" he shouted at the thing.

"Ah, oui," she nodded. "This is true, Lord Rais."

There was a moment of paralyzed silence as she hovered around him. Then, from the distant corridor, there came a sound they both knew well from days of battle. The sound of armed men approaching.

"The soldiers are coming, Gilles," she looked toward the corridor. "They will deal with you in blood and pain."

With this, the revenant raised her arms, and a powerful wind was summoned from the still, dank air and blew through the chamber like a gale. The pots on the walls teetered, then tipped, and the ocean of blood and gore that Gilles had amassed came pouring across the floor, washing away his protective circle in a crimson wave.

Standing there before the monster he had helped create, Gilles was defenseless, as naked as a child. He trembled, and in his trembling, the blade dropped from his hand.

"Vive la mort!" the Joan-thing howled and brought the sword of Fierbois up and slashed across his chest.

His tunic ripped open, and his flesh parted beneath the power of the holy blade. He cried out and sank to his knees, clenching his eyes shut in fear of the fatal strike that would follow.

The revenant floated high into the air and let go of the sword. It crashed to the stone below as she spread her arms and a great light appeared to seep from her eyes and mouth, the tips of her fingers.

In an instant, the body of the maid went limp and thudded to the floor. Above it, a dark shadow gathered into the shape of an impossibly large and pitch-black carrion bird. Fluttering in place for a moment as if to have a final look at him, the shadow bird then flapped its wings of smoke and went flitting out of the chamber.

As it soared down the passageway, it stirred the cave swallows that nested in the crevices of the catacombs and each one erupted from their roost to follow it down the corridor to the world outside.

Kneeling there, his own blood gathering about him and mixing with that of the innocents he had slaughtered, Gilles de Rais tasted hopelessness and defeat, and he wept madly.

6
Aftermath

Captain Laurent and his men struggled through the throng of swallows thick in the hundreds and emerged into the ritual chamber. They could hardly believe the sight of horror that greeted them. Without ceremony or comment, Laurent clamped the irons on the villain, Gilles de Rais. The duke's men took nothing from the carnage they found beneath Machecoul, save for a red-colored book full of faded and indecipherable writings that Jean Pelan explained to Captain Laurent may be of some historical value. He assured the soldier of his intention to turn the tome over to the Bishop in Nantes upon his return for study and safekeeping.

As they led him away from the catacombs, Gilles rambled on about a phantom Joan d'Arc, cursing her for some imagined treachery committed against him. While Captain Laurent put no stock in these fantastic claims, the cleric, Jean Pelan was not so easily dissuaded. To his mind, the strange red book itself and the lingering malevolence he had experienced in the chamber were cause enough for a man of faith to wonder just what had transpired therein.

After conferring with the captain and swearing those present to secrecy, both men agreed that it would be best to make no mention of either the catacombs or the peculiar circumstances of Rais' apprehension in the written record of the arrest.

Such dark matters should be left to the Church.

After returning to Nantes, Jean Pelan communicated his observations and fears of the truth of Rais' story to the bishop, releasing into his care the crimson book. The cleric hoped the bishop would see fit to lock the tome away forever, never again to be looked upon by the eyes of men, but he was given no such assurances.

Gilles de Rais continued to spew his bizarre story during his trial, though the Church—concerned that such blasphemous ravings might become common legend among the unlearned and oft superstitious population—agreed to create a more favorable and mundane record of Rais' testimony.

Along with his servants, Gilles de Rais was executed by hanging in the year 1440 for the crimes of heresy, sodomy and murder.

On that day, it was judged by all that a great darkness was dispelled, though in the years that followed, elders of the Church who lay dying in their beds would silently wonder if another darkness, unleashed, might still roam the countryside.

NIGHT OF THE NANOBEASTS!

1

Scientists have been creating technological wonders of immense power for some time and have been striving to make these creations ever smaller. The future is bound to a destiny where mankind will operate machines on a molecular level, or so they say. It was these same puffed-up scientists who jeered and laughed at Dr. Henry Breach for his peculiar quest.

In this world bent on miniaturizing everything, Henry Breach sought to make the smallest organism quite a bit larger.

The nanobe, a creature that, according to some, did not even exist as a living thing, had long held a fascination for Dr. Breach. His admiration of and longing for a greater understanding of this theoretical thing was all-consuming and—as many of his colleagues were heard to declare—left poor Henry a little unhinged.

But they would all soon know that Henry's madness was not merely the stuff of clichéd midnight movies. On this night, the scientist was on the cusp of a breakthrough.

He stood before his whiteboard and studied the mathematical formulas scrawled across it in his deplorable chicken scratch that was indecipherable to anyone but himself and his lab assistant, Jane Coffer.

Check and re-check. That was the key. The slightest inaccuracy in his formula would mean yet another in a long line of failures. Dr. Breach chuckled to himself. Science was, at its heart, not a science, but rather an art. Processes and logic could get a man only so far toward the brass ring of greatness. To grasp that ring required the unrefined, human quality of reckless imagination and instinct.

"Ms. Coffer," he called out to her, turning to find her leaning over the Veculizer's service panel with a precision screwdriver, making some final adjustments. Her pressed white lab coat greedily hugged her curves, and she unknowingly made the faintest of gyrating motions as she turned the zaropian dial on the machine.

Speaking of instinct.

"Yes, Doctor Breach?" she replied, standing straight in her blue polka dot pencil dress, her bosoms barely contained beneath the modest plunge of the neckline.

Not for the first time, Henry found himself a little flummoxed as he regarded her.

"Doctor?" she asked again after he gave no reply.

"Yes," he said, stammering a little. "Sorry, I was just thinking about the formulae. Is the Veculizer prepped?"

"I had some trouble getting it into the slot," she said, fingering the shaft of the screwdriver. "But I did manage to get it turned to the low setting like you asked."

"Excellent!" he replied.

He removed a handkerchief from his pocket and dabbed at the perspiration on his forehead as he looked over the lab, taking inventory of what still needed to be done. It seemed, however, that the preparations for the experiment were complete.

"The preparations for the experiment are complete, Doctor," Jane declared, slipping the long, slender driver into the pocket of her lab coat.

"So it would seem, Ms. Coffer. Very well then. Begin charging the Veculizer and I shall fetch the specimens."

"Right away, Doctor Breach."

Henry stole across the lab to the walk-in cold storage unit. Along the shelves there were sealed jars and slides of DNA specimens. Over the course of many months, Henry and Jane had painstakingly applied extracted nanobes to these slides. It was a new approach and one that Henry hoped would yield better results than placing the nanobes into the Veculizer unmoored.

What they were endeavoring to do was deceptively simple, really. The Veculizer, a machine conceived of and built by Dr. Breach himself, was a DNA fuser and rapid growth accelerator. The lynchpin of his hypothesis regarding the nanobe was that it was not merely a crystalline mineral structure, but a living thing, and therefore comprised of DNA. Unfortunately, even when isolated in the lab, the nanobes were too small to be properly studied.

Therefore, Henry needed to make them larger.

For the pairing of the nanobes, Henry had chosen DNA from the Japanese spider crab. He theorized that the exoskeletal nature of the animal would provide a welcome component to which the nanobes would bond. The long lifespan of the spider crab—easily a hundred years or more—would allow for the nanobes to exist in their larger state long enough to be documented and studied before breaking down. After an hour in the growth chamber, they would swell to the size of a quarter. Once the proper size was reached, he expected to have no more than a few minutes before they broke down entirely.

Henry plucked the specimens from the shelf and returned to the lab to find Jane dutifully waiting beside the Veculizer. The control panel indicated that the charge had reached over ninety percent.

"I see we're nearly ready, Ms. Coffer," he remarked as he set the specimens down on the steel table next to the machine.

"Ninety-seven percent, Doctor," she confirmed. "Nearly ready!"

They both watched the indicator gradually illuminate from left to right. Dozens of buttons and indicators on the panel flashed and beeped, though even Henry did not fully understand their purpose. They spoke not a word, the anticipation of this moment pervasive in the room.

The final indicator lit up green and the terminal monitor read that the Veculizer was ready. A wall of Tesla coils behind them sprung to life, buzzing and cracking with sparks as their tendrils of lightning snaked and shimmered.

"Open fusion chamber one, Ms. Coffer."

She reached up and pressed the button that opened the metal door to the first chamber. As it rose with a hiss, Henry unscrewed the cap on the specimen bottle. Inside, a blob of gelatinous material that held the raw DNA of the spider crab shimmied in his nervous, shaking hand. He slipped his hand into the chamber and turned the bottle over. The blob tumbled out and came to rest on the collection plate.

"Secure chamber one, please."

Her delicate fingers sought out the button again, and the door closed with another hiss as all the air was sucked out of the chamber.

"Now for chamber two, Ms. Coffer."

She pressed another button, and a second door opened on the machine. Handling the packet gingerly, Henry pulled the seal back and used a pair of tongs to remove the nanobe slide. He hardly even breathed as he lifted it to the open chamber and then set it down with a light *clink* on the collection plate.

"Secure chamber two."

With the press of a button, the chamber was sealed. The terminal indicated that the machine was initializing internal sensors, and after a moment, the screen announced the material had been received and the chambers stabilized.

Jane looked over at Dr. Breach, who stared at the machine's doors as if he could see through the half inch of steel.

"It's the deep breath before the plunge, Ms. Coffer," he said and then drew in a long, slow breath that raised his shoulders. "Are you ready?"

"I'm just thrilled to be plunging with you, sir."

He gave her a smile and nodded at the machine.

"Engage the machine for fusion and growth."

In the center of the machine there was a red switch housed beneath a clear, protective cover. She flipped the cover open and grasped the switch with her fingers, then applied some force. But the switch would not budge.

"Problem, Ms. Coffer?"

"The…uh…switch seems to be stuck, Doctor Breach. I can't get it up."

Henry searched his mind, then snapped his fingers like a jazz musician.

"It's the cool air in this lab, that's all. Let me help you."

Without thinking, Henry reached up and placed his hand over hers, his fingers atop hers. In this way, they both lingered for a moment longer than they should have. Then, with the combined effort, the switch was flipped up and the machine engaged. A low hum emanated from the Veculizer and the terminal displayed row after row of data being gathered by the sensors as the fusion process began.

Jane leaned against the table and watched as Henry carefully analyzed the data stream.

"Perfect," he whispered.

The fusion process was relatively short, and they would know in a moment if it had been successful because the green indicator light would light up and the terminal would announce that stage one had been completed.

At least that was how it *should* work.

Since they had never successfully fused the materials, they did not know for sure.

"Come on, girl," Henry said, his eyes scanning the screen. "That's it. Come on…"

Abruptly, the humming ceased, and the lab went dead quiet. The sudden silence alarmed them, and Jane leaned in next to Henry. Just as she did, the green indicator light came on and the screen went blank. After a moment, the Veculizer terminal beeped, and a single line of text was visible in brilliant white letters: *Stage 1 COMPLETE. Stage 2 ENGAGED.*

Henry went around to the sensor panel and stared at the monitor. He fiddled with the controls for a moment, adjusting the optic scope in the machine to the target area on the delivery tray inside the growth chamber. Once there, he zoomed in and adjusted for clarity.

"Phenomenal," he remarked, then looked over at Jane. "Successful fusion of specimens complete and viable growth already beginning. We've done it, Ms. Coffer!"

Her heart leapt with joy at this news, and she bounced on her toes, hardly able to contain her exuberance. She rushed toward the scientist and grappled him in a congratulatory embrace. As they pulled away from each other, though, something unexpected happened. Their hands met again. For a moment, they were suspended above the earth, staring into each other's eyes.

Jane didn't know what it was—maybe the streaks of gray in his wild, unkempt hair, maybe the crow's feet flanking his cold eyes from too many nights spent in the lab, maybe the slightly pervy mustache that sat atop his lip like a shorn, black caterpillar, or maybe the musk of pure genius and brilliance that radiated from him in that moment—but whatever it was, the feelings it brought out in her would not be denied, and she drew his face to hers and kissed him.

There they stayed for a long moment.

When they parted, Henry wore a stunned look as he struggled to find words.

"I...I'm...I'm sorry, Ms. Coffer. I shouldn't have—"

"Oh, Henry," she sighed and pulled him to her again.

"Oh, Jane."

Their lips met once more; their bodies pressed against one another. Roaming hands sought eager flesh through the starched white lab coats and layers of clothing.

"Ravish me, Henry," she pleaded with him, her loins afire. "Do what you will with me."

He looked around the lab. "Not here, though," he said. "It's a clean room. And there's nothing clean about what I'd like to do with you."

"Doctor Breach!" she squealed as he pulled her across the room toward the door that opened to the hallways of the university's science department.

With victory and lust in his eyes, Henry Breach rushed down the hall, his comely assistant in tow. They rushed toward his office and his seldom-used leather fainting couch. There they would adjourn as the growth process in the Veculizer ran through to completion.

Once in his office, they made rough, desperate love to each other, flinging themselves all over the room from the door to the desk to his chair, and finally to the couch. The radio was on, and Billie Holiday crooned, "Body and Soul" to the lovers as they gave in to long-unspoken longings and tension, conducting a fusion experiment of a very different kind.

Their moans and sighs were unbridled, for they knew there was no one to hear.

Outside the science building, dark clouds had gathered. Rain began to fall, and lightning created jagged fractures in the night as thunder pealed across the sky. The new lovers were oblivious to all of it.

2

For all her technical competence and her value as a lab assistant to Henry Breach, Jane had made one critical mistake that evening when she calibrated the zatropian dial on the growth accelerator. Counterintuitive to most all other things, the lowest setting was all the way to the right and maximum growth on the left. In what had been a simple and innocent mistake, she had turned it to the left. During previous experiments, it would have been no trouble at all—simply another failed result. But tonight, the brilliantly mad Doctor Breach's decision to place the nanobes in the chamber on a slide had made all of the difference.

They had succeeded.

Along with the successful fusion, there were some unexpected results occurring within the unattended Veculizer. The resulting creature did not render in the manner that Henry had anticipated, and where there was meant to be only one, there were many. It was reproducing, and the legion of creatures were growing at a frightfully accelerated rate.

Fox Bolton hated his job.

And why not? Who would actually like being the midnight janitor at some creepy New England college? His calling was to be an actor, he just knew it. To head out West and make it in Hollywood. After all, movies were his life, so it only made sense. Not to mention he had seen the lauded academy award-winning films that were rife with pedestrian acting and poor writing. Not like the director, Roger Corman's body of work. Now *that's* what cinematic gold looked like!

Sure, he was just a mop jockey at the university now. But when his ship came in, he was going to take Hollywood by storm. He'd turn his own life into an inspired biopic that would endear and terrify and draw both laughter and tears. Yes indeed, then Fox Bolton would show them some real movie magic.

He was halfway down the north hallway, mopping, wringing, and mopping more as he went when he heard a ruckus in one of the lab rooms. The painful screech of metal being pried open, glass breaking, and tables and furniture being overturned.

"What the—" he said and leaned the mop against the wall.

He walked down the hall, checking each lab until he was able to determine from which one the sounds emanated. The name placard outside of the door of Lab #21A read BREACH. The only thing he could figure was that some of the college students had broken in and decided it would be a fun Friday night activity to trash the place.

"Probably all red-eyed and hopped up on the Devil's lettuce, too," he grumbled.

He tried the handle, but the door was locked.

"You little punks better knock it off in there!" he hollered at the door as he located the proper key on his ring and slipped it into the lock. "You'll answer to Dean Armitage for this! Right after I put my foot up your—"

Fox pushed the door open and stepped inside, but what he saw there in the lab stopped him cold. He couldn't run, didn't even have the chance to scream before one of the things skittered across the floor toward him, a large crystalline spear of an appendage raised. Like a deer in the headlights of an oncoming car, he watched as that spear descended, following the arc through the air as it plunged through his abdomen.

The door shut automatically behind him and thudded repeatedly as the creatures began to feast upon him, arterial blood ejaculating from his torn throat in great bursts that covered the door and painted the portal window in a dripping curtain of red.

This is how my movie ends, Fox thought as he lost consciousness. *That's a wrap.*

3

Speaking of ejaculating, Henry lay on the couch with Jane atop him, having collapsed where she was when they finished for the second time. Sweat covered their bare bodies, and Henry clicked the remote to activate the ceiling fan as they lay entwined on the leather couch, smoking cigarettes from a pack of Lucky Strikes he kept in his office.

"Do you know how long I have waited for this night?" she asked him, running her fingers through his thick chest hair.

"I know," Henry replied, smoke rolling out from between his lips as he spoke. "It's extraordinary to think that in only a few more minutes, we'll have the opportunity to document the existence of the smallest organism known to man."

She raised an eyebrow. "I was speaking of you and me, Henry."

"Oh, *that*. Yes. Well, that was also extraordinary."

"It certainly was," she said, a twinkle creeping into her eye, her hand wandering down below his waist. "And there were no small organisms involved, either."

She was tempting him again; he wanted to yield to her and begin a third round of sweaty, wanton copulation, but the hour was nearly at an end, and they needed to get back to the lab.

Jane noticed him checking his watch and knew their interlude was finished. She rolled off of him and they both began to dress. After a moment, a loud noise echoed from beyond the door to Henry's office. They looked at each other in bewilderment.

"What could that be?" she asked as she reached over her shoulder to zip up her dress.

"I've no idea," Henry said. He was still buttoning up his shirt as he rose and went to the door. He opened it and leaned into the hallway for a look, but there was nothing to see. Jane joined him, leaning in close. That was when something rounded the corner at the end of the hall and came into full view.

Jane gasped and her hand went instantly to cover her mouth as she and Henry stared wide-eyed at the monstrosity.

Standing six feet tall with legs as long as a nightmare, the enormous creature bore a strong resemblance to the Japanese spider crab. But unlike the normal species, it was far greater in size and its exoskeleton appeared comprised of hard, quartz-like mineral.

As they took in every detail of the creature, they were all too aware that it was studying them, too.

Worse, as they ducked back inside and the thing began clicking down the hallway toward them, they saw other long, gigantic crystal legs coming around the corner directly behind the first. There were more of them.

When the door closed behind them and Henry slid the lock into place, Jane brought her hands to her face and let go a mind-rending scream. She then began to babble, clearly delirious.

Henry moved toward her, grabbed her by the shoulders. "Get a hold of yourself, Ms. Coffer!" he exclaimed and then pulled his arm back to give her a sobering slap across the face.

Instead, he doubled over as her knee connected with his groin.

"Oh, Henry," she said, "I'm so sorry. My mother is a rabid feminist who made me take all sorts of terrible self-defense courses. It was just a reflex!"

He groaned and stood. "That's alright, my darling," he said.

They needed to get out of that office. There were horrors the likes of which they had never seen coming for them.

"Oh, Henry, it was a horror the likes of which I've never seen!"

"I know," he replied. "And they're coming for us. We have to get out of here."

"But, Henry," she blubbered. "What are they?"

"My experiment gone awry, Ms. Coffer. That's what they are. An awful, bastardized combination of the specimens." He looked at the door to the hallway, pale with fear. "Like some kind of…*nanobeasts*!"

4

The academic offices were all connected, like a honeycomb of small spaces at the center of the Tillinghast Science Hall, and Henry and Jane slipped out of his office into the next just as an enormous claw of one of the nanobeasts ripped the door from its hinges and tossed it into the hallway like a soda can.

Seeing its prey disappear behind the other door, it let loose an awful inhuman howl. The other members of its brood answered in kind, their combined cries of rage shaking the very foundation of the building.

They continued to run from office to office, lab to lab, Jane following closely behind the scientist as he unlocked door after door and they drove deeper and deeper into the maze of academia, though to what end she did not know.

"Where are we going, Henry?"

"There's no time to explain!" he replied, reaching back to make sure she was close on his heels.

Behind them, doors and walls were being ripped apart by the nanobeasts as they closed in on the pair. Glancing back, Henry could plainly see that—astoundingly enough— the creatures were still growing. Like the phenomenon of centrifugal force, the accelerated growth process that had begun in the Veculizer had been assimilated by the growing creatures, like some kind of rapid evolutionary adaptation, and now the momentum simply continued. When it would stop…*if it would stop*…was anyone's guess.

The things had to be destroyed.

Henry and Jane had managed to get two or three doors ahead of the pursuing nanobeasts, and as they entered Doctor Pembrooke's office, they heard a roar of thunder from the storm outside and the crack of lightning striking somewhere close by. The lights in the office flickered, and then all went dark.

Behind them, the rending of brick and steel and wood ceased, and as Henry listened to the creatures clacking about behind them haphazardly, he knew that for whatever strange reason, the darkness confounded them, confused them.

"Doctor," Jane whispered, clinging tight to his arm. "It sounds like the darkness has confused them."

"Yes, I know."

Henry didn't think it would last long, though. The accelerated mutations set off by the Veculizer would soon cause them to adapt to their environment, to master it, and then there would be one less weakness to exploit.

"We must move quietly," he said, taking her hand and moving through the darkness to the door on the opposite wall of Pembrooke's office, which opened to the hall on the south side of the building. They crept out into the hallway and flattened against the wall outside of the office.

With the power outage, the backup generators had kicked in. But only critical systems and emergency lighting had priority, so the small, dim lights low on the walls did not provide much in the way of visibility, and for this they were thankful.

Across the way, taking up nearly the entire length of the south side of the building, were the chemistry labs. If they could lure the creatures there, it might be their only chance to be rid of them.

"Not much farther now," he whispered, giving her hand a reassuring squeeze. "Come, Ms. Coffer."

They stepped cautiously across the hallway, and when they reached the door, Henry turned the knob slowly. Opening the door just a crack, they slipped in and closed it silently behind them.

"What are we doing here?" Jane pleaded. "We need to get out of the building."

"I'm afraid, Ms. Coffer," he replied, pulling a pen light from his breast pocket, "that what we must do is prevent those things from leaving the building."

She clung to him. "But, Henry, how are we going to do that?"

He shone the beam of his light over the counters in the middle of the room. At each end there sat a star-shaped configuration of metal—natural gas valves used to power Bunsen burners for experiments.

"Those valves are on every counter in every lab on this side of the building," he explained. "We must open them up and fill these rooms with hydrocarbon gas."

"Then what?"

"We set the trap," he said. "And when the moment is right, we destroy this building, and the nanobeasts along with it."

She whimpered, the dark realization spreading over her face. "But what about us, Henry?"

"I'm afraid our survival is not paramount, Jane," he replied.

A heavy silence dwelled between them.

5

They moved stealthily from lab to lab, opening all the valves before moving on to the next room to do the same. They were more than halfway down the length of the building when the effects of the gas began to take hold.

"I don't feel well, Henry," Jane said as she leaned, woozy, against the counter and struggled to turn on the valves. Her vision was blurring, and her hand could find no purchase on the handles.

Henry, whose head was light and aching, was still managing. He opened the valves on his end of the counter and then clicked his pen light on and pointed it across the room onto the array of valves to help Jane see what she was doing.

Then Henry drew back in horror.

"Jane," he hissed. "Don't move."

But it was too late, and Henry knew it the moment the beam from his pen light illuminated the hulking shadow of one of the nanobeasts—a stealthy scout. It had been there, lying in wait to ambush them. As he beheld it and the creature acknowledged it had been discovered, its mandibles chattered together, dripping some clear, viscous fluid to the floor, and its crystalline armor began to radiate an eerie green glow.

This is its adaptation to the darkness, he thought. *Like the sea creatures of the deep, it has become a light unto itself.*

Its round, black eyes were devoid of any emotion and glittered in the muted light.

"Run!" he cried out to her.

She turned and began to shamble awkwardly toward Henry when a length of glowing appendage shot forth and grasped Jane in its enormous claw.

She was screaming. Henry was screaming. The nanobeast was chattering so happily that the noise had to be what passed for laughter among its kind. Then Jane was ripped in half and torrents of blood and gut-matter sprayed Henry, who stood there, wielding his ineffectual pen light like a sabre.

Jane's upper body fell away as the creature brought her still-kicking legs to its maw and began to eat. Henry dove forward and grasped her hand, turned, and went stumbling wildly out of the lab into the next, dragging her torso behind him all the way. Nearly slipping several times, he made it through two more labs before his gassed, fading mind gave out and he collapsed in a fog.

Henry pulled Jane's torso up next to him where he sat with his back against the cabinets. Above him, the open valves hissed. Lighting tore across the sky outside again and again, illuminating the lab with shocks of white, electrical light. In the hallway beyond, Henry heard the *click-clack* of the other nanobeasts closing in on him.

"Henry," he heard Jane say, her voice drowning as her lungs and trachea bubbled with her own blood and fluids.

"Yes, Ms. Coffer?"

"I'm all for you," she said, recalling the words of the Billie Holiday song playing on the radio as the pair had made love in his office earlier that evening. "Body and soul."

She gasped her last breath and then fell forever silent.

Looking at her shorn pencil dress covered in gore and the missing half of her below the waist, Henry supposed the sentiment was at least partly true.

He fished a hand into the pocket of his trousers and found the pack of Lucky Strikes there, as well as the book of matches. Resting his head on the shoulder of Jane's corpse, he waited until he could hear the things ripping apart the doors and bursting through the walls. These monstrosities he had created would be his end. Regrettably, though, it wouldn't be the first time an experiment-gone-wrong had run amok in the halls of this ~~thi~~ legend-haunted university, and tomorrow they would clean up the mess just as they always did. His death would amount to little more than another incident report in the Dean's file drawer.

And Henry Breach would still be a laughingstock to his New England colleagues. A sad and ironic footnote in the history of genetic science. A Shelley-esque cliché after all.

They were drawing near, his creations.

"Come and get it, boys," Henry croaked, striking the match and flaming up the end of his cigarette.

He even managed one good pull from it as the spidery, crystal behemoths came toward him.

The match still sizzled in his fingertips. Then the ignition took place, and the south side of the Tillinghast Science Building roared open in a plume of conflagration that blew out the windows of other nearby university buildings. Half of the roof collapsed into the pit of hellfire that was unleashed and, had anyone been present to witness it, they might have seen strange, gargantuan creatures with long and spindly legs climbing out of the rubble, covered in flames, and roaring into the night.

CRUEL MOON

1

Apart from squashing a cockroach or slapping a mosquito, Martin had never killed anything in his life. He knew that to be true, but in sleep, flashes of violence played behind his eyes. Visions of torn fabric and rent flesh, endless rivers of blood and the echo of a distant scream. The dream stirred him awake, his heart thundering in his chest and his sheets soaked in a sweat that could not be blamed on the balmy summer night alone.

In the dark, Martin squinted at his clock and discovered that the hour was ungodly late or early. He rolled over, bunched the pillow and buried his face in it, but the lingering reverberation of the nightmare would not permit him rest.

Wiping at the sweat that had gathered on his brow, he rose from the bed, slipped some boxers onto his bare ass and padded down the hallway to the living room of his apartment and found his couch was empty. The usual sight of his friend, Oscar, sprawled and snoring on Martin's couch was always a sure sign that it was the weekend. He supposed that he had gone on home late last night sometime after Martin had passed out, though he had a vague memory of Oscar helping him into bed.

He puffed his cheeks and blew out a long, whistling breath. "Must have gotten pretty wrecked," he remarked to himself and the empty room.

The old doors that opened up to the balcony were thick with years of paint jobs that had been applied atop the others as the hundred-year-old row house had welcomed new tenants through the decades. He usually left them open at night but on this evening there was no cool breeze wafting in to provide any sort of reprieve from the heat. He plucked his pack of cigarettes from the coffee table and stepped out onto the balcony, lighting one up.

The balcony overlooked Monument Avenue, a long and picturesque boulevard of towering trees and old homes that ran through Richmond's Fan District, dotted along the way with artisan crafted statues, most of them Confederate generals that had been erected long ago and had given the street its name. He leaned on the railing and blew smoke out toward the grand oaks lining the median. Just up the street, the Stonewall Jackson monument shone like a ghostly rider upon his horse, frozen in time. Across the street, the balconies of a sorority house were lined with Christmas lights just as they were throughout the year, no matter the season.

The avenue was lonely this time of night. An occasional car groaned by, heading west from the downtown area or one of the Fan bars that squatted for a time on every other corner among the old houses and the college campus buildings. Across the way, he could see the hot cherries of other cigarettes on the sorority house balconies flame and fade. Soft voices and inebriated laughter drifted into the warm evening. Stubbing out his cigarette, he shuffled back inside and cast a disdainful glance at the busted air-conditioning unit that showed its useless face from one of the windows along the side of his apartment. He shot the bird at the thing and muttered a curse as he passed by it.

The sheets of his bed were still damp with perspiration, but he sank down onto them. Lying there, he wondered if he would find sleep again before the morning came. The harsh light from a nearby streetlamp spilled into the room. He saw his cane leaning against the dresser. It had once belonged to his grandfather and wore its age well. The stained oak of its faded shaft terminated in the brass head of a duck that served as its decorative handle. Back in high school, he had been in a dirt bike accident which had left the ligaments and tendons of his left leg torn beyond repair. He would never walk normally again, they had told him. Certainly, he would never run. And they were right.

A peculiar realization settled over him then.

Martin had gotten out of bed, walked down the hall, out to the balcony and back, and he had done it without the cane. He sat up in bed and stared down at his bare leg, the scars of the injury and the surgeries from years ago still emblazoned on his flesh like a tattoo that he had always thought might as well have read *'gimp'*.

Now curious, he planted his feet on the floor and stood. He walked over to the dresser, reached for the cane, and closed his fingers around the handle. The brass was cool to the touch; probably the only thing in the apartment that was. But his leg felt strangely normal. He bent it at the knee, picked his right foot off the floor and stood there, the full weight of his body on his bum leg.

No unsteadiness. No pain at all. He looked down at his leg again and in the darkness of that ungodly hour, he grimaced. Such a thing would be regarded by most as a miracle, but for Martin it brought upon him a dark cloud of unease.

He lifted the right again, balanced again. Bent the left this time, lowered down easily. Nice and controlled as if he had done it every day of his life. His emotions swirled, stormy in his head and he struggled to take inventory of them. There was disbelief. There was amazement.

And terror.

There was definitely terror.

2

In the morning, Martin laced up his sneakers. He was going for a jog for the first time in twelve years. He stepped out into the hallway, locked his apartment behind him and then started for the elevator before realizing that was no longer necessary. He smiled as he went practically skipping down the three flights of stairs. Taking the rear exit of the building where the alley and gravel parking lot were, he could smell the heat of summer in the city the second he stepped out of the door. The heady mix of exhaust fumes and early morning warmth that promised a sweltering afternoon, grass clippings and asphalt, the faint aroma of someone's flower garden mingling with the sweet scent of cooking meat drifting in the air from some restaurant kitchen blocks away. The world seemed anew to him and so very alive.

He started out slow. It had been over a decade after all. There were others decked out in running gear who Martin recognized, having often watched them go zipping by from his perch on the balcony. Now he was out here among them, those agile creatures. In ripped jean shorts, with pasty white legs, and tattered Vans, yes, but among them, nevertheless.

Halfway through his jog down the avenue, he realized that if he were going to make this exercise thing a habit, he was going to need to quit smoking. There was a time when the curious phenomenon of the smoking jogger—a sight unique to the tobacco-centered economy of Richmond—was more commonplace, but these days if you jogged, you probably didn't smoke. The notion didn't sit well with him, though. He chuckled to himself. Jogging just might be a gateway to other healthy, granola tendencies, and the next thing he knew, Martin might find himself an emaciated vegan who sipped soy lattes down at Café Gutenberg while reading a dog-eared copy of Peter Singer's *Animal Liberation*.

As the J.E.B. Stuart monument came into view on his left, he made the u-turn that would take him back to his apartment. Admiring the lush green oaks and sycamores that lined the median and the young hipsters walking their dogs down the grassy lane, he spied a cluster of flashing lights up ahead.

As he got closer, he saw a group of police cars parked in front of the sorority house on the opposite side of the street. The house sported Greek letters painted across the pickets of the balconies. In front of the building, uniformed Richmond cops and others milled about, gathered into small groups, conversing or staring up at the building wordlessly, as if waiting.

Martin slowed, then stopped. He knew a girl that lived in that building—a girl from his Eastern European Anthropology class. A cute blonde with amazing curves, Morgan Wells had also been along on their class trip to do field work overseas. Another jogger approached—an older fellow with salt-and-pepper hair and the lean physique of a runner, looking like a young George Clooney. Martin nodded toward him and then back over to the sorority house across the street.

"Any idea what's going on over there?"

Clooney slowed down and then stopped, though he continued to jog in place.

"I heard they found one of the girls dead. Killed."

"Seriously? How?"

"Not sure, of course, but the word is she was found in the alleyway behind the building. Pretty gruesome stuff."

"Jesus," Martin gasped.

"Yeah," Clooney replied and then pointed his feet back in the direction he had been going. "Enjoy the day!"

Martin watched him go, thinking the latter part of their exchange a little inappropriate.

College girl murdered in an alley, yeah. Gotta get my miles done, though.

He walked the rest of the way back toward his apartment building, his mind a storm of thoughts and fears. There were probably two dozen girls or more who lived in that house. He had no reason to think the girl in question was Morgan Wells. None whatsoever.

And yet he did think that. He felt it in his gut with a dark certainty that came not from a simple fear of the possible but from something that felt like a memory. Unless he was imagining it all. Unless he was just going a little mad.

He hoped to God that he was going a little mad.

When he returned to his apartment, he turned on the television and scanned the local channels and the morning news shows for any mention of what had happened at the sorority house. The gathering of police cars was sure to have drawn some media attention. He smoked cigarettes and waited, suffering through inane news items of little interest to him. Finally, toward the end of the news hour, there was live footage of a reporter standing in front of the house on Monument Avenue and he watched with rapt interest as the attractive redhead in a conservative pantsuit relayed what was mostly hearsay to the camera and the morning news audience. There had been an assault, possibly in the alley behind the sorority house, and there had been one fatality. However, the police were not planning to release the victim's name yet. The news anchor then assured him they would be following this developing story closely and would update him with new information as it became available.

"Back to you, Gene, for the forecast."

Martin clicked off the television and sat there a moment wondering what to do. His nerves were frayed, and his mind was going a hundred miles an hour, making much hay of that horrible feeling in the pit of his stomach. Was eight in the morning too early for a beer? Maybe it was but these were extenuating circumstances. He fetched a cold can from the fridge and then went to the balcony.

Across the street, the RPD cruisers with their flashers on made it hard to discern any details of the scene.

It was already quite warm at this early hour and the cold beer felt good sliding down his parched throat.

He thought of Morgan and the trip the class had taken abroad. It had been winter and the depth of cold in that part of the world could not be overstated. There in the remote wilds of Eastern Europe, there was a constant and chilling wind ripping through the valleys of the Baltic Highlands. It drove the cold just a little deeper into one's bones. In that part of the world, the winter came baring teeth.

3

Martin had never been anywhere farther out of Virginia than the ass-end of western Kentucky, where his family had occasionally gone to visit some aunt of his father who lived on a farm. So, when the opportunity came up to go on an archaeological dig with one of his professors and a group of classmates, he jumped at the chance. It's not that he'd had a great interest in Eastern Europe, but he had a great interest in seeing a place which was utterly different from that which he had always known.

Lithuania sure as shit fit the bill.

They were in rough country northwest of Vilnius. The site of the dig was a very old, pagan holy site and settlement that had been occupied by one of the region's Baltic tribes. It was their first stop before spending the remaining few days in the city of Vilnius itself, although the dig had gone poorly up until the last night. The artifacts they had uncovered late that afternoon had greatly excited the professor and the other students with a keen interest in the project. For them, there had been much cause for celebration. That night, they had opened many bottles of vodka and beer.

Upon arrival, they had all been warned of the wildlife that populated the thickly forested highlands, but no one had seen any reason to be greatly concerned. So it was with no trepidation that Martin left a heated game of poker carrying on in one of the tents to relieve himself outside at the edge of the forest. Standing there, looking up with glassy eyes into the icy, bright stars and full moon in the sky, he heard a noise. A shuffling about in the snow and turf of the forest alerted his city-boy senses. He zipped up and backed away slowly from the looming darkness of the old trees. As he backed away, he heard a scrambling of the same noise. He didn't hang around to see what it was—only turned and hobbled with his cane as fast as he could towards the tents where the gambling and laughter and light were floating in the cold and endless wilderness. Behind him, heavy breaths snorted as he was pursued.

He couldn't have been more than twenty feet from the tents when the thing overtook him. His cane went flying from his grasp to land somewhere out of reach in the darkness. As he was thrown to the ground and the full weight of the creature bore down on him, there was a flash of searing pain as his flesh was torn open. The force of the attack spun him to the side, and he rolled before coming to rest on his back in the dirt. Recovered from its miscalculated lunge was a wolf, its pelt of brilliant gray and deep ash. It stared at him and bared its fearsome fangs as a low growl escaped its maw.

Martin was sure this was the end, but as the beast paused and studied him, as his side burned with agony from the bite, he noticed something quite strange and curious. Hanging from the thick mane of fur around its neck was a silver charm—a cross of the Eastern Orthodox Church.

What was an animal doing wearing jewelry?

He had no sooner formed the thought in his head than it was torn asunder. There was an explosion from the dark and the wolf crumpled, clawing along the dirt and howling its death song. Before he could understand what had happened, Martin saw the stout shape of Yuri, one of their guides, step into his field of vision and level a shotgun at the groaning beast. There was another explosion, and the air filled with fresh gun smoke as the head of the thing was almost entirely obliterated. A shower of bone and gore erupted from it and covered everything nearby, including Martin.

He looked up at the towering Russian who now stood over him and offered a reassuring hand up, a cigarette dangling from his lips.

"Does not need silver bullet," Yuri proclaimed in gravelly, broken English as he offered a massive hand to Martin. "Only good aim and no head."

Upon standing, Martin felt the burning pain in his side and wished for his cane as the burly Russian helped him into the nearby tent. As he was laid down on a cot, with many others poring over his wounds and calling for the medical kit, Martin remembered only muttering over and over again, "My cane. I need my cane."

Then he was swallowed by the merciful blackness of shock and unconsciousness.

When he awoke the next day in a Vilnius hospital, he was somewhat dismayed to find none of his classmates around him. As he stared through the window that looked out into a triage area, he saw only the hulking form of the old Russian who had saved him. Yuri was engaged in a heated conversation with one of the younger, white-coated doctors, yelling and pointing toward Martin's room. Though he could not understand what was being said, there was one phrase that the Russian man kept repeating with dire emphasis. Martin didn't know what it meant at the time but later asked the doctor.

The man regarded him darkly, then leaned in, and whispered, "The mark of the wolf."

Martin squirmed. "Is that like rabies…I mean, do I need a shot or something?"

The physician gave a laugh and smacked Martin's shoulder.

"Eh! Just superstitious country folk."

The mark of the wolf.

Assured by the doctor that had the animal gotten a better hold on him, its bite would have torn into his intestines, Martin left Vilnius with the distinct impression that he was lucky to be alive. On the plane, climbing into the gray skies, he had dearly wished only for home and to leave the terror of the Eastern European woods behind him.

4

They sat at a corner booth in the Village Café, one of the many venerated drinking and eating establishments in the Fan District that attracted the city's usual eclectic mix of folk; dirt-poor streetwalkers with just enough coin for a beer, off-duty cops, dolled-up trannies, West End slummers, and crusty, bespectacled hipsters. It was one of those many places in the city where one could really let their freak flag fly if they were so inclined, and that's why Martin and Oscar frequented the place.

"You look like hell," Oscar said.

Martin, who had been staring down into the golden depths of his beer rather than actually drinking it, looked up and smirked.

"You say the sweetest things."

"I'm serious," Oscar insisted, lifting his pint glass and draining it. "You haven't looked this bad since your brush with death in Latvia."

"Lithuania."

Oscar waved it off.

"Whatever former Soviet Union shithole it was," he teased.

Martin gave no retort, no reply.

"Is this leg thing really bugging you that much?" Oscar asked.

Martin took a long drink of his beer and nodded his head. He had told Oscar about waking in the middle of the night and walking down the hall to grab a smoke, about seeing the cane. He had not mentioned anything about the fitful dream or his concern regarding Morgan Wells and what might have happened to her. Martin had even given him a demonstration of his newfound mobility by pirouetting on his bum leg like a bearded ballerina. Oscar had howled with laughter.

"You know, I know you don't believe in miracles, you godless heathen," Oscar said. "But most people in your situation would be over the moon."

"But how is it even possible? You're the pre-med student. Tell me how I go from twelve years of leaning on the stick to moonwalking like Michael Jackson?"

Oscar snorted.

"One day of being normal and suddenly you're Michael Jackson."

"I think you're missing my point," Martin pressed.

Oscar sighed.

"No, I read you loud and clear. Listen, I'm not a doctor-"

"Yet."

"That's right, *yet*. But I've heard of stories like this, even read of them in textbooks. Lifelong injuries suddenly repairing, cancer patients on death's door going into remission. This stuff happens sometimes. I consider it a miracle of the human body and maybe something more. I know that's not your thing, though, so why don't you just think of it as a medical anomaly...a particularly beneficial one...and just take it for what it's worth. Some of us would do almost anything to have your *problem*."

Martin glanced down at the midnight blue frame of the Wildcat powered wheelchair that got Oscar around these days. As a child, the poor guy had suffered a severe spinal injury at the hands of his abusive father who, after finding his seven-year-old son tricking out the walls of his bedroom with some paint, had seen fit to toss him down the half-flight of stairs in their split-level house. The doctors had said that it was a one-in-a-million chance that Oscar could have hit those stairs like he did: in precisely the worst way. Talk about anomalies. Suddenly, Martin really did feel like a shitheel.

"You're right," he conceded. "The next round's on me."

"Ha!" Oscar retorted, raising his empty glass to get the waiter's attention. "And the next and the next and the next after that." He tapped the chassis of his Wildcat. "If I don't get pulled for a DUI going back to the dorm in this thing, you will have failed me."

Martin grinned. "Deal."

5

By just shy of nine o'clock that night, they had gotten good and tight. Oscar had managed to fill up two piss bags and had to change it out for another. They would have stayed longer but as the place got more and more crowded, Oscar pushed for leaving and going back to Martin's apartment to drink. It happened sometimes, Martin had noticed, when Oscar was feeling self-conscious about his disability and the wheelchair. As he often put it, he wasn't fond of "being the biggest gimp in the room."

They stopped by Oscar's dorm room so he could pick up another bag for his catheter and Martin stood outside and smoked while he waited for his friend. Moments later, Martin stumbled, pie-eyed, into his apartment and went immediately down the hallway toward the kitchen. Oscar rolled in behind him, closed and locked the door. He opened the doors to the balcony and went out onto it. The summer sky had darkened to well past twilight and, in the east, the moon had begun to rise. It was a beautiful evening.

The friends sat there and talked of girls and music and college life. In this merciful time, Martin's thoughts were not drawn to nightmares or miracles or the murdered girl across the way. It felt good. It felt normal.

"Want another one?" Martin asked Oscar, having just returned from the bathroom.

"Sure," Oscar replied, draining the last of his beer.

He pointed at Martin's bottle.

"Tsk-tsk," he said. "You still got a swallow or two in there. If you don't finish it, that's alcohol abuse."

Martin smirked and upended his bottle, then walked back into the apartment to fetch more. Halfway into the living room, he stopped. He was woozy, feeling too light, and his guts wrenched into a knot. The apartment glittered and faded, then came again. The room swam before him with unnatural motion.

"Oh, damn," Martin said, then dropped the bottles, and ran for the bathroom.

He nearly fell making the hurried turn from the hallway but was on his knees in front of the toilet within seconds. He vomited. The ill feeling came in great waves and in between was a lull of nausea and blurred vision. Martin couldn't remember the last time he had gotten this sick from drinking.

"Martin, you okay?" Oscar called from the living room as he rolled toward the hallway.

He leaned over and spewed chunks of bar food into the bowl, then sat back. His head was swimming.

"I don't know, man," he replied. "Pretty sick all of a sudden. I don't feel right."

The shape of Oscar in his Wildcat chair rolled into view beyond the threshold of the doorway.

"It's gonna be all right," Oscar said as he closed the bathroom door.

"Yeah, I got this," he said, then lurched forward to offer another round of puke to the porcelain gods.

The world spun like a wheel, and he grabbed hold of the toilet bowl to steady it. He was adrift, on his way to passing out.

Amid that journey, Martin heard an odd sound. So out of place was it that he thought for sure his drunken, sickened mind was manufacturing it.

A mechanical whir and whine followed by the cracking of wood.

Screws from Martin's toolbox being driven into the door and the jamb.

"Oscar?" he called out. Martin was fading, to be sure. "Oscar, what the fuck are you doing, man?"

"It's gonna be all right," Oscar replied again, with an icy calm.

6

Oscar sat in the darkness of the apartment listening as Martin stirred in the bathroom on the other side of the living room wall. He heard him get to his feet, heard the porcelain top of the toilet tank shift as he stumbled into it. A moment later, after Martin had no doubt steadied himself, he shuffled across to the door and tried it. Oscar listened as the brass knob turned and jiggled but of course the door did not open.

"Oscar?" Martin called out, muffled from behind the wall. "Oscar, I think I'm locked in here, man."

"I know," Oscar replied.

Martin snorted.

"Well, you gonna help me out here?"

Oscar wheeled into the hallway, stopped in front of the bathroom door.

"No, Martin. I'm not."

In the bathroom, Martin leaned against the door. Was this some kind of joke? The vomiting was over, but he still didn't feel right.

"Come on. I think I'm really sick."

"That'd be the lobelia extract. They call it pukeweed. Can you believe that?"

"You poisoned me?"

"Yeah, sorry about that," Oscar replied through the door, glancing down at the empty vial of extract that he'd had in his dorm room as part of a homeopathy kit. "I needed you in there. Contained. And it's not like I could drag you in myself."

"Contained?" Martin whispered.

"Oscar!" Martin screamed. "What the hell is this?"

"You really don't remember, do you?"

"Remember what?"

In the hallway, Oscar shook his head and sighed.

"What you did last night. What you became. What you *are*."

Martin's world was beginning to spin again, his mind crashing in on itself. He sat down on the edge of the tub and cradled his head.

"Tell me."

Oscar recounted the early evening of the previous night. They had gone to see one of the dollar movies at The Byrd Theater, then to a bar for something to eat and a couple of beers. The moon had just come to full that night and it had been high and bright all evening. Tired, they had returned to the apartment and managed one more beer before calling it a night.

Later, around midnight Oscar had been awoken from his deep slumber on the couch by what he thought was a dog outside. As he sat up and slipped his glasses on, he saw Martin come stumbling out of his room. The apartment had been dark, so he hadn't seen the whole of it but there was no denying the hunched, canine shape of the thing that staggered toward the apartment door and fumbled with the latch even as Martin's hands were changing into the clawed pads of an animal. And the reek of him had been foul, the whole place smelling at once like a dog wet with afterbirth. He had called out to him, but Martin made it out of the apartment and went bounding down the steps.

Oscar got himself into the Wildcat and rolled out onto the balcony. From the open main door below, he saw a solitary animal emerge. An enormous wolf—like the dire wolves of prehistory with dark, matted fur—padded onto the sidewalk, stuck its nose into the air and sniffed a moment. Then it bolted across Monument Avenue headed for the house down the street. Oscar hadn't wanted to abandon his friend in case he returned but then what if he returned as the beast? He rolled into Martin's bedroom, to his dresser drawer where he kept his gun. A Colt Python .357 revolver. He took the gun and sat there in the living room for what seemed like hours, just waiting to see if his friend would return.

Martin returned all right. He fell in through the open apartment door in a naked heap. Oscar came to his aid and found him unconscious and covered in blood and gore that was not his own. Oscar had then spent the rest of the night cleaning Martin up, scrubbing the floor where he had landed and wiping down the apartment door smeared with bloody prints. He had managed to awaken Martin enough to get him into bed. When Oscar left the apartment, he did so with a trash bag full of bloody rags, clothing, and paper towels that he chucked into the dumpster of a 7-11 on the way back to his dorm room.

That morning, Oscar had seen the story about the murdered sorority girl on the news and he knew that it had been Martin who had done it. Not Martin exactly, but the beast that he had become. He wouldn't breathe a word about it, though he was not sure what would become of his friend. This thing that had been visited upon him in the wilds of Lithuania was not over. It would come back.

The old myths didn't ring true in every aspect, though. Or so it seemed. It had been six months since Martin's encounter with the wolf and full moons had come and gone without incident. Oscar's only guess was that it took that long for the fundamental portions of his friend's physiology to accommodate the ability to shift between the two forms. Still, even knowing all of this, what he was and what he would always be, Oscar intended to help Martin. To learn to live with it if necessary, to cure it if possible. It was—to his mind—simply another form of disability.

"But then," Oscar growled, "you came into the Village all mopey, whining like a brat. 'Oh, woe is me…my leg is healed and it's a miracle but it ain't natural.' And I was supposed to do what? Sympathize with you?"

Martin hung his head.

"You selfish prick, Martin," Oscar spat.

A long moment of silence passed between them and the enormity of it all settled upon Martin with the weight and burn of a crown of molten iron. Guilt and anger. Remorse and betrayal.

"So, you locked me up in here with the thing that I'll become."

Oscar glanced at his watch. It was five until midnight. "We'll find out soon enough."

Martin stood and pounded on the door, rage and anguish having swelled into clenched fists.

"I wish it would have just killed me," he groaned, nearly weeping.

Oscar watched the door rattle with Martin's blows and found the screws were holding just fine. For now. Against the wiry frame of his friend, the extra measures were certainly adequate to the task. But against a four-hundred-pound wolf it was likely to give way.

In fact, he was counting on it.

Fingering the cold steel of the Colt Python in his lap, he melted back into the darkness of the living room, never turning his back on the hallway or the bathroom door.

7

A few minutes later, he sat in the Wildcat, listening to Martin thrash about in the bathroom. The sound of plastic ripping and metal clanging as the shower curtain and rings were ripped from the rod. The transformation, he surmised, must be extraordinarily traumatic, though he never heard his friend cry out in pain. The whole affair took no more than two and a half minutes to complete.

Then there came the growling.

After the first lunge at the door brought the sharp sound of cracking wood, Oscar switched the safety off and brought the revolver up. The assault on the door continued and with each lunge and crack, Oscar's hands shook more and more. The enormous gun was heavy in his grip, and it wobbled.

A loud crash and most of the heavy oak door was ripped free, swinging open into the hallway. The wolf's momentum carried it forward and it crumpled against the far wall but righted itself instantly and turned its snout in Oscar's direction. It crept forward, the moonlight coming in from the window spilling upon it as it came. The wolf's golden eyes flashed in the half-light, and it bared its mouthful of teeth at him, a string of saliva stretching toward the floor from its dark gums.

His hands and the pistol were shaking wildly. Oscar couldn't hit the beast from this distance even if he tried. In his mind, he urged the thing on, but it only stalked forward slowly, its eyes never leaving his. God help him but Oscar could not escape the feeling that there was still something of Martin behind those lupine orbs. Some last measure of friendship that stayed the attack.

Oscar bared his own teeth at the thing.

"Come on," he screamed at it. "Come get me, you sorry-assed sonofabitch!"

The wolf cocked its head to the side a moment and whatever loyalty had remained disappeared in that movement, for the beast took a few strides and then leaped. The weight of the beast would have toppled Oscar if not for the Wildcat. The chair was a piece of machinery with considerable heft. What surprised him, though, were the gears being rendered useless against the force of the thing and before he knew it, they were all rolling backward; Oscar and the wheelchair and the wolf.

They hurtled past the doors that opened onto the balcony; the plastic lawn chairs knocked aside as they came. When they hit the railing, it slowed their momentum quite a bit. But as Oscar heard the old, weathered wood crack and splinter, he knew it would not be enough. A second later, they were falling backwards through the air, the man and the wolf locked in a fatal embrace.

The long, ivory daggers of the beast's teeth missed Oscar's throat but found purchase in his shoulder and they bit deeply. He cried out from the pain but also from the sudden terror that gripped him. They were falling from three stories up and the ground was coming.

When they hit, the wolf slammed into him and the gun pressed up into the animal's belly. While his senses were still about him, Oscar commanded his trigger finger to contract.

There was a muffled blast between him and the wolf and a sudden flow of warmth that spread out across Oscar's torso in a rush of dark blood. The wolf whimpered from the shot and from the impact of the fall, then rolled off of him. Oscar looked over at it and he could plainly see that although it was wounded, the injury was not mortal. He recalled Martin's tale of the attack in Lithuania and the words of the shotgun-wielding Russian guide.

Does not need silver bullet. Only good aim and no head.

The breath had been knocked out of Oscar and the searing pain of the bite on his shoulder made it difficult, but he reached over and placed the tip of the Colt's barrel against the ear of the beast even as it began to get to its feet.

"Thank you for this, my friend," he whispered to the wolf. "You sure as hell don't deserve it."

Then he pulled the trigger and shattered the top of its head into a hundred pieces of blood and bone and bits of golden eye.

It wasn't long before people came to see what had happened, before they were standing over him, calling the paramedics on their cell phones and gawking at the whole scene. It seemed that there were a great many things the old stories had wrong about these magnificent beasts, Oscar reflected. The need of killing silver and the immediacy of full transformation were among them.

Six months, he thought, smiling. *Six months.*

The dead wolf beside him remained just as it was, never shifting back into the form of his friend. The myths taught that, no matter how much of the monster there was, deep inside, the man always remained…that it was the man who would emerge at the moment of death. But that just wasn't true.

Once the mark of the wolf had been made, the man became nothing more than camouflage for the hunting thing within—a long and tedious interlude of self in between the nights when the full face of the cruel moon would rise, high and reigning in the sky.

Maybe it was just his imagination, but even as the wound in his shoulder ached down to his bones, Oscar thought he could sense a tingling in his legs as severed nerves in his spine began to rebuild their connections to each other.

Oh, the places he would go.

DARK ROSALEEN

1
5 February 1847

Having stood on deck and watched as the harbor at Liverpool disappeared behind us in the heavy morning fog of the Irish Sea, I affirm that we have set our course due south to sail around the Dingle Peninsula of Ireland where we will then turn northward. If luck and the weather is to be on our side, we shall be making port in Quebec, British North America by the middle of March. It is a journey that we have undertaken many times before under the leadership of Captain Redway, hauling cargo of dry goods and other wares to the North American territories. This time promises to be quite different, I am afraid, for rather than tea and spices and textiles, our cargo consists of seventy-eight human beings—yet another small portion of the exodus of souls from Ireland's shores and the famine that continues to decimate her people.

Many captains have refused to take on such work and I suppose the reasons that we have agreed to do so are largely sentimental. I was born near Athlone in County Westmeath, though I was later moved to and raised in London. For Captain Redway's part, he has always maintained a great affection for his Irish mother, whose name was given to our vessel some years ago. So, it is out of a sense of compassion and duty to the island of our origins that we take on the woeful task of becoming yet another "coffin ship" as such vessels have come to be called.

Indeed, they are a pitiful lot—these famine refugees. A great many of them outwardly suffer the effects of starvation forced upon them by the potato blight that has all but destroyed the crops across the entire island. It is my understanding that, as a result, the meager amount of potatoes they are able to harvest are sold and go to pay for, in most cases, only a portion of the rent that they owe their landlords, leaving them little or nothing to eat for themselves and no means by which to acquire other foods. The health of some of these folk is so poor, and their malnourished bodies so riddled with sickness that they appear to me as little more than wraiths. What has been allowed to happen to these people is a damnable sin in the estimation of this former soldier and one that will forever be a stain upon Britannia's soul.

Regrettably, though, my opinions on such matters are of no consequence to anyone. They shall therefore be relegated to the pages of this journal given to me this past Christmas by my betrothed, Margaret, whose warm company I will no doubt soon long for. As ever, I remain James Robert Tilleigh, First Mate of the Brig Rosaleen. I am merely a man of the sea and nothing besides.

-JRT

There was a knock at his cabin door followed by the gruff Cockney voice of midshipman Poole.

"Mister Tilleigh?"

"Aye?"

"Begging your pardon, sir, but the captain is requesting you on deck."

"Thank you, Mr. Poole."

With that, he heard the midshipman go plodding back down the corridor. Sitting on the edge of the bed, Tilleigh closed the journal and slipped it beneath his pillow. He rose and donned his coat and cap, then headed topside.

When he emerged on deck, he noticed the sky in the west lightening from gray to blue and took such a change in the weather as a good portent for their journey. The wind was in the sails and half of the crew were on deck bustling about in their duties while the other half were below in the mess room. A few of the Irish had come topside and leaned against the starboard railing, perhaps waiting to see bits of sandy strand, jagged cliffs, and green fields when the ship rounded the peninsula, though that would not be for some time. It would likely be the last that most of them would ever see of their homeland and the drawn, bony faces of these folk openly displayed their despondency.

One of them was a young lad who stood against the railing and drew forth small bits of lead shot from an unattended box on deck. One after another, he flung them into the ocean, judging the distance of every throw. Tilleigh started toward him.

"Boy!" he cried out. The box of shot, commonly used in cannon to maim men and destroy the sails of an enemy vessel, was of no real importance to the ship. They had not sailed with cannons on board in quite some time. However, the men used the shot for purposes of amusement, much in the same way as the lad was doing now.

The boy started and swung round, shot clutched in his fingers, his fist drawn back as if he might lob a blow at Tilleigh.

"What do you want?" the boy asked, one eye staring dead on at Tilleigh, the other one lazy and slightly askew.

Tilleigh could not help but admire the boy's spirit. "That's ship's property there, if you wouldn't mind."

"What's it to you?"

With astonishing speed, Tilleigh reached out and snatched the bit of shot curled into the boy's fist and tossed it himself into the lapping waters. The boy stared down at his hand, gobsmacked.

"Jim Tilleigh, First Mate," he replied, offering his hand.

The boy regarded him a moment, though his suspicion waned, and he clasped the sailor's hand.

"Gerard Flynn."

"Pleased to meet you, Gerard. Are you alone on this journey or is your family below deck?"

The boy shook his head. "Just me and my sister, Moyna. She's in the hold with the others."

"What about your Mam and Da?"

"Constable took Da when we couldn't pay the rent. He's on a prison ship halfway to Australia by now."

"And your Mam?"

"She was sick with consumption. We left Donegal and Mum took us back to her village in Down. But the place was deserted, and no kin were about. She died while I was away in Newcastle lookin' for work."

Tilleigh pursed his lips and shook his head. "I'm very sorry to hear that. Very sorry indeed. How old are you, Gerard?"

"Fifteen. Moyna's to be thirteen in the spring." Gerard then eyed the first mate with renewed suspicion. "You some kind of peeler?"

"A policeman?" He shook his head. "No."

"You ask questions like a peeler. Army, then? Navy?"

Tilleigh smiled. "At one time, I served in the British Navy, as did nearly every man here. However, we came to part ways, owing to ideals and practices of late. So, we are no friend of the Queen's military if that is what you are wondering."

Gerard managed a cautious smile. "Brilliant. Then I won't have to kill you."

Before Tilleigh could inquire as to the root of the boy's hostility—though he could guess—the lad was blowing by him, headed below deck. "Have to check on my sister," he shouted. In a moment, he disappeared from view and Tilleigh made his way to the quarterdeck to meet with the captain.

He nodded a greeting to the captain as he approached.

"How fare the spirits of our passengers, Mr. Tilleigh?"

"As you can see, Captain, a great many are hoping for a last glimpse of home, I'm afraid. And are rather sullen for it."

Redway looked out at the few scattered Irish on the deck and nodded. "Who was the boy with the lazy eye?"

"Ah, young master Gerard Flynn, sir. Aged fifteen years. Quite a lad, though. Brash and full of vigor and quite ready to brawl with the next British enlisted man that crosses his path."

"That so?"

"Aye, sir. Threatened to kill me. In a manner of speaking."

The captain had a good chuckle at this.

"Very well, Mr. Tilleigh. Get the men topside. We shall be rounding the Dingle peninsula within the hour. And spread the word down in the hold as well. They deserve a last look."

2

The hold of the ship was dark and the air more than a little foul with the smell of the many unwashed and ailing refugees. Gerard walked among them, careful not to step on the limbs of the sick and sleeping, whose numbers were many. Those of better health sat with their families, eyeing others with suspicion and dread. The dim light from the wall lanterns made it difficult to see. After a moment, he heard his sister's voice shout to him from the far corner of the hold.

"Gerard! Over here!"

The boy continued on through the huddled masses and saw his sister seated on the floor across from a tall, scraggly fellow of middle age and they were engaged in a game of jackrocks.

"Moyna," he said as he approached.

"Gerard, there you are! Come and sit!"

"Moyna, did you forget what I told you?"

Looking up at him, she waved him away. "Come sit and play with us."

The man looked up at the boy and smiled. His teeth were cracked and yellowed. His grin seemed more that of a beast than a man. Even in the dim light, Gerard could see that his complexion was sallow and dark circles of thin skin hung below his eyes. The man stretched out his hand.

"Greetings. Boyle's the name."

Gerard looked down at the offered hand and shook his head.

"No, thank you. Mr. Boyle, I thank you for taking the time to play with my sister but for the rest of the trip, we'll be keepin' to ourselves. Understand?"

Boyle nodded silently and the boy stood there, staring him down until the old man turned and walked away.

Moyna sat alone, pouting.

"Come now, Moyna, you don't need to be knockin' around with strangers."

She cut her eyes at him. "He was playing jackrocks with me. At least someone was. You never play games with me anymore."

Gerard rolled his eyes. "I know. I know it's been bad for us since Mum passed. I just been tryin' to keep us going is all. When we get to Quebec, things'll be different. You'll see. I promise."

She turned to look at him, the hardness of her blue eyes softening. "Because you're my big brother, I forgive you."

Gerard smiled and wrapped his arm around her neck. "That's right, I am your big brother, and I love you." With his other hand, he reached around her and grabbed the brown leather satchel she carried.

"Now, let's play some jacks!"

Turning it upside down, he emptied the contents of it onto the floor. Several jackstones and the polished wooden ball went skittering across the floor, followed by a tin cross-shaped pendant, a few pence, crumbs from bits of bread long ago eaten and her peculiar doll. The latter object hit the floor with a dull thud, such was its weight. Gerard picked it up and studied it as he had several times before. It was a strange, almost hideous thing and each time he looked upon it, he found its form more confusing than the last. Hewn from some kind of dark stone, it was a figure, bloated and somewhat man-shaped sitting atop a column. Its head was adorned with long, dangling strands of what Gerard thought might be a beard. Subtle details in the smaller crevices and gouges were covered by hardened dirt and thick, barnacle-like growths. There were indecipherable marks all about the base that might have been some kind of writing but were more likely scratches worn onto the surface with age.

"This is absolutely the worst doll I've ever seen; you know that?"

She wrinkled her nose and snatched the figure from his grasp, slipped it back into her satchel. "It's mine and I like it."

"Why?" Gerard asked as he pulled the jacks together to play.

"Because, you eejit, the *murúch* gave it to me."

Gerard smiled at this and shook his head. "Next time, ask the bloody fishman for some food, yeah?"

Moyna giggled but said nothing.

They set about their game of jackrocks, neither one aware of the eyes staring from the darkness across the ship's hold.

Such a pretty polly, Boyle thought.

Younger than her mouthy brother. Curly locks of dark hair, pink lips and supple flesh hidden beneath the drab stitches of her clothing. Lust and a thousand black notions slithered through his mind.

Boyle wore his wolf's smile back to the forward of the hold where he sat gladly amongst the ill and starved and dying. There he perched, like a stone gargoyle, leering.

3

The captain had commanded an announcement to all of the refugees that if they wished a last look at Ireland, the time was now. Tilleigh stood on deck, doing his best to be of good cheer in welcoming the folk who came up. Many ascended the stairs to the deck in a slow march, their withered limbs and gaunt faces shaking, and their shoulders slumped as if the weight of the entire world was upon them. A few who were in better health managed a courteous smile or nod, but most said nothing and returned no gesture of greeting. They only stared out across the Irish Sea with ghostly longing. After a few moments, someone shouted.

"Look! There she is!"

There was a stirring as the passengers bunched up, craned their necks and scanned the blue horizon. A small tip of black could be seen at first, then grew larger. Captain Redway was steering them closer to the shore than he might otherwise have done and soon they could see the emerald fields shining in the winter sun. The meadows crowned the rocky cliffs that the sea had broken itself upon since time unremembered.

An old woman, bent with time and hunger, sang a lonesome dirge in her native tongue. No others joined in, nor did they sing a song of their own. Though Tilleigh could not understand the words, one thing was clear: this dark melody, this dirge, belonged to all of them.

After too brief a time, the singer went quiet and they were drifting away, the island receding from view.

Tilleigh watched as many of the people began dispersing from the deck and back down toward the hold. There was not much more to see. In a few moments, the shores of Erin's Isle would disappear and be nothing more than a memory.

As the last of the refugees made their way down into the belly of the ship, Tilleigh heard the sound of shouting and turned to see the boy, Gerard, fighting his way against the flow of people. He burst out onto the deck, a small, leather satchel in his grip and his head turning this way and that, searching frantically.

Then his eyes settled on Tilleigh, who looked at the boy with concern.

"It's Moyna!" he cried to the First Mate. "She's gone!"

4
6 February 1847

I have never been so loathe to make an entry into my journal as I am this morning. As we departed the waters off the coast of Ireland, a boy by the name of Gerard Flynn alerted us that his sister had gone missing. Upon further investigation, I found this claim to be both credible and troublesome, as one of the other refugees, a man reputed to suffer from insanity named Nester Boyle was also missing. I assembled the crew and formed a search party. After a quarter of an hour or so, one of the men shouted that they'd found something of suspicion.

I made my way from the crewmen's locker and sick bay to the gunroom where the captain and I normally take our meals. Of the few coat and broom closets that are in this room, it was discovered that one had been barred somehow from the inside. I quieted the men and put my ear to the door. I could hear muffled sounds from within, though as to their exact nature, I could not be certain. I commanded the brutish midshipman Poole to break down the door. What we found I am hesitant to even record here. The madman Boyle was indeed in the closet, as was the young girl. Boyle had her on hands and knees with a rusty blade to her back and the folds of her dress were bunched about his waist and his trousers at his knees. The girl was sobbing quietly. It is unclear to me how long the rape had been going on when we found them, though it matters not. The damage to the young girl has been done and the experience will likely haunt her for the remainder of her life.

Mr. Poole wrestled the knife from Boyle and clasped the irons on him. I then instructed that they take the madman topside and lash him to the deck.

Both Captain Redway and I offered Moyna and Gerard shelter in our personal quarters and on her behalf, Gerard accepted mine. Eschewing my bunk, he insisted they would be fine bedding down on the floor of my cabin. Since being attacked, Moyna has not spoken and cannot bear to look on any man other than her brother. I could hear her gentle weeping all through the night.

-JRT

5

When Tilleigh stepped out onto the deck that morning, he was immediately struck by the unseasonable warmth of the air. As he ascended the steps onto the quarterdeck, he greeted the captain who stood near the wheel taking his morning tea. The navigator, named Jacobs, was poring over his charts. The warm air was nearly entirely without so much as a breeze and the waters all around them were oddly still as far as the eye could see in all directions. The sails hung limp on the masts.

"We won't be making our arrival date if this keeps up," Tilleigh observed.

Captain Redway took a sip of his tea. "Can't last. Never does."

"What does Mister Jacobs calculate our position to be?"

The captain looked over at the frantic navigator. "Mister Jacobs can calculate nothing at the moment. The sun has been hidden behind these clouds all morning, making it impossible to get a bearing."

"What of the compass?"

Redway shook his head. "None are functioning proper. Blasted things can't make up their minds which way is north."

Tilleigh nodded. These phenomena by themselves were not uncommon. On the sea, one was likely to come upon odd weather and dead waters, even areas that rendered compasses useless. These peculiarities often passed quickly, however, so Tilleigh was not concerned.

Just then, Tilleigh heard a racket coming from the forward of the ship and realized it was the voice of Nester Boyle, screaming out to be released.

"It'll take us! Take us all! You'll see!" Boyle spat at the men who stood around him, all of them gawking and having a good laugh.

"What will take us, Mr. Boyle?"

"The kraken, you puffed-up twit!"

At this, the men roared.

"So, it's your assertion that a kraken will come and take the Rosaleen down below the waves, is it?" Tilleigh asked, bemused.

Boyle's face wrinkled with disgust. "Not the kraken, no. The kraken sleeps. Sleeps down in the cold and deep."

Tilleigh narrowed his eyes.

"But the kraken takes in other ways," Boyle said, looking calmly up at Tilleigh, an evil glint in his eye. "And that's how it'll come for us. For you."

Something about the look he fixed Tilleigh with chilled the First Mate and he ordered the men to secure Boyle in some dark hole below decks where he could rant to his black heart's content.

Once it was done, the deck was suddenly quiet but for the moaning of the spars.

"Let's hope that's the last we see of Barmy Boyle," Redway commented.

"Amen, sir."

Redway nodded and looked out at the calm sea.

"Still waters and strange weather make me uneasy, Mr. Tilleigh," he said as he took up the spyglass and scanned the horizon. "Just where in God's name are we?"

As no man could manage so much as a guess, the question was met with silence.

6
10 February 1847

Again this morning we find ourselves on still and breezeless waters, surrounded by a fog as thick as any I have ever seen. I have made no entry for the past several days as there has been little to report. I have never seen such strange circumstances in all my years at sea.

To make matters worse, Mr. Harrison, our cook, has shown me something both disturbing and perplexing. He took me this morning to the galley storage room where we are holding Nester Boyle to show me that the foodstuffs are rapidly decaying with some form of rot or mold. Mr. Harrison further explained that the same blight was upon all of the food on board. I fear it will not be long before it is inedible.

At the moment, the water that flows from the tanks seems drinkable, though it has a faint, earth-brown cast to it. Attempts by the crew to supplement our food by fishing from the deck have thus far been unsuccessful. There has not been a single nibble on a line, though the men have said they have seen weird, dark colored shapes break the surface from time to time and then slip back down into the still, stagnant waters.

-JRT

Tilleigh and Redway sat in silence at the table in the gunroom, each man cutting around and scraping away the bits of rot from the salt pork before him. The tea, having been made with the ship's supply of darkening drinking water, had a foul taste not unlike seawater. Redway poured the tea from both cups back into the pot and reached under the table and drew forth a bottle of whiskey. He filled each cup halfway and made a perfunctory toasting gesture, then sipped.

"Well, there's some good news. Seems the spirits are the only perishables on board that are not…perishing."

Tilleigh snorted and threw his cup back, feeling the warm liquor slide down into his belly.

"Cheers," he offered, as sardonic a toast as ever there had been.

Redway nodded and sipped more.

"Captain, you've not said much in regard to the peculiarity of our circumstances."

Redway eyed Tilleigh over the rim of his cup. "And?"

"Well, sir, the men…sailors that they are…are beginning to talk. Outlandish rumors, of course. Supernatural imaginings. Some say we are cursed."

The captain smiled, took another slug of whiskey and eyed Tilleigh with his leveling gaze. "What makes you think we are not?"

Tilleigh sat, mouth agape at the notion that the captain would lend any credence to such superstitions. "Sir, I hardly think that—"

The door to the gunroom swung open to reveal a sailor named Granby standing there, his eyes wide and pallor gone cold and pale.

"Beg your pardon, Captain, but there's something you ought to see."

The captain and first mate rose and followed Granby down the corridor and into the sailors' mess. Something had the men in an uproar. Granby parted the crowd, and they stopped outside of the storage room where Boyle was being held. The ship's physician, Dr. Brown, leaned over Boyle, who lay prone on the floor.

"What's this about?" Redway demanded.

Doctor Brown looked up and moved to the side. Tilleigh could see the face of the criminal and he recoiled, unable to censor himself. "Dear Lord!"

Boyle's face was covered in blood and raw skin that hung in sinewy threads around large patches of his flesh—flesh that had become dark in color and scaly in appearance, resembling the scalloped tiles of a roof.

The doctor rose and explained that for the moment, Mr. Boyle was sedated with laudanum.

"But there's no telling how long it will last. He was quite agitated. Bloody mad, to be honest, Captain. He was on and on about his hunger and how he was going to kill us all. It took six men to subdue him." Doctor Brown meant to continue but the captain silenced him.

"We should speak in private," he said and waved them back down the hallway.

Back in the gunroom, the doctor continued.

"I don't know what it is. Never seen anything like it before. The man was completely maniacal. He tore his own face to ribbons, Captain."

Redway looked somber.

"And that's not the worst of it," Brown said. "Three other men came to me this morning with small patches that look identical to Boyle's scaly rash."

"A sickness?"

Doctor Brown nodded.

"So, it's spreading?"

The doctor nodded again, and they both glanced over at Tilleigh, who had gone white.

"What is it, man?" Redway demanded.

"Moyna," the first mate said. "The young girl, Captain. I checked on her this morning…she was sleeping and looked well enough… but I noticed the same thing. I thought likely it was bruising from the assault, but now…."

Redway sighed and growled his frustration. He tore the cork from the bottle of whisky and poured himself a glassful. "Can we expect the others to react the same way?"

"I've no reason to suspect otherwise."

Redway took a few sips as he thought through the next course of action.

"Doctor Brown, instruct the crew to assemble topside by the mainmast. Mr. Tilleigh, go to your cabin and gather up the girl and her things. Quarantine her down in the sail room. The doctor and I will identify all men and refugees displaying the condition and quarantine them below decks as well."

Both men looked at their captain with long faces. He could feel their doubt.

"I will not risk this madness spreading through the ranks of every man, woman and child on this ship. I will do what must be done."

7

When Tilleigh arrived at his cabin, he found the door locked from the inside. As he put his ear to the wood, he heard strange sounds emanating from within. Sounds of sobbing and low, guttural hissing.

"Gerard, are you in there?"

There was a long moment of silence. "I am."

"Gerard, open the door."

"I can't. There's somethin' wrong with Moyna."

"I know. You need to open the door so that we can let the doctor help her."

"I don't think he can."

Then there was a commotion and a panicked sound that Tilleigh recognized as coming from the boy. He began searching his coat pockets for his keys.

He pulled the key from his pocket and slipped it into the lock. He turned it slowly but before he could complete the rotation, the door burst open, swinging into the passageway and knocking Tilleigh to the floor.

He could hardly believe what he saw. The thing that had been locked in his cabin—the thing that had once been Moyna Flynn—was leering down at him, wide-eyed and its mouth turned up in a snarl to reveal rows of jagged teeth. Although the thing was utterly inhuman and the stink of the deep sea emanated from its frog-like skin, some features of the face still bore some resemblance to the young girl. The rest of its powerful, wiry frame was covered by flesh stretched over bone and muscle and was marked by patches of scales.

"Moyna, no!" Gerard called from inside the cabin.

The thing looked back at Gerard and then down at Tilleigh. It hissed, then went bounding off down the hallway with incredible speed. Tilleigh watched it disappear around a corner and then reached out, grabbing the ankle of the boy as he rushed by, meaning to give chase.

"Let go of me, ye bastard! That's my sister!"

Tilleigh yanked him down and took him by the shirt collar, pressing him against the wall.

"That's not your sister any longer, boy! Now get yourself right!"

"But I've got to find her!"

"I will, Gerard. Stay here and I will find her."

He stole carefully through the passageways of the ship, following the stench of ocean rot. He soon found himself outside of the threshold of the galley. With all the sailors having been assembled on deck, the galley and adjoined mess room were empty and should well have been silent but there was no mistaking the sound that Tilleigh heard coming from within the galley.

Something inside was eating.

Unknown 1847

We are adrift on a sea of strange horrors that dwarf even the worst of a madman's dreams. After being nearly attacked by the thing that was once Moyna, I followed its smell through the ship and into the galley. Once there, I looked on as the Moyna creature bent over the still-living Boyle and feasted without particularity on his flesh. I addressed it by name, tried to appeal to it, but it was apparent that the last vestiges of Moyna Flynn had fled entirely from the beast before me. It managed only a few words uttered in a watery voice. "So hungry" it said, again and again in between gnawing. Moments later, the captain appeared with the doctor and Mr. Poole. The captain's face was covered in specks of crimson, though I saw no wounds upon his person and found this curious. He ordered Mr. Poole to draw his pistol and instructed him to shoot both Boyle and the creature, an order with which Mr. Poole complied swiftly and without hesitation.

I later learned that it had never been the captain's intention to sequester the infected below decks. He had assembled the entire crew topside and after the infected were identified and removed to the foredeck, Captain Redway and Mr. Poole drew their pistols and executed every last one of them. Their corpses were quickly discarded overboard, forever given to the sea.

I was given a fool's errand, it seems, to keep me below decks while the executions were carried out.

Captain Redway knew I would object.

Later, the captain saw fit to do the same with the refugees down in the hold. I voiced my protests before he carried out this action, but it became clear to me that should I stand in the way, there would be a bullet put in my brain as well.

I have never doubted the captain's judgment in the past and in these matters, I can imagine only that he felt there was no choice. The captain must have known that if we ever made it to our destination, he was sure to be brought up on charges of murder.

However, that was not to be his fate.

I am saddened to report that a short time ago, Captain Redway stood at the bow of the ship and blew out the back of his skull with his own pistol.

This turn of events now leaves me in command of the Brig Rosaleen, but I ask of the Almighty, what is there to command? We are a sailing vessel without wind or waves and an unearthly darkness is ever creeping through the ranks of those still living on board. When we set sail from Liverpool, we were eighty-seven refugees and twenty-three crewmen, including myself and the captain. We now number fifty-two in all. We are without food or drinkable water. The casks of spirits seem to be the only provisions on board not spoiled and so the men have taken to drinking away the hunger and the despair.

The only good news I can report is that neither myself nor my cabin-mate, the young Gerard, show any signs of the scaly infection. We are nothing more than partners of necessity now, though, I am afraid. Since his sister's execution, he has been cold to me. Whatever foundations of trust and camaraderie might have been laid were obliterated with a single pistol shot. He regards me now as a stranger and spends a great deal of time staring at the strange statue that belonged to his sister. He knows nothing of its origins apart from her fanciful tale that she received it from a merman who crawled out of the sea in Kilkeel near the Mountains of Mourne.

Until recently, I would have given no credence to such a tale but considering the things I have witnessed, it is as likely as not. As for the statue, or idol—she called her "doll"—it is a grotesque thing to look upon and has the strange habit of being perpetually wet with seawater even after I have dried it well. While Gerard has voiced his belief that the idol may be our salvation, I am more inclined to believe it is the root of all the black things that have befallen us.

I am spent and in need of rest. Before I retire, I will again check the boy and myself for any signs of infection.

For the record, I shall not hesitate to continue the good work of Captain Redway and put down any man, woman, or child exhibiting signs of infection, even if one of them is me. Grim are my duties of late.

-JRT, Captain of the Brig Rosaleen

8
Unknown 1847

*T*o the best of my ability, I reckon that it has been more than a week since my last journal entry. It is impossible to tell the night from the day. Conditions aboard the Rosaleen have become dire, and I have been forced into hiding. In the captain's cabin, there is a false bookcase that opens to a ladder leading down to the smuggler's hold, a feature of the ship left over from Captain Redway's days as a rum runner. In this compartment are a few bottles of spirits, an arsenal of weapons, several barrels of black powder, and various items of personal and monetary significance. For the last few days this has been my home. Before I retreated into the secret confines, I managed to steal from the bread room and galley a few items that were not entirely rotten, and on them I have subsisted.

For days, Gerard and I remained barricaded in my cabin as the monstrous transformation swept through those on board. They killed amongst themselves wantonly and even talked of cooking and eating the dead.

The boy, whose behavior had grown ever more peculiar, agreed to a plan that I hatched to sneak up on deck and lower one of the dinghies into the water so that we may escape, though it would be to whatever unknown fate awaited us. Once above, we crept along under the overhang of the foredeck. All was going to plan until one of the creatures—I believe it was Doctor Brown—spotted us and sounded the alarm. In our flight back down below deck, I was separated from the boy, and he was lost to me.

Though I should have mounted a search for him, I shamefully confess that I was also glad to be rid of Gerard. His stone-quiet and brooding demeanor had begun to unnerve me. And the attention which he paid that statue! His obsession had become so all-consuming that I was forced to secret it away in a place where he could not find it.

I saw in his eyes that he hated me for doing so.

Silently, I made it into the captain's quarters. To the smuggler's hold. The very spot where I had hidden the idol. I do not know if Gerard is also in hiding elsewhere on the ship or if he has since met with a worse fate.

In the days since, I have kept my use of the lamp to a minimum and have spent much time in darkness. It wears on me, seeps inside my heart, rots my hope and dulls my wits. My only companion has been Moyna's terrible idol. Though it is hidden in the satchel from my sight, even in the dark I feel as if it watches me. The few times that I have slept, I have dreamed things I cannot explain. Dreams of a black and faceless figure, tall and thin, walking a strand of beach beside a forest of thick and lush vegetation that, along with all the world, falls into decay as the figure passes. It leaves no footprints in the sand. Hordes of mermen…fishmen, if you will…crawl from the surf. Always it is the same dream and always I wake trembling and in a sweat with the unmistakable sense that in the dream I am witnessing a future that has not yet come to pass.

I am becoming weaker in mind and body with every hour and if I have any hope of escaping my circumstances, the time to act is now. I have formulated a plan and intend to see it through. I hope to see the day when I will be rid of this cursed ship, though I fear it is but a fool's hope.

This will be my last entry. I am not even certain why it is I have written all that I have of late. I suppose it has given me something on which to focus, to drive back the terror and panic that is rapping at the door of my mind.

To my darling Margaret, know that here at the end, you are still a bright light in the darkness of my thoughts. As ever, you inspire me, and I adore you now as I always shall. If I never have the privilege of becoming your husband, know that I will be less a man for it.

This is the final account of the Brig Rosaleen, a trusted vessel of many years, gone dark with misery and murder. It is the tale of her wise Captain Redway and loyal crew; of eighty-seven souls that will never make it to the shores of North America to build a new life. I know not to where I am bound, but I go gladly and with my wits about me, with courage in my heart, and trust in the Almighty. Only in Him can we know that our hunger will be tamed, that our thirst will be slaked, that our immortal souls will be guided to safe harbor from these weird and deathly waters.

-JRT

9

There had been no indication of movement in the captain's cabin since Tilleigh had hidden himself in the smuggler's hold. With as much stealth as he could manage, he emerged from the hold and into the room above. There were windows all along the aft side and for the first time in what seemed an age, Tilleigh looked outside and beheld the beauty of clear blue skies crowning the horizon. The air was stirring again and the sea moving along with it, whitecaps and waves dotting the surface of the water. To see such a change buoyed his spirits and summoned tears to his eyes. He was reluctant to tear himself from the sight but the guilt he felt for abandoning the boy had been eating at him. Tilleigh reckoned he owed it to the boy to make one last sweep of the ship in search of him.

Tilleigh lit the oil lamp and left it burning on the table. With a revolving pistol in his hand and Moyna's satchel containing the strange idol hanging about his neck, he eased into the passageway. Moving quietly, now aware of every creak and groan of the Rosaleen's timbers, he crept forward. He passed the mess room and galley, stood for a moment, listening. There was no movement, no sound to be heard.

"Gerard?" he whispered in the darkness.

When no answer came, he took the steps further below deck to the hold and the sail room. As he neared them, he smelled the rot of flesh and the pungent, salty odor of the sea. He suspected the chambers were littered with the putrid remains of those who had fallen under the gnashing teeth of the fishmen.

"Gerard?" he whispered again, but still there came no reply.

Satisfied that the boy was not there, he climbed back up a level and stood at the bottom of the stairs that led topside. Laying his body flat against them, he crawled up until he could just peek over the edge. From this vantage point, he could see the masts and the torn and rotted sails as well as the deck, where he beheld a sight that he would never be able to burn from his memory.

The creatures had gathered amidships on the deck and were lounging about quite close to each other as pack animals might. They intently picked over the flesh and bones of the dead—even their own kind, from what Tilleigh could see—and those not eating were sleeping or mating. The wantonness with which they went about their orgy of devouring and fornication was beyond even the sordid legends of Caligula himself and Tilleigh felt he would vomit. He swallowed it down and steadied himself. There was no sign of the boy, though if he were still alive, the deck was certainly not where he would be hiding. As Tilleigh looked on, he began to recognize some of the creatures, many of whom still bore some physical attributes of their previous human form. He again saw Doctor Brown as he lay, nibbling flesh from the leg bone of some unfortunate refugee. He also spotted the old Irishman from Sligo named Kilmartin coupling with another of his kind, though the thing appeared inert with death. The longer he watched, the more faces he recognized, and this only served to deepen his revulsion.

Tilleigh had just decided to retreat back to the captain's quarters and execute his escape when one of the creatures, perched atop and feasting on the body of another fishman, caught his attention. It looked up from its eating and fixed Tilleigh with a lazy-eyed stare. The boy had not evaded the blight but had succumbed to it and had been transformed. Tilleigh rose up to begin backing down the stairs when the Gerard-thing hissed at him. Immediately, the eyes of all the creatures fell on Tilleigh, suddenly exposed.

He did not wait to see them come for him but turned and ran down the stairs. He'd gotten no farther than the bottom of the steps when he heard the many footfalls of his pursuers, their webbed feet slapping against the wood.

He propelled himself forward with more speed than he thought possible for his racked, starved body. The narrow passageways worked to his advantage and the resulting bottleneck slowed their pursuit. As he approached the door to the captain's cabin, he turned and fired the pistol at them. Many shots blasted forth from the weapon with deafening force.

One or two of the creatures fell and there was a moment of hesitation. Then more fishmen were clambering over the wounded toward him. It had bought him only a few seconds, but that was all he needed. Once inside, he slammed the door shut, locked it and toppled a heavy case of books against the door.

Taking a chair from the captain's secretary, he smashed the glass windows that opened to the outside. It was then that he heard the wood of the door splinter and saw the shape of one of the creatures come powering through, landing upright on its feet and leering hungrily at him. The thing bore the last of Gerard's features; one black fish-eye lolling to the side as it opened its maw and bared its teeth.

Tilleigh brought the pistol up and squeezed the trigger but there sounded only an impotent click. Looking down, he saw the pistol was out of rounds and tossed it to the floor. He stumbled backward and reached for the oil lamp on the table but the creature, seeming almost to have discerned his intent, flipped the table. The lamp went to the floor, rolling gently to the port side of the room. Without the lamp, he might well escape, but the ship would survive and whatever evil had swallowed the bodies and souls of those on board would survive with it.

"Gerard!" he cried to the thing, hoping to appeal to the boy if there was anything of him left within that horrible form.

The thing seemed to recognize its name and cocked its head to the side, pausing for a moment. Tilleigh dove to the floor and snatched the lantern up in his grasp. He tried to raise himself but felt the cold, amphibian flesh of the creature on him then, grappling at his body with uncanny strength. Webbed claws closed around his limbs and the reeking breath of the beast was in his face. Drawing back from its snapping jaws, fighting it tooth and nail, Tilleigh edged ever closer toward the shattered window. Out of the corner of his eye, Tilleigh could see the wide blue sky through the shattered windows and hear the lapping sounds of the sea below. With the last bit of fight he could muster, he kicked out at the thing and sent it reeling across the floor toward the far side of the room. The others were starting to make their way in then, squeezing through what remained of the door and the fallen bookshelf. Tilleigh stood and took aim, hurling the burning oil lamp at the opening to the smuggler's hold. It shattered, the flaming oil spilled down into the hold, then Tilleigh turned and dove out of the window.

As he plunged into the sea, he was surprised to feel the warmth of the water. As he swam toward the surface, he wondered if his newfound freedom was nothing more than a continuation of the torment he'd endured for so long. Shaking the water from his head, he saw land in the distance. To his surprise and confusion, he recognized it as Chandeleur Sound on the American gulf coast of Louisiana. Under Captain Redway, the Rosaleen had brought many a shipment of cargo here to the port of New Orleans. How the ship had diverged so far south from the intended course in so short a time, he could only wonder at, but then the entire voyage had been the stuff of surrealism and nightmare.

Tilleigh looked up at the stern of the Rosaleen and saw the Gerard-thing hanging halfway out of the shattered window, holding something aloft in its claws. It let loose a terrible sound—a song, from what Tilleigh could reckon—that celebrated victory and triumph.

His hands went to his neck, and he discovered that Moyna's satchel containing the idol was no longer there. He must have lost it in the struggle with the creature. His heart sank and he began to lament his failure when he saw a bright flash flare up from below the creatures that stood there cheering with glee.

Before he could brace himself there was an explosion as the burning oil from the lamp reached the first of the barrels of black powder in the smuggler's hold. A rain of charred and obliterated wood and glass and metal followed, and Tilleigh felt the shockwave in his chest. Then there was another blast and another as the barrels of black powder were exploded one after the other and the Brig Rosaleen was consumed in a ravenous fire.

Tilleigh paddled his way to a large piece of wood that had once been a door on the ship. Grasping it, he belly crawled his way atop it and felt his muscles go limp with fatigue. He looked on as the last bit of the Rosaleen's main mast sank below the waves and he breathed a sigh of relief.

Then there was a splashing nearby. He turned to see the monstrous form of Gerard raise its terrible head from the water. Clenched in its jaws was the black stone of the weird idol. Tilleigh went skittering backward and nearly tipped off his floating sanctuary. He grabbed hold and centered himself again, eying the creature warily. Tilleigh was cursing the fact that he was without any means to defend himself against this foe when his hand slipped and was sliced open on the edge of something sharp. Looking down, he saw his weapon; the black iron clasp of a door hinge that had been torn free in the explosion. The weapon hung limp from the door by only a few loosened iron nails. Taking care to wrap his fingers around the dull edge on the backside, he pried and pulled it free. He steadied himself, then brandished it at the fishman, slicing through the air and growling savagely.

The two of them drifting with the flow of the tide toward New Orleans, he watched the thing with a panicked heart. For the first time he noticed that the creature was wounded. A slash across its shoulder and chest had opened its flesh and its black blood was leaking into the bay water. Shards of glass and wooden splinters as thick as a man's thumb were embedded in its flesh and in the eyes of the creature he saw reluctance.

It looked to the shore and back to Tilleigh many times before it shook its head in defiance, the idol clutched in its maw. It then dove beneath the waves and swam toward the shoreline.

Tilleigh felt an elation sweep over him and he was brought to tears, clasping his hands together and bowing his head. Why the Lord had chosen to deliver him to safety after so much death and toil, Tilleigh could not know but he was nonetheless thankful for it. He trembled, the fight still coursing through his veins, his heartbeat thundering in his ears.

He watched as the form of the fishman shrank toward the shore, becoming nothing but a dark speck against the glinting blue of the gulf waters.

Though he was glad to be rid of the creature, a new fear filled him. It crept over him like a cold shadow—a fear for all mankind at the devilry that Tilleigh now knew lurked beneath the surface of the ordinary lives of men and thrived in the dark spaces.

He wondered if grace would see the world through the coming darkness as it had seen him through the last voyage of the Rosaleen. Shaken but not broken, Tilleigh held fast to his faith as he clung on to the bit of wreckage that would bear him to safety.

Even so, looking long to the stretch of shoreline the creature swam toward, he could not shake the notion that it would crawl from the waters with the fell idol safely in its grasp and the seeds of a darkness unimagined would find purchase in the bayous and bays perched along the edge of the loathsome sea.

THE DYING PLACE

1
TODAY

The darkness soaked the mountain in its suffocating, inky embrace, punctuated only by the rolling and shifting rivers of shadow, borne by the wind, which slithered among the highest branches of the trees. On the porch of an old cabin there sat a man in a rocking chair, sipping generously from a bottle of corn liquor with a shotgun lying across his lap.

With grand determination, the man had come to this place—his ancestral home in the Blue Ridge Mountains of Virginia. He had come here to die, and die he would, though not in the way he had intended. As the shadows in the trees shifted and grew closer, he rose and slowly shuffled his way inside. Leaning the shotgun against the door, he took a seat in a nearby chair in the common room and picked up the dog-eared spiral notebook in which he had shakily scrawled the events of the last few days. As he flipped through its pages, barely able to read the words within, he felt his attention drawn to the family quilt that lay folded over the arm of the chair next to him. Its seemingly random patterns were the result of generations of his kin having repaired it, adding new pieces as the years drove on. The last square bit had been added by his own mother when he was a child, years ago in a time that now seemed like another man's life. Her contribution would prove to be the last.

He reached out, ran a finger over the stitching that held every square together. Seams that bound one generation to another.

Something grated along the metal roof above and he looked up as if he could see through the ceiling to the other side.

Out there, in the woods, in the world, the seam had frayed and loosened. It was coming undone here and now—these last moments of his life.

2
Some Days Before

The perils of old age had long since descended upon him. He'd suffered the terrible ache of old bones, the nearly complete loss of his sight, the dulling of his mind, and the myriad other indecencies customarily visited upon one who'd stubbornly persisted on this planet for eighty-nine years. He'd suffered them in the confines of a retirement home, a place of putrid-smelling halls inhabited by other old ones in varying states of decay, many unaware that the rooms for which their loved ones paid a king's ransom were nothing more than a luxurious facsimile of the tomb that would be their final resting place. A place that served not the old so much as it did the young, who themselves could not face the slow and downward spiral of their elders under their own roofs. Howard Martin had endured the place for the sake of his son until he saw the flesh of his own flesh, his one and only child, laid in the ground just over a month ago. It was on that day he had resolved not to meet his end staring upward at the cheap drop ceiling tiles, hooked up to machines that invaded his body in order to prolong a life already spent.

He'd been craftier than most and with the help of Brenda, a sympathetic nurse, and a handful of cash he kept locked in his wife's jewelry box, Howard had managed to engineer his escape. As agreed, she had picked up a meager amount of food and supplies for him at the grocer's in Thrushton and had driven him up the winding roads on the south face of the mountain named the Priest. It had begun to snow earlier that day and Howard watched as the majesty of the mountainside passed by his window, being painted whiter by the moment with winter's brush.

She had carried his things into the cabin and said a reluctant and cautious good-bye there on the gravel road. He'd assured her that despite his failing sight, he knew the grounds and the cabin well enough to navigate it blindfolded, and as she pulled away, he heard the final groans of her four-wheel drive disappearing down the mountain as he stepped into the old homeplace.

Once inside, a flood of memories overtook him. In that moment, it did not seem so long ago that he was there as a young and able-bodied father taking his boy on a week-long retreat from their life in town. The smell of the place, although dulled with the stench of vacancy, was ever-present—the earthy preponderance of the wood stove, the scent of the last pot of coffee that had lingered on its surface, the sweet and sour aroma of old pipe smoke. These scents triggered memories of days now disappeared. However, he reminded himself that there was presently no fire and no coffee and no tobacco to be had. The afternoon sun was disappearing over the mountain, so he'd best get to work.

Fishing through his coat pocket, he removed his spectacles and slid them over his face. The bottle-thick lenses afforded him some amount of improvement in his vision, though it was meager. Nevertheless, he set about unpacking his supplies and soon went out the cabin's front door to the woodpile that sat off the east side of the cabin. Removing the snow-covered logs from the top of the pile, he slowly hauled a few armfuls of dry, split wood into the cabin and set them by the stove. He rested when he needed to, which was often these days, but finally, the chore was done.

Crouching before the stove to start the fire did his back no favors, but after a few moments, he'd gotten a good flame going, and he closed the black iron door on the mouth of the stove. Going about the small place, he supplied all the lamps with fresh oil and lit their wicks. Soon the cabin was ablaze with light and warmth. He quickly washed and filled an old coffeepot with some bottled water and packed the infuser with dark grounds, set it on the stove, and waited. Sitting on the couch, he drew the family quilt about his shoulders and stared at the flames leaping behind the grate of the stove. Between the couch and stove there sat a TV tray and, on it, a chessboard. Its pieces, covered with a thick layer of dust, were immobile and seemed frozen in time. He smiled, for the memory of that last chess game with his son was fresh in his mind, though he could not recall who had been winning or who had been which color.

After a bit, the coffeepot began to sing, and he removed it to the cooler part of the stove and poured a cup of deep, black liquid into a mug from the kitchen cabinet. He wrapped himself in the quilt and shuffled out the front door onto the porch where he sat down in one of the age-worn rocking chairs he'd built as a younger man when his mind was sharp and hands steady. Though creaky and covered in a thin layer of moss, it seemed as sturdy as the day he'd nailed it together so long ago.

He rocked there for a moment, sipping his coffee and immersing himself in the mountain night. In an old notebook, he penned disjointed recollections and memories as they came to him. The old homestead had always been a place of peace and calm, a refuge from their noisy lives in town. A place where he watched his boy, Lynn, chase fireflies in the summer. On those humid nights, it was as if the stars themselves had come down onto the mountain to play, flitting this way and that to the delight of the young boy and his parents. Howard had loved it so well, and he was happy to dwell there in the embrace of memory, but something drew his attention away from reminiscing. The strangeness came first in the shape of a shadow among the trees.

The snow drifted down from the clouds, although they were thin, and only partially cloaked the moon, diffusing its ghostly light upon the world below. As he narrowed his eyes in the darkness, he reminded himself that the mind—especially one as old as his own—was wont to be tricked. This he learned as a young lad when the cabin had belonged to his great-grandfather. The mountain was full of odd noises and movements, and the boy who saw demons in its shadows was no different than the fool who saw an oasis in the sands of Arabia. Still, he was unnerved by the shapes that formed in the dark vestiges of the forest, seeming to appear in an instant and then swallowed by the deeper darkness. Howard rose from his chair and crept inside, slipping the lock and the bold on the front door into place.

He took a seat in the rocker by the stove and sipped the last of his coffee. He wrote more in the notebook, then began to doze. Sleeping near the fire like on old hound, he dreamed.

Lynn is sitting in the creek and playing in the water at the bottom of the towering, cascading waterfall called Crabtree Falls. The hills and trees of the mountain loom over the creek, crowding the sky. Yards downstream, Howard is looking on in curiosity. He trudges up the shallow creek toward his son, who seems blissfully unaware of his presence. The closer Howard gets, the icier the water becomes. The trees, earlier green with the suppleness of warm weather, transform into empty, skeletal things that lean toward the falls with menace. When he is a stone's throw away from his child, the boy turns and seems to recognize him.

The child seems cold; tinges of blue sweep over his pale skin. The pace of the water quickens dangerously, and Howard's curiosity turns into panic.

"Daddy?"

"I'm coming, Lynn," he cries as he edges his way toward the deepening, icy rush of water. The boy appears not to notice. A chessboard, laden with ice, surfaces in the water in his son's lap.

"Rook takes king, Daddy," he hears him say. "You win!"

With that, the boy raises up one of the rooks. A long and terrible black needle protrudes from the base of it. As Howard fights to gain ground upstream, his son drives the needle into his own flesh at the crook of his arm and a blackness creeps through his veins and overtakes him, painting his skin the color of tar. Howard struggles against the swift and foaming waters but before he can reach his son, the boy's form begins to crack and peel, becoming dry as a husk. Like gray ash, bit by bit, he falls by clumps into the rush of the freezing water and is swept away while Howard goes slack against the tide.

When the old man woke, he cried aloud and found himself sitting up and gasping for breath, draped in the quilt that now felt alien against his skin. The light from the new day poured in from the world outside, and it was this that brought about his slow return to consciousness. The cabin was chilled, the fire having given out over the night.

Shivering, he sought to rid his mind of that sorrowful dream. It did him no good to think of his troubled son, who had gone from the world well before nature would have commanded it. As any father would, he felt a fresh and pointed anguish at not being able to save Lynn's life. This he felt even though his rational mind knew there was little that Howard could have done. In the years that he lived at the rest home, his son's visits became increasingly less frequent and during the times when he had come around, the young man was of sallow complexion and dark, sunken eyes. His patience and demeanor had grown short, and Howard had seen in Lynn's blood-streaked eyes a nervousness for which there was no reason. What person or thing had drawn his son into that sleepless, bent existence was no doubt the same thing responsible for the needle tracks that decorated his arms and feet like constellations of stars.

Being of a different time and such, Howard had barely heard of heroin or what it did to those who "chased the dragon," but Brenda, his nurse and confidant, had explained it to him. She'd even tried speaking to Lynn about it in private, but her warnings were met with indignation and self-righteousness and had clearly fallen on deaf ears. Whenever Howard pressed Lynn about it, he would respond with a dismissive smile and shrug it off, saying it would never get the better of him. Eventually, though, it did.

The dream had left Howard tired and spent. He drew the quilt tight around him and sank down into the chair, imagining that the smells of a stiff black brew and sweet hoecakes would greet him upon waking just as they had when he was a child. Some part of him knew, however, that there would be only the smoldering remains of the fire.

That afternoon, he stood in the doorway and gazed down at the dark, narrow passage that descended into the earth. It had been constructed long ago by his great-grandfather in the time of prohibition for the purpose of storing illegal liquor and, through the generations since, had been improved upon. In the old days, its entrance had been concealed underneath a wool rug, nothing more than a trapdoor and a ladder that reached down into a hole in the damp dark of the mountain soil—a bootlegger's hideaway. Later on, as the menfolk had expanded the space and added timbers for support and wooden planks for the floor, a proper cellar door had been constructed along with wooden steps. In Howard's own time, he had helped his father string the cellar, along with the rest of the cabin, inside and out with electric light fixtures and bulbs. Along with the other inhabitants of the mountain, his family had always insisted that electricity not creep up its slopes from the town beyond since the days of the WPA. Rather than breaking with tradition, his father had favored using a gasoline powered generator for the cabin's lights. Even so, his father was reluctant to make use of such power except on particularly dark nights when the lanterns strung about the place were no longer sufficient for his father's failing sight—or when the menfolk would spend time down in the cellar, playing cards, smoking, and drinking from their stores of corn whiskey.

Howard was no fool; at his age, he was not about to go feeling his way down into the dark cellar to take a few bottles of white lightning for his last days. He'd been wise enough to ask nurse Brenda to purchase a few cans of starter fluid as well as a few gallons of gasoline. There was no guarantee, of course, that the generator he had left shielded from the elements and in perfect working order years ago would be sound, but there was a hope. And to free himself from the rest home, a hope was all Howard had needed.

The snow had accumulated a bit more than a dusting overnight, so he slipped his boots on and went trudging around the cabin to the plywood housing that sheltered the generator. He found it in much better condition than he had feared, wrapped in a plastic tarp and the proper parts well-lubricated with oil. To his surprise, even the pull-cord on the thing was limber and strong. From this observation, he could figure only that Lynn had come here some time over the previous year and used the lights, taking care of the generator just as he'd taught him. It made him smile just a little.

He reveled in that knowledge for only a moment before he got to the business of making the thing work. With some tinkering, a fresh infusion of gasoline, and some starter fluid, Howard managed to get the old engine of the generator humming. When it sprang to life and he saw the lights under the eaves turn on, he said a quick prayer of thanks not only to God but also to his late son. It brought tears and, for a moment, he leaned against the wall of the cabin and cried.

It had been many years since he'd seen the cellar. The lights now illuminating the darkness, he descended the steps and found himself surrounded by stores of the old mountain liquor. Some were in dark, molded casks that lined the walls and had leaked their contents into the dirt floor, and others were scattered about in several dozen glass bottles, large and small. The thick layer of dust on everything told him that it had been a very long time indeed since anyone had set foot down here, apparently not even his son. There was a small collection of rusted woodworker's tools piled in a corner next to the grime-covered remains of his grandfather's workbench. Atop it sat scattered boxes and moldy books whose spines could now scarcely be read at all. Among the tools and fasteners, there was even an old box of TNT that had been down there as long as Howard could remember. Shying away from it just as he'd been taught to as a boy, he ran his finger over the liquor bottles, scraping away years of mildew. Grasping them by their necks, he picked a few bottles and held them up to the light. Judging their worth just as he had seen his father do, he took for himself a few bottles of what looked to be the best of the booze and climbed back up the steps. He closed the door behind him.

Howard wrote in the notebook and spent most of that second day slowly bringing in a good stock of firewood to last through the evening. After his venture into the cellar, he had shut off the generator to save fuel in case there was a need to light the cabin at night. Such was the way of his upbringing. The uneasiness he'd felt on the porch the night before ate at him and as he lumbered out to the woodpile and back, he did so looking often over his shoulder. Without any particular reason, he felt a sense of trepidation at going too far afield. It was a worry that he assured himself could be attributed to his failing sight, though in his heart he knew that was not the whole of it.

After the day's labor, he rested in the rocker on the porch with a blanket covering his legs, sipping his family's corn liquor from the bottle. Even in the light of the day, Howard could not shake the sensation that there was a presence about the place that was not his own, as if he were being watched. He dismissed it out of hand as the fearful imaginings of an elderly mind. To pass the time, he brought out a battery-operated radio and tuned it to a station out of Charlottesville that broadcast songs he recognized from his youth, songs from the likes of Lefty Frizzell, the Carter Family, and Hank Williams. The sounds of music gave him some comfort and soothed his mind as it wandered down through the years past, dwelling on certain memories as one might stop to take in the beauty and aroma of flowers in a garden. He drained the last of the moonshine from a bottle, set it down, and stood to retrieve another from inside. As he turned his back, he heard a great noise of fluttering and scattering. He snapped his head around to look out at the forest, his eyes searching the boughs of the tall hardwoods, but he saw nothing. Uneasy, he turned and shuffled into the cabin. "By God, the trees have all gone mad," he grumbled to himself.

When he returned to his rocker, it was not only with a fresh bottle of liquor but also the pump action Winchester shotgun he kept in the broom closet. Something troubling was going on out in the woods, and it set him ill at ease. Mumbling to himself, he ran through the list of animals that could be blamed for the disturbances. Other things, which he could not name but that lingered at the edge of his fears, were not mentioned. Content, he rocked back and forth for the remainder of the afternoon, the weapon with which he intended to do himself in laid across his lap. *Perhaps tonight's the night*, he mused, though he was undecided.

As the sun sank from view, he ambled around to the side of the cabin and coaxed the generator to life once again. He hurried inside as best as his old bones could manage, then stoked the fire and set about heating a simple meal of beans and cured pork on the top of the stove. He followed that with a few crisp slices of a Winesap apple. When his belly was full, he sat down in the chair next to the fire and cracked open the top on another small bottle of moonshine.

He drew a cigarette from the old pack he'd found in a drawer. Next to the pack had been a flattened stone with a curious, branch-like pattern engraved upon it. He presumed the stone to have belonged to his son, just as the cigarettes had. He looked at the pack and smiled bitterly. Howard hadn't smoked in fifteen years or more, but his son had, and he recognized the pack as his own favorite brand.

"Chesterfields," he muttered, placing one between his lips. "Chip off the old block."

Striking a match, he puffed on the cigarette and closed his eyes with a smile as the nicotine mingled with the alcohol in his veins. Just as he began to enter a deep sense of calm, a noise came raging from the night outside. Sitting up, he tossed the cigarette into the pot of cold pork and beans and grabbed the shotgun.

He listened as the noise lessened, then stopped altogether. For a moment, there was only silence. Then it came again, a crackling noise as of spindly-legged things crawling about the cabin. It came not only from the roof but from the walls around him also. The tip-tapping sound was accompanied by the occasional drag and thud of something heavy, then silence once more. Listening, he heard the constant drone of the generator beginning to idle down and sputter as it sometimes did, though the timing could have been no worse. Panic leapt into his throat as the lights flickered off. During this darkness, the sound returned, though it seemed tenfold, and Howard felt his finger caressing the Winchester's trigger. Outside, the generator struggled to regain its momentum. His vision, however poor, was fixed on the wide window that looked out the front of the cabin, and he brought the weapon up to aim in that direction. Again, he had the feeling of being watched, and he slowly approached the window. With renewed vigor, the generator roared back to life, and the lights blazed back on. A terrible form that loomed just beyond the window crackled, then fluttered and was gone. He'd not seen enough of it to describe it even to himself, but it was big. Big as a man and its shape and presence was not that of any creature that God had made for this world.

Casting aside the bottle of moonshine, Howard spent the remainder of that second night wide-awake in the chair, his weapon at the ready, and his mind unable to dispel the memory of those sharp and inhuman sounds or the great, black shadow that had stalked him just beyond the window in a moment that may have been the darkest night of the old man's soul.

3
Today

He spent most of the day on the porch, writing in his notebook of the last days. It was a chronicling interspersed with memories and observations of the past as well as confessions of his grieving heart. Surely, it would make little sense to anyone but him.

Nodding with resigned satisfaction at what he'd written, Howard scrawled a last few parting words. He had no one to whom he might address them, but certainly at some point, someone would find them.

Many years ago, his father had brought a family safe up to the cabin and kept it under the drape of a table in the common room. Even now, with his feeble mind, he remembered the combination and gently eased the dial right and left and right again to the secret numbers and unlocked it.

In it, he placed the notebook along with two chess pieces—a rook and a king— from the chessboard. Until now, the safe had been empty except for a stack of faded old Confederate bills that had been passed down through the generations.

The safe was a kind of time capsule now, it occurred to him.

Musing on this, he took the family quilt from the chair, folded it, and slid it inside, filling the space. There was something sacred about the act of preserving the remnants of things that had come before. Whether or not those things were worthy of preservation was another matter.

Having sealed them within the thick steel walls of the safe, he rose and trudged down the steps into the cellar.

Seating himself in a rickety old chair he'd dragged down earlier in the day, he took a bottle of moonshine in his grip and lit up a Chesterfield to pass the time. Some men wished for eternal life, but what life was there when all that was dear to his heart had passed before? Time does not heal all wounds but makes some injuries into suffering boils upon the soul that eat away at a man until memories were the only thing left of him.

Howard waited there in the cold of the cellar, though he would not have to wait long.

The hum of the generator outside ceased, and it began to spit and sputter as the last of its fuel was spent. The two remaining cans of fuel he had dragged down to the cellar sat on either side of Howard's chair, spouts open, and smelling high of petroleum. With a last gasp of protest, the engine quit, and the cabin and cellar were plunged into absolute darkness.

He took another drag of the cigarette as he listened to the noises that began outside. Now emboldened by the darkness and entreated by the stench of his final resignation, the things breached the windows and doors of the old homeplace. He heard them as they skittered about the floor above, searching. There was a brief pause, for only a moment, as they sensed his presence down in the cellar. Stairs did not seem to be their normal method of conveyance, and they clicked their way down them clumsily.

Now merely a few feet away, Howard was unable to see them, though he suspected they could see him very well. He knew not when or why these terrible shadows had come to cover the mountainside but concerned himself only with ridding it of the scourge.

He struck the match on the seat of his chair and ignited the old, dry rag stuffed into the moonshine bottle in his hand. In that light, he saw more than he ever cared to see of the gaunt, winged minions of the night that hovered over him. He could smell the rot of their breath. Great, twisted horns crowned their heads, beneath which was a faceless black visage. Their tall, skeletal forms were hunched forward in the confines of the cellar, leaning toward him hungrily.

Despite the terror of what he saw, Howard Martin managed a defiant smirk as the rag burned close to the bottle's neck, and he tossed it onto the old workbench where it shattered, and flames licked the surface. He was not certain that these monstrosities from some shadowed otherworld could understand what was happening, but it was of no matter. It took only seconds for those fingers of fire to find the moldering old box of dynamite.

He closed his eyes, content to have the horror that he'd just beheld cast away forever. In a blinding flash and with the roar of a thousand terrible winds, the fury of the sun was loosed upon the night, and it shattered the old cabin, consuming every corporeal thing in a rush of force and fire. It was well that in that moment, Howard Martin was gone and could no longer hear, for the anguished cries of the dying creatures was a sound not meant for the ears of men.

STATIC

1

The industrialist, Cole Winfield, was on the cusp of turning seventy-five years old, an event apparently worthy of an elaborate celebration and one that called for Hank Mackey to drive halfway across the south to wish the old sonofabitch a happy birthday when, truth be told, all he wished him was dead.

After leaving their home in Macon, Hank had done little more than rue the trip down to Carol's hometown of Gulfport, Mississippi, where his father-in-law would hold court at his estate that overlooked the waters of the Gulf of Mexico. Far as Hank was concerned, this party was nothing more than a typical Winfield display of self-importance.

Nevertheless, dutiful husband that he was, he packed his wife and newborn child into the pickup, took a few days off from work, and struck out southward to the birthday gala of a man who had never cared to be even so much as courteous to the husband of his only daughter.

The day that Carol Winfield had become Carol Mackey, she had married down. The old man knew it and Hank knew it, too. Hank had been a minimum-wage construction worker at the time and lived in an apartment above the garage that belonged to his boss. He hadn't owned much back then besides a rusted Ford pickup and, perhaps most importantly, the love of a privileged girl from Mississippi attending Georgia Tech.

He had met Carol for the first time in some bar in Atlanta. He'd watched as some yankee tourist got handsy with her, so he'd stepped in and ruined the fucker's hopes and dreams with a few punches.

They left the bar together that night, holding hands, with the handsy tourist bleeding on the floor.

Six months later, they were engaged to be married.

The wedding had been a grand affair on the old man's tab, but Hank had seen the disdain in not only Carol's father but all their posh, high-society friends as well. When the old man came to congratulate them, his eyes and forced smile bespoke the truth. Who was this rabble from Macon, Georgia and what did a proper girl like Carol see in such a roughneck?

"I'll never know what it is that makes my baby girl want to cleave to you, Henry," Cole Winfield had said, taking Hank aside for a moment under the guise of having a friendly father to son-in-law chat, "but I can promise you that this wedding is the last of my money you'll ever see. And I'm confident that in time, she'll come to see what a mistake she's made because, Henry, I know your kind."

"My kind?" he had asked.

"Henry, do you honestly think I would even indulge such a union without first having my people investigate you and your family?"

Hank had stared blankly at the man, unsure if the question was genuine or just rhetorical. A breath later, he had his answer.

"Lowcountry laborers, beggars, and thieves, the lot of you Mackeys... and the no-good, gypsy micks from whom you descend," her father had said to him, smiling all the while.

Hank then thanked him for his well wishes and, smiling in turn much wider than he should have, told the family patriarch to go fuck himself. He then stood by as he watched the old man dance with his bride.

It wasn't until much later that Carol removed her blinders and noticed the animosity between the two of them. Funny enough, it was around the time the checks from Daddy Warbucks stopped coming in despite their financial strains. Even then, she placed the blame on her husband for not being ambitious enough to ask for a position in her father's employ. Hank valued his pride, though, and had no inclination to lose it to the likes of Cole Winfield.

"Hank!" came the shout from the passenger seat.

"Yeah?"

"You're veering over, honey."

He saw that he was indeed riding the double line a bit. He gently guided the truck to the right and back into the lane. Carol relaxed a little in her seat.

"I sure hope you drive that big old truck better than you're driving this one," she remarked.

There she was again, always tearing him down. Like father, like daughter, he thought. Hank glanced up at the secondary mirror that allowed him to see the car seat in the back and saw that Jacob was sleeping peacefully if only for the moment.

"Where's that gas station?" she wondered aloud, staring out the window into the inky blackness.

"Should be coming up soon," he speculated, glancing down at the odometer. "Sign said it was five miles and that was three miles back."

"I Hope so. I sure got to make water."

Piss. You gotta piss, Hank thought. He hated such polite euphemisms.

After a few minutes, the darkness of the landscape was broken by the blazing neon sign of a DixieQwik.

"It's about time for him to eat, too," Carol said, glancing back at the car seat. "I'll feed him when we stop."

Hank nodded and a few hundred feet later, he was pulling the Chevy into the DixieQwik parking lot alongside one of the pumps.

"Oooo! Wish me luck," he heard her whimper as she jumped out of the truck and ran toward the building in hopes of a public toilet.

Hank looked in the mirror at the sweet, sleeping face of his child and smiled.

"Guess it's just you and me, hoss."

He stepped out of the truck and set about gassing up the behemoth, dual-cab Chevy. He watched as the numbers on the gas pump flew by, siphoning money from his pocket, and glanced up at the price per gallon.

"Hells bells," he remarked.

As the pump motored on, he glanced around it to see inside the gas station. After a moment, Carol appeared from around the aisles with a couple bottles of water. She stood in line and when it was her turn, he watched as she traded banter with the clerk, a svelte, young Latino boy. Too many seconds and too many smiles passed between them before money changed hands and Hank felt his blood begin to simmer. The boy was hitting on her, no doubt. And why wouldn't he? She had the body of a swimsuit model, something she had gotten back in record time after Jacob's birth, and she was dressed for the heat and the long drive in a tank top and cut off jean shorts that didn't leave much to the imagination. Not the sort of attire that her father would have approved of, but the dirty truth was that Carol, for all her proper upbringing, had a love for slumming it. Deep down inside, Daddy's little princess had a white trash streak wide as a country mile. That was part of the reason she had fallen in love with and married Hank and he was smart enough to realize it. So, while even he didn't always approve of her manner of dress, he said nothing about it. To do so would put him on common ground with Cole Winfield and he would be damned if he let that occur.

She came out of the DixieQwik just as the gas pump finished reaching into his pocket and he hung the nozzle up.

"You find a bathroom?"

She nodded.

"Got you some water and a pack of No-Doz, too," she said, offering him a sweating plastic bottle.

"What was *that* about?"

She cocked her head.

"What was what about?"

"You and the clerk," he said, punching one of the little, yellow pills from the envelope and twisting the cap off the bottle as he took a swig. "He ask for your phone number or something?"

She waved it off.

"Aw, you know, just a boy being a boy."

She tucked her bottle between her legs, fished a hair tie from her pocket and pulled back her long, golden locks, twisting them up in the elastic band and baring the nape of her neck. Hank felt himself begin to stiffen beneath his jeans. Back in their courting days, he would have pulled the truck into the farthest, darkest spot in the parking lot and screwed her right there. They would have started in the front seat but ended in the back, fogging up the windows with the wet heat of their lovemaking. But those days had long since passed. Instead, he would pull the truck into the farthest and darkest spot in the parking lot and when she pulled her breasts free of that tank top, it would be for Jacob's benefit, not Hank's.

My, how the times do change, he thought as they climbed into the vehicle, and he drove it into a lone spot by the DixieQwick's dumpster.

The feeding of his son was quite an ordeal as Carol struggled to pull Jacob from his car seat in the back and bring the abruptly woken and now crying infant to her to nurse. Hank's stiffness had not yet subsided, and it left him feeling awkward, so he decided to walk it off until the feeding was done.

"Gonna get out, stretch my legs, and grab a smoke," he grumbled.

She nodded and he stepped out of the cab, closing the door behind him.

The gas station sat adjacent to an open field of blooming cotton. He approached it and pulled a cigarette from the pack in his jeans pocket. Lighting it with the same Zippo his father had used to smoke himself into an early grave, Hank walked the edge of the field. The moon was high, full and bright in the night sky and the way it shone down on the white flowers of cotton made the field seem as though it were a breadth of snow in the middle of the summer night's heat. He smoked and looked on with a sense of wonder. When he was done with the first smoke, he lit another. As he neared the end of his second cigarette, the sky brightened in the distance with flashes of lightning. Each eruption of light bathed the world below in a striking and ghostly glow and the cotton field radiated as if infused with a powerful and electric energy.

Behind him, he heard the Chevy's motor start. He knew that the nursing was done, and they were ready to head on down the road. As he stubbed his smoke into the ground, preparing himself for a few more hours of driving, another flash reigned over the sky that was followed by a low and distant rumble of thunder.

2

When he had climbed into the cab outside the gas station, he had remarked to Carol that there looked to be a storm on the horizon, a thing which had given him no pause. After all, he drove a big rig for a living these days and had driven through every variety of storm, be it rain or snow, sleet or hail, that the I-95 corridor had to offer from Florida to Maine. But this wasn't the rig, and his wife and baby boy were passengers. Had he known the little bit of lightning and thunder he had seen at the DixieQwik were shaping up into a *hell of a storm*, he might have chosen to wait it out.

As it happened, though, they were winding their way through the maze of back roads and hairpin turns toward the highway when Hank missed— or misread, rather—the sign pointing toward the salvation of the highway. While Carol would blame the oversight on her husband for many miles, in truth it was no one's fault. There was an old road sign with arrows that pointed in one direction toward I-10 West: Biloxi, Gulfport. In the other direction it pointed toward two towns, the name of one being mostly unreadable but looking something like Leakesville and below that Locust Hill. The road sign had become soft in its earth weeks before during a soaking rainstorm and was leaning to the point of almost falling over. The powerful winds of the storm that swept across the lowlands of Alabama and Mississippi that night had twisted the sign and pointed its arrows in the exact opposite directions. After Hank Mackey and his family made that wrong turn, a stray but strong wind pummeled the road sign one final time, and it unearthed itself entirely and fell flat and useless on the roadside gravel. Serendipity, some call it, when such an unforeseen chain of events works in their favor. Bad luck, it is called by others.

3

"Hank?"

"Yeah?"

"Where the hell are we going?"

"Gulfport, baby," he replied, sensing her frustration but not inclined to give it any credence.

A few moments of silence passed before she spoke up again.

"I don't remember it taking this long when we got off the highway."

Hank nodded but didn't take his eyes off the road. He found himself lurched forward like a hunchback over the wheel. A storm raged around them, battering the truck with its winds and covering the windshield in sheet after sheet of thick rain.

"Well, one thing I learned driving the rig is that a rainstorm can mess with you something fierce. Make you think you're headed in the wrong direction when you're right on target."

She nodded and said nothing, but Hank could feel her quiet disdain. He was about to mount an argument, a further justification for their route when a set of headlights appeared on the road.

"See?" he said, smiling and smacking the steering wheel, "There's a sign of life, baby."

She flashed him a forced but confident smile as they drove on and the lights got closer. Then the lights wandered into their lane.

"Hank?"

"I see it, honey. I see it," he said as he brought the Chevy to a gentle stop, intending to let the other vehicle pass him by. Better to not indulge them, he judged. "Likely just some kids is all."

They sat there, unmoving for a few seconds before it became clear to Hank that the oncoming vehicle was fatally serious about playing chicken. They were headed right towards them at no more than a hundred yards and closing fast.

"Hank?"

His eyes were fixed on the headlights barreling their way. He heard Carol's voice but tried to tune it out.

Seventy-five yards and closing.

In his glory days, back when Macon was rural, he had played chicken with friend and foe alike and he had done it more times than he could count. Of course, the first to swerve had been saddled with the moniker of "chicken shit" but in those days he could count on a sort of gentleman's agreement when it came to the commitment of those engaged in the competition. No one was in it to die or even maul their heavily waxed, super-charged muscle cars in the contest. It had been nothing more than a test of teenage machismo. Inevitably, both drivers always swerved. But these jackasses?

Fifty yards now. With these kids nowadays, Hank couldn't be so sure. To him, they all seemed to live with reckless abandon and no regard for others.

Too many movies, he thought. *Too many video games. Too little reality.*

Twenty-five yards now, at the most.

"Hank!" Carol screamed from the passenger seat.

In a moment of utter clarity that seemed to transpire in slow motion, Hank looked to his wife and nodded.

"Relax, babe," he said.

He then whipped the wheel to the right and jammed his foot deep into the gas pedal. The Chevy tore off the asphalt with screeching tires and fishtailed as it went. His experienced hand guided them to the right, toward the water-filled ditch at the side of the road and as the teenagers passed in what Hank recognized as a pathetically souped-up Toyota with rebel flags and KC lights on the cab, he heard them screeching a rebel yell that he thought sounded like a bunch of girls watching a slasher flick at a slumber party. Carol's face had gone ghost-white, and he heard her squeal from the passenger seat as they headed toward the deep slope of the roadside ditch. Hank had it well in hand, though, and pumped the brakes twice gently before slamming on them and whipping the wheel left. The Chevy spun around and landed squarely back on the asphalt of the road facing the direction in which they had come.

He felt a smile lift his face and looked over at Carol.

"Now watch this."

The Confederate Toyota, which was already out of control, spun to face them as the driver slammed on the brakes but continued for a few screaming yards, down and down, before it came to a stop in the ditch.

Three feet of water bogged the teenagers down in the ditch and all the revving of the Toyota's engine couldn't free the vehicle. After a moment, with Hank and his family sitting there watching them, the boys began to pile out of the truck.

Hank was still consumed with adrenaline as he watched them. Some set to digging the Toyota out of its predicament and others with stern faces made their way toward the Chevy. He had seen at least one of the boys grab a shotgun from the truck's gun rack.

The baby was screaming now, and Carol was in his ear.

"Hank…" she said, hoping he would hit the gas and eject them from this incident right away.

He nodded.

"Just gonna teach these young bucks a lesson, honey."

Hank reached under the seat and found the butt of the .44 caliber Smith & Wesson automatic pistol he kept there. He pulled it and stepped out of the truck.

Figuring that they were little more than misguided, volatile, teenagers who hadn't the courage to pull on him first, Hank stepped free of the truck's open door and aimed at the Toyota's radiator. He fired twice and his shots were true. The Toyota began leaking coolant into the ditch and the boys that advanced on them took several steps back, hands up and shouting insults at him all the while. *"Crazymotherfucker"* this and "Georgia peachfuzz faggot" that and so on.

Satisfied, Hank climbed back into the Chevy and holstered the pistol, slid it back under the seat. He revved the truck's engine just for show and then peeled out, guiding them back in the proper direction. Until then, neither one of them had noticed that the driving rain of the storm had stopped. The absence of raindrops clicking on the metal skin of the truck was barely noticeable, lost in the mind-shearing wail of the screaming child. Still, they drove on, Hank and Carol both hoping that baby Jacob would exert himself to the point of exhaustion and sleep, granting them some small amount of peace and quiet for the rest of the trip.

4

By Hank's count on the odometer, they had gone twenty-one miles beyond the trouble they'd encountered with the teenagers. They both felt better as the miles disappeared behind them and so they said nothing of it, the kind of unspoken and shared sentiment that only married couples know. After the DixieQwik, the night had taken a troubling turn. First with the unwelcome rain and wind, then the Confederate Toyota and now, forty miles later, Jacob still screaming in the back. Carol rested her head against the passenger window, singing every tune she could think of in hopes that one of them —or all of them— would soothe the child.

Twenty-one miles, Hank reflected. He couldn't decide if they had come this way or if, somehow, they had taken a different road to return to the I-10. These rural roads were populated with crops and creeks and tucked-away farm homes. Proper road signs were a rarity.

Somehow, though he knew not how, he had taken a *very* wrong turn somewhere and plunged them into an unfamiliar maze of long, curving, paved and unpaved roads without numbers or names. He tried to puzzle it together, to back-track the road they had taken, but with his son screaming behind him, he couldn't manage a coherent thought. Not to mention Carol's singing, well-intentioned though it may be, was also starting to grate on his nerves. He cocked an eyebrow and glanced over at her.

"Maybe he just don't like the sound of your voice."

She turned her face from the window and shot him a narrow-eyed, humorless glare.

"Try the radio," Hank suggested.

Carol leaned forward and flipped on the truck's stereo. The garbled sounds of some kind of music came blaring through the speakers and she turned down the volume. After another pause, she hit the button to continue scanning the band. Up and down the FM band she searched but could find nothing that wasn't scrambled by the hiss and crackle of poor reception. She even switched to the AM band only to find it was even worse. Everywhere it was static, static, static.

Exasperated, she turned away from it and cursed the radio, letting the whispering, crackling sound linger in the speakers.

"Can't find a damn thing. Must be the storm clouds going through." Then she shot another disapproving look in her husband's direction. "Or maybe it's just wherever in Bumfuck Egypt we are."

"Carol, listen—"

"No, Hank Mackey, you listen!" she hissed at him. "We best be in Gulfport come the morning just like you promised because I'm gonna need a full day's sleep and a few hours at the spa or else I'll look like polished shit at Daddy's party and I'm not going to- "

Hank slammed his open palm down on the steering wheel where it rang out a quick slap, startling Carol out of her rant and she paused for a moment.

"Listen," he whispered to her.

"Listen to what, Hank? I don't hear anything but the goddamn radio."

"Exactly," Hank nodded, cracking an uneven grin.

Carol turned and looked into the back seat and saw, with great joy, that baby Jacob was out like a light. His eyes were closed, head slightly to the side, fists balled and mouth hanging open.

"Think it's the static on the radio?" Hank asked.

She nodded.

"Yeah, I do. Now that you mention it, I do remember reading something in one of those maternity magazines about white noise and babies. I think it even said that on a long road trip, you could tune the stereo to the static to help them sleep. How about that?"

Hank smirked.

"Yeah, how about that. Too bad you didn't have that handy tidbit of information about twenty miles back."

She swatted his shoulder with her hand, and it came to rest there on his arm. She couldn't help but grin just a little. For all his social lacking, Hank had a nice, thick build and his shoulders and arms were rock-solid to the touch. When they were still dating and in the early years of their marriage, it had been one of those tells that couples have. Just laying a hand on his shoulder or bicep in a certain way, providing just the slightest squeeze had conveyed that she was in a frisky mood. Hank had his tells also. Usually, a firm grasp on her hip while she stood near to him, pulling her closer just a tug with a breathy sigh that escaped his lips. But it had been a long time since either had felt those subtle touches. She let her hand linger there for a moment before dropping it back to her own leg, wondering if Hank remembered.

"Woman," he whispered and placed his hand on hers, "Once upon a time, I'd be climbing across this seat and have half your clothes off by now for a little move like that. Don't test me. I'm of a mind to pull over and take a chance on it anyhow."

"Don't you do nothing to wake that baby, Hank." She blushed, though he could not see it in the dark of the Chevy's cabin. "First you get us to Gulfport. Then maybe I'll show you how thankful I am. Then, and only then, maybe we'll take a little trip in the bed back to *once upon a time*."

Hank shook his head and grinned but said nothing more. That was a classic Carol move, though Hank had always reckoned she had learned such a tactic from her old man. It must have been how he had shown love and affection for his only daughter. Everything came with conditions.

5

Hank glanced at the truck's clock, then had to look again.

Only 1:32 in the goddamned morning? he thought, rubbing his eyes. *Jesus.*

Carol was fast asleep in the passenger seat, her gentle snoring just barely audible over the sound of the static on the radio.

The night was passing with impossible languor. Even with the wrong turn—or turns—that he had made, he figured it to be much later. They had left Atlanta early that morning and had driven across Georgia and, he was reasonably sure, most of Alabama if not all of it. He knew only that when they last stopped for gas and Carol had had her flirtation with the clerk, they were somewhere close to the Alabama-Mississippi line. Because he was a truck driver, Carol expected him to know all of the roads big and small that crisscrossed the South. While Hank had not confirmed that expectation, he had also done nothing to discourage it, happy to be regarded by her in such a light. It was a rarity. Anyway, he was confident that he could find his way anywhere so long as he had his trusted map book handy. He wished he had it now but knew to a certainty that it was sitting idly behind the driver's seat of his Kenworth parked in the driveway of their home. Every bit as vital as his underwear, he had meant to pack it for the trip but getting out of the house with the baby had been a confusing ordeal and in the flurry of activity, he had missed grabbing it.

Still, his trucker's sense of the road told him that they were somewhere in Mississippi, even if he could not confirm it.

The static from the radio was beginning to wear on him. The constant hiss was punctuated only seconds at a time with barely recognizable things. Bits of songs, snippets of sports radio, the broken words of midnight preachers. These were the things that filled his ears to an almost maddening degree. On top of that, he was getting sleepy. He recognized it in his own subtle movements. For a while now, he had been shifting restlessly in his seat, blinking his eyes as if trying to clear them of some obstruction. Humming to himself. Reaching down for his water bottle, he found the bit of fluid lacking and knew that he had one, maybe two swallows in the bottle. Not about to waste them, he dug into the pocket of his denim jeans and fished out the last two yellow NoDoz pills from the gas station. He tossed his head back and swallowed them with a gulp of water.

Damn. What I wouldn't give for a quickie mart, a map, and tall cup of black coffee right about now.

The headlights of the Chevy illuminated something in the distance. There was a bit of a shine coming off something up ahead, a glinting. Most likely the eyes of an animal, he knew. Hank slowed the truck a bit and proceeded with caution. He would rather not have to swerve to avoid it and risk waking Carol and the baby. As he came closer, he could make out the shape of a deer, though the headlights were not reflecting back the usual brown and white coloring of its body.

Even the animal's eye shine was dim and muted in the dark of night.

He slowed the truck to a crawl as the full shape and details of the deer emerged. The best he could figure, he was looking at a buck. It was tall and broad in its carriage just like every buck he had ever seen. That's where the similarities ended, however, as the creature in the road was not crowned with regal, branch-like antlers. Rather, the antlers were dark and misshapen, growing down the deer's face instead of away from it. There was no soft brown fur covering its body. Its matted hair was the color of spent embers in a cold fire. So dark was the animal's coat that the deer had seemed to materialize from the darkness itself as the Chevy drew closer to it.

The deer did not leap and run into the fields of tall corn that stood on either side of the road. It did not seem bothered by their presence at all. In fact, Hank noted, it was as though it had been waiting there by the road for him, for it never took its gaze off of the truck.

He was very close to it now, about to pass it by, and noticed that not only were the thing's antlers malformed and growing downward, but portions of them had grown *into* the deer's face. Like a thick thread of bone, sections of the antlers punctured the snout of the animal on one side and emerged from the other only to find their way back in again.

Hank felt his stomach tighten at the sight. A look of absolute revulsion passed over his face. The deer raised its maw to the starless sky and bellowed a low and agonized sound so loud that Hank worried it might wake Carol or Jacob, or both. It did not.

Looking back at the animal in the rear-view mirror, Hank watched as it turned its back to him and sauntered down the side of the road in the other direction, eventually melting back into the black of the thick summer night.

Hank ran his hands down his face as if the motion of doing so could erase from his eyes and his mind the eeriness of what he had just seen. The night had been strange and was becoming ever stranger. They were lost in the middle of nowhere. For the first time since making that wrong turn, Hank admitted to himself that they would not make it to Gulfport on time. For the first time, he felt tired and peculiar. The dark roads unfolding before them and the ever-present drone of the static were grinding on his mind. Hank was seriously considering pulling the Chevy onto the side of the road just so they could sleep through the night.

That was when a voice, fiery and impassioned, emerged from the static on the radio.

"When things get hard—and they do get hard, don't they, people?"

Hank thought the voice sounded like that of an old, black Baptist preacher. It continued on.

"When things get hard and that road don't make for easy going, you gonna be tempted. Tempted to turn around and go back the way you come! Tempted to tuck tail and head for the hills but I'm gonna tell you now, boy, you got to drive on. You got to keep down the hard road and see where it takes you. You got to drive on."

Hank listened as the voice faded out and was again replaced by the static. He was struck by the clarity of what had come through the white noise but most of all he was struck by the timing. Hank Mackey wasn't one to place great significance on coincidences, nor was he the type to see the Virgin Mary in a piece of burnt toast, but this was different. He felt it, knew it in his bones. It had been a message meant just for him. With any luck, there would be more, Hank found himself hoping. His mind weary and beleaguered, there had been a sudden disconnect from critical thinking. Hank's mind did not, in the least, question the absurdity of the notion that random radio signals surfacing through the static would help guide him out of the endless night.

6

Hank drove for another hour before pulling off for a smoke. He tried to be as gentle as he could when he brought the Chevy to a stop in a barren spot just off the road at the edge of a kale field. He stepped out, leaving the motor running and the radio on, but rolled down the window so he could still hear the radio.

Lighting up his smoke, he leaned against the truck's fender and looked up at the sky. The clouds that had brought the storm earlier in the evening were thinning out and a crack had opened up in them, revealing the stars and light from the moon still cloaked behind the clouds.

At first, jumbled among the flurry of thoughts in his head, Hank hadn't even noticed the music.

A man's mind is a cacophony of many things. Images, thoughts, words, sounds, all bursting forth simultaneously like a barrage of cannon fire. As the last few bars of Aerosmith's "Slow Ride" faded out and he heard another voice, Hank nearly spat the cigarette from his mouth as he turned to look into the cab of the truck. Mercifully, both Carol and Jacob were still sleeping.

"Take it easy, take it easy, man," came the voice, smooth in its timbre with just a touch of rasp that made Hank think that whoever the voice belonged to was puffing on a smoke at that very moment, just like he was. "Words of wisdom from one of rock's greats, the legendary Steven Tyler."

There was an audible exhale that came through the speakers and Hank's strange and only thought was to wonder if the man smoked reds or lights.

"Two forty-four in the A.M. here on WLCS the Locust. From Leakesville to Locust Hill, you're listening to the night program and I'm your DJ, Johnny Scratch. I'm feeling a little native tonight so brace yourself for a long night of offerings from the deep South. In a little bit, we'll get into a deep cut from Skynyrd and then a live track from the North Mississippi All-Stars."

"Skynyrd," Hank whispered aloud, nodding with approval and lighting up another smoke.

"But before we get into that, we got to talk. What are you doing out there in the middle of the night listening to the radio anyway? How come you ain't home asleep in your own bed or out hauling up and down I-95, making that money?"

Hank bit down on his cigarette, narrowed his eyes and looked back at the truck's radio.

"This ain't the life you wanted for yourself, is it? And where are you headed to? Some place you don't really want to be, that's where. And why?"

Hank shook his head, shrugged his shoulders.

"I'll tell you why. Because like the saying goes, when you lie down with dogs, you get up with fleas, fella."

Hank wasn't sure what the DJ meant.

"What I'm talking about is your number one—your main squeeze."

There was a pause.

"That woman," the voice of Johnny Scratch came again, those two words dripping with venom. "That harlot you took for a wife. That's the dog that's making you itch."

Hank was still staring at the radio, his mind racing to find some kind of logical reason for what he was hearing. Something to ground him in reality. Maybe he had just been awake too long. Driving too long in this strange night and all of it was getting to him, playing tricks with his mind. But as the DJ on the radio began speaking again, the signal waned and was replaced by squelching tones that dwindled down into the uniform hiss of static.

Hank slid back into the truck and worked the dial on the radio, running it up and down the band to try and find the signal from that station again but there was nothing now but the constant sound of static.

He looked over at his wife sleeping in the passenger seat, his son sleeping in the back.

It was nothing short of a lunatic idea, he knew. The idea that some man he had never met was sitting in a radio station somewhere and broadcasting to him alone! And yet something in the words of the DJ resonated with him as if fingers in his own mind had peeled back the layers of assumption and laid bare a very real fear that he had always had about Carol.

That harlot that you took for a wife.

Somehow, some way the DJ knew what troubled Hank's sleep and set him on edge during the nights of his long hauls away from home. Somehow, he knew, and Hank decided that he would like to have a word or two with the man…this Johnny Scratch…about it. Lunacy or not, Hank had to find that radio station.

He blinked his eyes hard a few times and rubbed the stubble on his chin, glancing in the mirror as he did so.

"Shit, that's just crazy," he said aloud to no one but himself.

All the same, when Hank pulled the Chevy's door closed and eased back out onto the dark road, he was no longer chiefly concerned with making it to Gulfport in time for his father-in-law's birthday gala. Whether or not he was honest with himself about it, his objective had changed.

7

Hank slipped along the back roads for another thirty minutes or so and still there was nothing to be seen other than crop fields and thickets of dark woods with gnarled, leaning trees draped in Spanish moss. As he took his time with a hairpin turn, however, he came upon an intersection at which sat a small Texaco station. It was lightless and appeared to have been defunct for a number of years. The wooden slats of the station's exterior were covered in peeling, cracked paint and, at first glance, it looked as though the station's front window was missing entirely. It was of no matter to him. His bladder was demanding a pit-stop and so he pulled up under the overhang and eased the truck to a stop by the old pumps. He left the truck, careful to close the door behind him, and walked around the side of the station. A Coca-Cola sign was still just barely visible through the thick wall of wild blackberry bushes that grew there, choked with other weeds and vines. Hank relieved himself and glanced about in the darkness nervously, half expecting to hear a possum or some other vermin as they tramped through the nearby woods. When he finished, Hank zipped up and was digging in his pocket for his cigarettes as he rounded the corner and noticed that the station was not quite as defunct as he had thought. The front window was intact and, though the station was closed, a few lights from refrigerators and other signage glowed softly inside. The cash register sat on the counter next to a display of packaged nuts and candy bars.

Hank took stock of his surroundings and found that, similarly, the fuel pumps were not as faded and rusted as he had thought and out front, the Texaco sign was dim but most certainly lit from within. He had been on the road a long time but not so long that he would have confused such details. Unless he had been trucker-tripping on all the No-Doz. Neither possibility sat well with him. More than that, there was a cold feeling in his gut that leaked into his bones. His truck still sat where he had parked it, engine running along and the cabin dark inside. He stole over to it and opened the driver's door, half expecting to find his wife and child missing from the interior as if they had never been there at all. For some reason he could not name, it would not have surprised him in the least.

Inside, Carol was now sitting up and rubbing her eyes because he had woken her when he threw the truck door open.

"Hank, what's going on? We still lost?"

He sighed and tapped his fingers on the door frame as he looked around.

The sounds of static drifted from the cab. No music, no DJ Scratch. Only static.

"Yeah, still lost," he said. "But it looks like I found a filling station. Looks closed, though. Maybe."

Carol looked out of the window.

"I'll say it sure does."

"I'm gonna knock anyway, though. These little places, sometimes they got a night man who stays just to watch the place.""But Hank, I don't think— "

"Be back in a few. Just try and go on back to sleep," he replied, cutting her off and quietly closing the driver's door.

He stood at the station's front window and rattled the locked door and rapped on the glass. He did this for a couple of minutes before he heard the sound of metal grating on metal—the moan and grind of a garage door opening up.

Hank walked around the other side of the station where the service entrance was and saw that one of the service bay doors had opened. From inside, he could smell the aroma of frying catfish and as he came around closer, he saw an older man standing by the open bay dressed in the greasy navy-blue coveralls of a mechanic's uniform.

"Help you?"

Hank waved and smiled as he approached.

"Boy, am I glad to see you, sir," he said as he approached the man and stretched out his hand. "Name's Hank Mackey."

The old man clasped his hand, his firm grip rough with years of callouses and thickened skin.

"Gabe," he replied. "You in some kind of trouble, mister?"

Hank gave a nervous laugh.

"No, not…uh…not exactly. We got a little turned around a ways back. I was hoping for some directions."

"Where you headed?"

"Need to get back to the highway," he said, then added, "but I wanted to stop by this radio station first. I think maybe it's somewhere close."

"Radio station?"

"Yeah."

"In the middle of the night?"

Hank's hand went to his face, where he rubbed his stubble.

"Yeah, my wife thinks maybe she knows the night DJ," he lied.

Gabe looked at him with one squinted eye and the brow of the other raised, as if deciding if Hank was on the level or if he was after something else entirely.

"Got some fish fryin' up. Would you…?" the old man asked, motioning back into the service bay where an electric burner sat heating a cast iron pan that sizzled with oil and breaded catfish.

"It sure does smell good. Thank you, but no…if you could just tell me how to get to the radio station…"

"How about a beer, then?" Gabe pressed. "You look like a man could use a bottle of suds."

Hank looked over his shoulder in the direction of the truck and figured Carol and the baby were both sleeping soundly.

"Uh…sure," he replied, "I'll take a beer."

He followed the old man into the service bay. Gabe the mechanic disappeared into the store for a moment and returned with a cold bottle of High Life. As he twisted off the top and handed it to Hank, the old man sat down on a gnarled old chair and sipped from his own bottle.

"You must have got mighty turned around, friend. You a good ways from the highway now."

"Oh yeah?" Hank asked as he gulped down the beer, its icy cold effervescence waking up his taste buds and relieving some of the summer night's heat.

"Just a couple more turns and then it's just a long, straight shot, though."

"How about that radio station? Transmission came in through the static a little while back. I think it was called the Locust?"

Gabe nodded and squinted his eyes as he thought about it.

"Not too sure about that, but the highway's just up the road a piece. All you gotta do is— " the old man said and leaned forward to gesture at the nearby road.

"Right," Hank said, interrupting, his patience growing thin. "And that's great news. It is. But what I really need to know more than anything is how to get to that station."

The old man sat back, taking stock of Hank.

"I don't mean to pry, Hank, but if you heard something on the radio from that place, I can't imagine that anything good could come of it."

Hank was in the middle of a swig when the old mechanic offered the comment, and he turned the bottle up to drain it. This old coot wasn't interested in helping him out and it was just pissing him off. When the bottle was empty, he set it on the table and stood.

"Well, I thank you for the beer. Reckon I'll just have to find it myself."

He was striding toward the open bay door when the old man's voice came again, though it seemed to resound not only in the empty space of the garage but in the dark spaces of Hank's own mind.

"You know my father," he said.

Hank turned and stared at the frail old man sitting there on the stool, his shoulders slumped and a half empty beer dangling from his fingertips. Weak and old as any a man he'd ever see. Yet, despite all of that, he felt a sudden awe of him. His knees went weak. He almost stumbled but reached a hand out to the wall and steadied himself.

"As I was saying, Hank," Gabe continued, "you know, my father... he used to have a great deal to say about temptation."

"How...how... how's that? I don't know your—" Hank stammered. It was as if his tongue no longer obeyed his thoughts.

The mechanic waved away his protest.

"It's a hell of a thing, Gabriel, my father used to say to me..." The old man drifted off for a moment. "Come to think of it, he used to say that a lot..."

Hank's view of the world swerved this way and that. He breathed but could not quite catch his breath.

"It's a hell of a thing. Hell of a thing. A man is always provided another path, a way out, you know? Before he gets too far gone. Problem is that most times, he can't see the other path."

The old mechanic stood and folded his hands together before him, something suddenly regal and commanding about his presence, as if he had grown taller and somehow greater.

"Hank, the best thing you can do is get back in that truck, take a left, your third right, then go straight for about thirty miles to the highway. Get back on it and lay the hammer down. You might even find yourself in Gulfport just in time for the party. Right now, you look to be a man deep in pain and anger—even deeper than you are in Mississippi."

Hank stood there, his mouth agape, his mind searching for words of reply but finding none that would have made any sense.

"I...I have to go, mister."

The old man dropped his head and looked aside at the road.

"It's your choice, Hank. But believe me when I tell you—you're deeper in it than you know."

"Right…into Mississippi, you said."

The old man smiled.

"That, too."

On his way back to the truck, with the taste of the beer turning sour in his mouth, Hank shook his head like a wet dog. Everything tonight had been so weird, and he needed to be shut of it. He wished he could brush the strangeness from his mind like dust from his shoulders but it seemed to have seeped into everything now. He climbed back into the cab of the truck and pulled it onto the road, not heeding the directions of the odd old mechanic but forging his own path down another dark lane that bent its way farther into the land.

8

Later, as Hank continued the drive, looking all around for the blinking lights of a radio tower or any sign of the station at all, the static began to squeal and whine and after a moment, music came ringing through the speakers. Old blues music, the twang and pop of a single, clumsily strummed guitar and the alto crooning of the singer.

"My girl, my girl don't lie to me, tell me where did you sleep last night…"

It was a recognizable tune, though Hank couldn't recall just who sang it. After a moment, when the song had ended, the gravelly voice of the night DJ came back on.

"A little Leadbelly for those of you joining us in the small hours," he said. Then, after a pause, continued, "Like you, Hank."

If there had been any lingering doubt in Hank's mind about what he had been hearing all this time, it evaporated just then as the DJ addressed him personally over the airwaves. He stared down at the glowing tuning knob, the eyeball of the truck's radio.

"And what about her? Where did *she* sleep last night? Metaphorically speaking, of course. I mean, do you really know, Hank?"

He glanced over at his wife.

"She's a good woman, my Carol," he spat at the radio in a whisper, but deep down, he wasn't sure he believed it.

"Oh, she's *good*, Hank. I'll give you that. But that's what drew you to her, ain't it? She might be from money but that girl's pure Mississippi fucktrash and you know it. What kind of *nice girl* behaves the way she does when you get her between the sheets?"

It was true that Carol had always been a firecracker in the sack, a bold contrast to her demure mother whose demeanor was so frigid and unwelcoming that Hank had long ago dubbed her the Ice Queen of Gulfport.

"Fucktrash, Hank. Pure and simple."

Hank's eyes darted about, and he desperately wished he could light up a smoke.

"That's the mother of my boy you're talking about there, hoss, so you best watch it."

There was a modulated chuckle that was almost lost in the slight static that ebbed and flowed.

"That's what you think? Boy, I never took you for such a fool."

Hank's hands were shaking now.

"What the hell's that supposed to mean?"

"Come on, Hank. I ain't telling you nothing you don't already know. You know it deep down in the marrow of your bones. Wondered about it the first time you looked at that little boy, all brand new, red-faced, and screaming. And not a trace of your face in him, was there? You know it now—every time you look the little bastard right in his cold, blue eyes. But you know something else, Hank?"

"What?"

"He knows it, too. Because he's looking right back at you. You with those shit-brown orbs stuck in your head like a couple of cow patties from an old Irish heifer. *Shit*, Hank. Like all the Mackeys. The no-good, gypsy micks from whom you descend."

Hank bristled at hearing the familiar phrase. Cole Winfield's words to the letter.

"Whatever made you think someone like you could have had a part in a gorgeous, blue-eyed slice of perfection like that little boy?"

Hank felt his knees going weak and he leaned forward into the Chevy's steering wheel. He lingered there for a moment, considering everything the radio was telling him. "*With truth comes a pang*," Hank's father used to say. Usually after his father had said something to chastise or berate him or one of his brothers.

"I know it's a lot to swallow," said the voice from the radio again, Johnny Scratch's tone more conciliatory now, static eating at the edges of every uttered word. "But you deserve to know the truth about your so-called *loved ones*. And I'm fixing to tell it to you."

9

Trooper Corbin Coolidge of the Mississippi Highway Patrol had found himself a good spot under some trees where he could pull off of the endless labyrinth of backroads that was his assigned territory. In this part of the county, there wasn't much to police except for the occasional speeding ticket or youngsters drag racing down the dark, country roads. Nothing much ever happened here, and that was precisely the reason he was often assigned this territory. Back at the base, the other troopers called him Porkchop because he had a weight problem. He also had a pronounced lack of professional ambition.

He had been there for many years and watched as the new boys came in, lean and muscled with their high-and-tight haircuts. Many of them—most of them—were former soldiers fresh back in country from Iraq and in need of a means to make ends meet. That being the case, most of them had both the ambition and the almost pathological need to lay down the law on someone or anyone…and they had it in spades. To them, Porkchop Coolidge was just a fat, unmotivated, donut and fried chicken-eating cop content to spend an uneventful night in his air-conditioned cruiser. He was a walking Southern cop cliché.

Trooper Coolidge knew this and, for the most part, had no problem with it. The ribbing and the shame got to him on occasion, but his Momma was eighty-nine years old and in a retirement home and what would become of her if he should be killed in the line of duty?

Easy and non-eventful was just fine by him.

Still, he always dreamed of the chance to prove himself as a lawman and, though he had just woken up from a nap in his cruiser and stepped outside to relieve himself at the edge of a cornfield, tonight would prove to be his opportunity to do just that.

Coolidge still had his fat little pecker in his hand when he heard the throaty growl of an engine coming his way down the road. He had just barely turned his head in time to see the truck go rushing by in a flash of white.

"Aw, shit! Holy Moses!"

He tried to squeeze it off but at middle age, such things did not come so easily as they once had. After a few more seconds, he finished up and climbed into his cruiser. Coolidge knew these backroads pretty well and knew that there was now a good bit of road between himself and the speeder, though he was confident that he could catch up. He was still buckling himself in as he mashed the pedal to the floor and peeled out of his spot, muddy earth spraying in the air and all over the cruiser's fenders until the rubber met the road.

Coolidge tore through the winding roads, running over eighty miles per hour and doing so with sweaty palms grasping the wheel. The times he'd had the chance to pursue someone at this speed were few and far between and he had never been comfortable in high-speed situations. After a few minutes, he closed in and could see the red taillights up ahead on the back of a white Chevrolet pickup.

He hit the siren and the lights and closed the gap enough to recognize the peach shining at the center of the license plate and knew the vehicle was from Georgia. They had come to a straightaway in the road and the truck had picked up speed, so Coolidge laid it down to the tune of ninety miles per hour and sweated bullets in the cool, blasting air of the police cruiser.

By the time he could clearly read the numbers on the plate, he had decided against calling it in. This was his moment, dammit. Time for Porkchop Coolidge to shine.

He was going to chase the speeder down and pull him over. Then he would cuff him and haul him to the county lock-up his damned self. Proud as a peacock. His fellow troopers would see it. The entire station would roar with applause.

When they gathered at the bar, they would toast him.

10

When Carol woke. it was to the sound of a police siren and the spastic glow of flashing lights. Bouncing off the interior of the cab. It frightened her and, with a gasp, she turned to Hank to see what was going on, but what she found there was even more disturbing. Her husband was not regarding the policeman behind them warily, slowing down and looking for a spot in the road where he could pull over. Instead, his eyes were fixed on the road ahead, which disappeared beneath them, the fields of crops zipping by the window at an alarming pace. He glanced into the rear-view mirror only once and did so quickly.

"Hank," she began to scold him, leaning over for a look at the speedometer to see how fast he was going. But she was stopped midway by his hand on her shoulder and pushed back into her seat.

"Sit back, Carol," he spat at her, devoid of any tenderness or understanding.

The sound of the static on the radio was still blaring and, amazingly enough, Jacob was still sleeping. She was about to demand an explanation when Hank glanced down at the radio and spoke toward it.

"Yeah, she's awake now."

As they tore down the road, swerving here and turning there, the tires of the truck screeching every so often, he nodded and cut his eyes at her. There was something in them that she had never seen before, and it chilled her.

"Uh-huh," Hank spoke aloud, though not to her. "All right. How many…no, no. I see it now."

They had lost the policeman behind them for the moment, hidden by a tight curve the Chevy was hugging but he would soon come into view again.

"Who are you talking to, Hank?" she cried, somewhere between a whisper and a scream.

He looked over at her, studied her for a few seconds with his eyes that were so full of ice.

"Don't you fucking move, you goddamned jezebel."

With that, he reached up and killed the headlights, the running lights and then the cab lights. There were plunged instantly into darkness.

The next thing Carol saw was the edge of a stop sign as they went sailing through a T-shaped intersection and barreled forward into a field of tall, leafy corn. With the stalks whipping against the exterior of the Chevy, Hank still had the accelerator buried to the floor. The truck was fishtailing a little in the soft earth but kept onward. The policeman who had been pursuing was now completely out of sight and she thought she heard the last wailing tones of the siren fading off into the distance.

Then, just as suddenly as they'd entered it, the corn was gone and Hank slammed on the brakes, bringing the truck skidding to a halt on a gravel road that had given up most of its rocks a long time ago. He switched the lights back on and in the multi-colored glow, she could see the dust as thick as fog around them.

"We made it," Hank said, breathing a sigh of relief, though his comment was not directed toward her. Once again, he was staring down at the glowing face of the truck's radio.

Then he paused, as if listening.

"Damnit, Hank, who are you talking to?" she finally managed, her voice shrill and shaking.

His head snapped over to her, a look of astonishment on his face.

"You don't recognize him, huh?"

"Recognize what…who?"

Hank reached down and turned the knob all the way up, the static now blaring in the cab at an uncomfortable volume.

"You're telling me you don't hear that voice, Carol?" he hissed at her, leaning in close.

She drew back with a whimper and shook her head.

"That figures, don't it? I reckon the truth just hurts too damned much."

She was still shaking her head, pressed against the passenger door.

"What truth? What are you talking about?"

Hank sat back and smiled. His madly grinning face was altogether alien to her in the glow from the dash lights. Her husband then reached under the seat and pulled his pistol from the holster, cocked the hammer back and pointed it squarely at her.

"By God, then, woman, let's have ourselves a talk."

11

Trooper Corbin Coolidge cursed himself in the darkness of his cruiser. Maybe the hucksters in his Troop were right. Maybe he was too old, too slow, too goddamned dumb for this job anymore. He'd had the speeder in sight when a tight but long curve in the road had gotten between them and when he came to the intersection, with only two ways to go, Coolidge had chosen left. One was as good as another, he had reasoned, for the road led to nowhere in either direction for many, many miles. But it seemed that Porkchop had made the wrong choice.

The futility of his hot pursuit now dawning on him, he backed off the gas pedal and slowed. Again, he considered calling in the plates he had seen but to do so would mean admitting to the dispatch—and thereby the rest of the troop—that he had lost his quarry. That was something Coolidge could not bear at the moment. So, he resigned himself to scouring the back roads until he came upon some sign of the speeder. Considering how fast the subject had been going, Coolidge wouldn't be a bit surprised to find the truck upside down in a drainage ditch or crushed around the base of a tree. He had been on the job long enough to know how these things ended. Hotheads behind the wheel, likely boozed, generally ended up in either the hospital or the morgue. Either way, Coolidge figured, he would eventually catch up to the old boy. Either way.

12

Hank had ordered Carol out of the truck, and they were standing in front of it now. He leaned against the front and smoked a cigarette, the gun in his other hand still pointed in her direction. She stood there with her arms closed around herself and watched him regarding her with eyes darker than she had ever seen during even the worst of their knock-down-drag-out fights, conflicts that were the stuff of legend among their friends.

"What is going on, Hank? Honey, you're scaring me."

He nodded but said nothing.

"Who was it you were talking to in the truck?"

"You should know, shouldn't you? Or were you so soused on margaritas and Cuervo that you wouldn't even recognize the sound of his voice?"

"Who are you talking about, Hank?"

"Johnny."

"Johnny who? I don't know any Johnny."

Hank shook his head in disbelief.

"Your fuckbuddy, Carol."

"I told you. I don't know any…" she began but drifted off into silence as memory caught up with her. It was impossible, though.

How could Hank have known? And, of all the times to bring it up, why *now*?

"There's that light bulb clicking on in that empty head of yours," he said with a sinister grin.

Her instinct was to play dumb, to deny it. But there seemed no point in going that route now, with the two of them standing at the edge of a cornfield in the middle of the dark nowhere and Hank with a gun trained on her.

"I'm sorry, honey," she said, her voice beginning to crack, tears coming to her eyes. "It was one night. Didn't mean anything, I swear."

"You must think I'm as unworthy of respect as that sonofabitch father of yours."

"No. No, that's not what I think," she stammered, the tears rolling down her cheeks now, her face flushed with heat. "You were just… you're gone all the time, Hank, and I got lonely. I had one night of weakness. One bad decision. One night."

"Jezebel!" he screamed at her, the cigarette falling from his lips.

He raised the gun and advanced on her and she sunk to her knees in the dirt, sobbing. She felt the cold muzzle of the pistol on her temple.

"You betrayed me," he said again, this time with an awful sense of calm. "Twice."

This surprised her and she put her hands up in protest.

"No, Hank, it was just the one time. I swear. I swear!"

The muzzle disappeared from against her skin, and she opened her eyes to see him standing over her pointing the weapon toward the cab of the truck.

"I'm talking about Jacob! I'm talking our baby, Carol! Only he ain't *ours*."

"No, that's—" she began only to be cut off again.

"Don't tell me you don't know. Don't tell me you never thought it. Boy don't look nothing like me."

She continued to sob. Hank was right. It had occurred to her. She didn't remember much about the man she had been with that night, but she did recall the blue of his eyes. They had been so different than Hank's. *He* had been so different than Hank.

"Look at me and tell me I'm wrong, woman."

She raised her head and intended to lie but when her eyes met his, she could manage nothing more than a trembling lip. Hank saw it.

His face screwed up in disgust as he turned away from her and whispered something under his breath that she could not hear. Then he turned back to her, lowered the gun, leaned in, and spat on the ground at her knees.

"Get in the goddamned truck, Carol."

She did as he commanded, pulling herself along the hood and fender, opening the door. She thought for a moment about making a run for it, but that would leave their son— *her son*— in the care of this man who she no longer recognized.

"Where are we going?" she asked, sliding into the cab.

"We're going to see your Johnny, honey," he said, the bitterness oozing from every syllable. "We're going to see Johnny Scratch."

13

They had driven another thirty or forty minutes by Hank's reckoning. He wasn't sure because he had forgotten to check the clock. It was of no consequence, though, because the radio had been on all the while, and he had followed Scratch's directions to the letter. Sure enough, ahead in the distance, he saw the glow of neon lighting up the dark.

"There it is. Right up ahead," he nodded and pressed deeper on the accelerator.

Carol leaned forward to see but couldn't pick anything out.

"There's what?"

Hank glanced over at her, his eyes narrowing, an expression of disdain carved into the stone of his face.

Moments later, Hank was pulling into the gravel parking lot of the WLCS radio station. The only structure that stood at an unnamed cross-roads, it was a plain, flat-roofed building with poured concrete walls. The station's call letters shone above the main entrance door in dazzling white and red, dimming and brightening like a heartbeat. At the rear of the station, rising above the landscape and reaching into the dark sky was the radio tower. Lights atop it blinked and the early morning mist gathering before dawn soaked up the light. That red fog pulsated all around them.

The parking lot itself was empty except for a burnt-orange Dodge Roadrunner— 1969 by the look of it, Hank thought— with a white vinyl top. Hank pulled the truck up close to the front door. Carol looked at him warily as he turned to her once more. His face was grim but betrayed no other emotion as he shut the truck off. The lights, the motor, the fans of the air conditioning were suddenly gone. For the first time in a long while, the permeating static ceased its assault on their ears and in that moment, for the both of them, the quiet was a thing unremembered, suddenly resurrected by the simple turn of a key.

Hank opened the door and stepped out of the truck. He patted his jeans pocket in search of his cigarettes but realized he had left them on the hood when he and Carol were having their heart-to-heart. He muttered a curse under his breath and turned toward his wife.

"You sit tight. I'm going inside and talk to Johnny myself first." He winked an eye at her. "Then we'll see to you."

Carol nodded but her brow was furrowed with confusion. She didn't understand how the Johnny she had met in Smitty's Bar back in Atlanta could be out here. Why would he be?

Hank paused for a moment, though it was not in response to Carol's bewildered expression. In that brief moment, Carol thought she caught a glimpse of the man she had known all those years. In the absence of the noise, the night song of the crickets and toads conveyed to the ear the romance of a quiet country evening that might be enjoyed by lovers. But not by these two, not ever again. The darkness had washed back over Hank's countenance as he stepped toward the front of the building. In the back seat, the child still slept. Somewhere far beyond in the misty fields, a hound bayed at the moon still hidden by clouds.

14

Walking into the lobby of the small radio station, Hank found it brightly lit and cool. Framed pictures of rock and blues legends adorned the wood-paneled walls. The vibrant photographs ran the gamut from Chuck Berry and Led Zeppelin to Howlin' Wolf, Johnny Cash and even KISS in their early days in full regalia and makeup. A water cooler sat between two black leather couches and copies of music and recording magazines littered the end tables. An empty coffee pot sat in the cradle of its maker, the burner still on and the smell of burnt coffee hanging in the air. There was a large window next to a door with a glowing sign that read "On Air" above it. Through the window, Hank could see the DJ seated behind the mixing board and turntables and various racks of electronics. He was speaking into the microphone, though Hank could not hear him. When he looked over and saw Hank, he raised his head in greeting and held up a finger, then continued speaking. A few seconds later, he flicked the switch on a turntable and the sounds of Son House bled quietly through speakers in the ceiling as he stood and came to the door.

"I see you made it," Johnny Scratch said as he stepped through the door, closing it behind him and offering his hand.

Hank took in the appearance of this man who had come to know his wife in the biblical sense while he was out earning a living. Johnny Scratch was tall, the chiseled features of his face framed by a head of long but neatly groomed blonde hair. He wore a dark, collared shirt and slacks that were neatly pressed all the way down to his snakeskin cowboy boots. He had a refined look, and his ice-blue eyes regarded Hank happily as his outstretched hand lingered in mid-air. It was a hand never scarred or calloused by hard labor, tipped by fingernails without a speck of dirt beneath them. He was, in every way, different from the mid-sized scrapper, the blue-collar mick with dark brown hair and eyes that was Hank Mackey.

Rather than return his hand in greeting, Hank pulled the pistol and held it at waist level, pointed in Scratch's direction.

"Didn't have much of a choice, did I? What with you in my ear all goddamned night long."

"C'mon, Hank. You heard what you did because you wanted to hear it. Hell, you *needed* to hear it."

Hank had noticed the arrogant son of a bitch hadn't even so much as flinched when Hank pulled the weapon.

"That may be, Mr. Scratch, but that ain't no excuse for you taking liberties with another man's wife."

The DJ held his stare but said nothing.

"Did you even know?" Hank asked.

"Know what?"

Hank clicked the hammer back.

"That she was married, asshole. Did you even bother to ask?"

Scratch held up his hands, though it seemed more an action of playing along and less motivated by any actual fear.

"Of course I did. At first, all she could talk about was you. Though," he leaned in and looked coy for a moment, "she hardly had anything nice to say at all."

"You sonofabitch," Hank growled and gripped the pistol just a little tighter in his hand.

"Hey, Hank," the DJ said, "don't shoot the messenger."

He saw Scratch crack a smile, quite pleased with his little joke.

"You said she talked about me. She tell you the baby doc told us that I'm shooting blanks? That having a child by me would be nothing short of a miracle? She told you all about that, I bet. Is that what put the idea in your head to get her in the family way?"

Again, the man regarded him without concern, without emotion. Stone-faced.

"You know, I made her listen to you," Hank said. "On the radio. I made her listen. But she didn't seem to recognize your voice. I figure that means it couldn't have been all that memorable, now could it?"

Hank wasn't sure if the purpose of those words was to take a dig at the stranger or if it was more to convince himself, but it hardly seemed to matter.

"Oh," the DJ scoffed, "she remembers, Hank. She remembers."

About to offer a retort, Hank suddenly found his senses unavailable, and he was pitched forward into the fog of a vision that had the taste of a memory, though not one of his own.

Like a movie, the scenes played in his mind but with the added benefit of touch and smell. Carol was on her back, her head shoved up into a group of pillows as Johnny Scratch leaned into her. They were naked, the both of them. The scent of sex was in the air and the sheets beneath their bodies were coarse and thin. He heard her moan over and over again as the blonde man took her in this way and then that. The headboard of the motel bed smashing against the wall with every thrust. What must have taken much longer flashed through Hank's mind in a matter of seconds and as the sex neared its apex, Hank could feel in his own flesh the sudden tremors and release of climax. Then there was quiet, and he watched as Carol lay on her side, the stranger spooning her and kissing the gooseflesh of her bare skin. "Goddamn, Johnny," she whimpered, almost breathless. "I'll never forget this. Never ever."

When Hank came to, he found himself lying prone on the floor. It took a moment for him to realize he once again had control of his own body. He could smell the stench of burnt coffee and could feel the pistol still grasped in his hand. Then, reflexively, he did what he wanted so badly to do as a prisoner in that vision. He sat up and raised the gun to the figure standing in front of him. Without a second thought, he squeezed the trigger again and again, firing a half dozen shots into Johnny Scratch's chest.

The adrenaline was still coursing through his veins and the smell of gunpowder now thick in the air when he realized that Scratch had leaned forward, unscathed in any way, and was offering Hank a hand up.

"I was hoping we could be friends on this, Hank."

Hank scrambled backward until he was up against the wall and then stood, though his legs were shaking. The pistol dropped to the floor as he regarded the man who, by all rights, should be dead on the floor and bleeding out. Yet somehow Scratch seemed larger and more invigorated. Then he noticed the lobby had changed. It was darker than before; the ceiling lights having dimmed. On the walls, the photographs had changed. The picture of Jimi Hendrix at Altamont now portrayed a rotting corpse slumped over a burning guitar. So real was this image that Hank could feel the heat of the flames. Looking at the others, he found they had transformed in a similar, macabre fashion.

"What do you want?"

"Right to business, then. Very well." Scratch nodded. "What I'm after is the child. We've got important plans for him. And more than that, he's *mine*. And I want him."

Hank's eyes narrowed as his head swam with conflicting notions. Even if the boy wasn't his own flesh and blood, he wasn't of a mind to hand over the child to the likes of Scratch, whoever and *whatever* the hell he was.

"Unfortunately for all of us, Hank, there are rules to this sort of transaction."

"Transaction?" Hank asked.

"That's right. The rules say the little mudskipper has to be given up freely. By the mother."

Hank snorted. That wasn't going to happen, no way, no how.

Scratch's lips tightened and he nodded.

"Unless, of course, the child is orphaned by the mother. *Or in the event of her death.* Then it's up to the child's caretaker."

A smile crept over Scratch's face with the utterance of that last bit.

"If I can't have him, then nobody gets him. Especially not Carol. So, it all comes down to you, Hank," he said with real solemnity. "You have to choose which way this goes."

Hank nodded and glanced down at the pistol still on the floor. He was still eyeing it and turning the options over in his head when the gun flew up from the floor and into the waiting hand of Johnny Scratch.

Scratch popped the clip out to check for bullets, chambered a round and then held the weapon out to Hank, offering the thing as easy and cool as he had offered his hand in greeting.

"So, what's it gonna be? Carol or Jacob? Dead cheating bitch-of-a-wife or dead little boy?"

If Hank could have burned holes through Johnny Scratch's eyes with his own, he would have done so in that moment.

"Come on, Hank. Your choice. Tick-tock."

His lip snarled. "What are you? The devil?"

At this, the blonde man seemed genuinely taken aback, though Hank couldn't be sure if it was from apparent insult or flattery.

Johnny Scratch waved a dismissive hand.

"Me? Naw," he said, then flashed a sinister and inhuman grin, his mouth suddenly full of sharp, discolored teeth. "But I do work for him."

15

Carol had taken Jacob into her arms and waited while Hank was in the building. She couldn't be certain how much he could see from inside, so she had tried to move as little as possible. There was no sense in provoking someone who had gone so completely out of his mind. Keeping cool and playing along might be the only way she and baby Jacob would make it out alive. So, she waited, though she knew not for what. All of her imagining and the many scenarios that ran through her panicked mind did not end well for either her or her baby. There was nowhere to run from Hank and even with the miles and miles of fields that might hide her, Jacob would surely continue screaming just as he was now, and it wouldn't be long before Hank found them.

In the darkness, she could make out what looked to be the shadow of a payphone just at the edge of the parking lot. She decided it was the best option and she thumbed through the console, snatching up coins to use. She was sitting there in the dark, heart racing in her chest to which she cradled the crying child, when she heard the shots ring out from inside of the building. For a second, she wondered what it was he could be shooting at but then decided it didn't matter. Carol realized then that the payphone was the *only* option. Their only chance.

Fumbling with the door, Jacob held against her with one arm, she climbed out of the cab and scurried across the dusty gravel parking lot toward the shadow. As she got closer, she could see for certain that it was a payphone. The light which had once illuminated the sign emblazoned with the Bell South logo had burned out but as she approached it, she fingered the coins in her free hand. When she reached it, she collapsed to her knees in order to stay low and hopefully out of sight. Clutching Jacob to her, she reached up and pulled the receiver from the cradle and let it dangle while she plunged the coins into the slot. It occurred to her just then that to dial 911, she may not even need the coins and so she dropped the remainder of them in the dirt at her knees. Grasping the receiver in one trembling hand, she brought it to her ear and listened. Hoping for a dial tone or operator or even a busy signal, she instead received nothing. No sound whatsoever came, and that silence slaughtered the last bit of hope she had been holding onto.

"Please, God, somebody help me," she moaned into the phone, though there was no one on the line to hear.

She sat down in the dirt and both mother and child wept. She was still sobbing, still holding tightly to both Jacob and the phone receiver, when she heard the front door of the radio station swing open.

Hank came staggering out of the radio station, pistol in hand. He walked as a drunkard might, weaving this way and that, but always with his eyes fixed on Carol's position. He found her cowering at the foot of the payphone with the child in her arms, crying uncontrollably. When she looked up at him with blurry, tearful eyes, she pleaded with him to let her go. He looked down at her and the child, then surveyed the dark country around them as if making some cold and calculated assessment. As he did so, she thought she might have seen momentary flashes of her husband, but the prevailing look in his eyes was that of a man walking in his sleep.

Hank glanced back down at his wife and raised the pistol. There was a flash and a thunderous roar as she felt the bullet tear through her abdomen and she crumpled, the warmth of life leaking out of her belly and into her lap and down her legs.

Then the muzzle of the gun was pointed at Jacob, the weapon shaking in Hank's grasp.

"I'm so sorry, Hank," she whimpered, clawing at his legs. "Don't hurt him, honey, please." If she could touch him, if he could feel her, then maybe he would return from whatever black place he had gone. Not that he would forgive her, no, she didn't expect that but hoped that he might see his way clear to spare the child.

In his eyes, she saw a conflict. A pitiless stare traded places with glints of remorse and the two extremes danced across his face, one leading and then the other.

"I love you so much, baby," she whispered.

He nodded and she saw tears well up in his eyes.

"I loved you, too," he croaked. "Once upon a time."

It was the last thing she heard.

16

It was just after five in the morning when Porkchop Coolidge sighted the white Chevy pickup in the parking lot of the old radio station. He called it in but didn't request any backup. He suspected that he would find the driver sleeping it off in the truck or passed out inside next to a lady friend. He turned into the parking lot slowly, switching on the lights but leaving the siren off. As more of the scene came into view, though, he knew this would be nothing so simple.

Stepping out of his cruiser into the wet heat of the morning, the only sound was the roaring song of the locusts in the trees. The sky was growing brighter by the minute, the clouds from the night before having moved on. All in all, it looked to be the start of a beautiful Mississippi day except for the aroma of blood hanging in the air. The truck sat empty with the passenger side door wide open. At the far edge of the parking lot there was an old payphone. Near to it were two bodies on the ground. One, a woman, was crumpled at the bottom of the payphone itself and the other, a man, lay face-up in the gravel just a few feet away. He thought that the term face-up may not be fitting, however, as the man didn't seem to have much of one left. He had seen a few self-inflicted gunshot wounds in his time and that certainly seemed to match the look of the man's body from the neck up. The .44 caliber pistol which had been used lay on the ground a few inches from the body. Surveying the scene further, he noticed the front door to the radio station was open.

He approached the front of the building warily, his heart thrumming all the way up to his throat. The old building, like the parking lot, was pretty well eaten up with weeds and vines. Kudzu and Virginia creeper and honeysuckle enshrouded it like a cocoon. In its heyday, it had been a radio station run by black folks, playing mostly blues and country. He recalled hearing something about a firebombing and death threats issued by local Klan thugs. Those events had been the demise of the radio station. Later, in the early 1970's, some self-styled hippie types had turned it into an acid-rock station but that hadn't lasted very long out in these parts. Ever since then, the building had continued to decay, steadily being consumed by the unforgiving country that surrounded it. The neon tubes of the station's call letters, WLCS, were still visible but dark and hanging askew above the front door. The radio tower behind it, once tall and proud and rising up above the fields, had given in to decades of rust and the glancing blows of too many Gulf hurricanes. While the base of it still stood erect, the top half had snapped off long ago and lay on the ground, almost invisible now with the vegetation that covered it.

As he crossed the threshold into the lobby, he called out the customary warning.

"Highway Patrol trooper on site and I'm armed! Anyone in here, come out now and let me see your hands."

He waited a moment but heard nothing inside; not even so much as the scurry of a Mississippi rat. Stepping farther in, he drew the flashlight from his belt and shone it into the dim confines of the building. Bits of framed pictures still hung on the wall, though their contents were long gone and most of the walls displayed graffiti markings; poorly rendered rebel flags, curse words and caricatures of sexual organs being the most common. A thick dust had collected on everything, especially the floor, and it was there he found evidence that someone had been in the building recently. The tracks of a man's work boots littered the lobby area along with several wide swaths of disturbance which told him that the man had, at some point, been sitting or scooting across the floor. Coolidge reckoned that the man must have come upon a deer or something inside the building that startled him because mixed in with all the other signs were the odd tracks of some cloven-hoofed animal. There were spent brass casings on the floor and the smell of gunpowder lingered in the air, though it was almost imperceptible among the curious and overwhelming, sulfuric stench permeating the place—as if someone had been boiling *one hell of a lot* of eggs in the room.

Stepping back out of the building and surveying the scene with a little less nervousness, Coolidge found that the rear cab of the truck had an infant-sized car seat in it, though it was empty. Suitcases and bags of child paraphernalia were packed into the back seat also, and the trooper suspected that the husband and wife had been on a road trip of some kind when, for whatever reason, things had gone horribly wrong.

Whatever had happened, the child was unaccounted for. The age of the child was unclear, and he reasoned that perhaps it had been old enough and mobile enough to crawl or toddle away and had simply become lost in the surrounding fields. He stepped away from the truck and closed his eyes, listening for even the faintest cry or cooing. Hearing nothing, he could only hope that the car seat had been vacant all the while. Perhaps they had been on their way to retrieve a child from an aunt or uncle somewhere.

He checked the vehicle registration in the glove box and found that the truck was registered to a Henry James Mackey of Atlanta, Georgia. It was at this point that Coolidge decided it was time to go ahead and call this in. The scene would soon be overrun with state cops and forensic personnel. Knowing this made Coolidge smile because it meant that they would all be looking to him for answers and input.

"First on the scene," he grinned as he opened the door to his cruiser. "Kiss my fat porkchop ass."

Coolidge had the radio in his hand when he heard the sound of groaning coming from somewhere in the parking lot. He dropped the radio and pulled his weapon again, spinning around to see where the noise was coming from. The man's body was still prone on the ground in a wide spot of dark blood. Unbelievably, Coolidge saw the woman pitch forward in an attempt to stand, though she reeled and landed on her side in the dirt.

He rushed over to her and knelt beside her. He placed a gentle hand on her shoulder.

"Mississippi Highway Patrol here, ma'am. You've been shot."

She struggled to get her breath.

"It's best if you don't move too much," he said.

Nevertheless, the woman tried, but only ended up rolling onto her back. It was then that Coolidge saw the bullet wound in her abdomen, just below the edge of the tank top she wore. He was no EMT but for what it was worth, the wound looked to be through-and-through. Glancing behind her, he saw the bullet smashed and rippled into the base of the payphone stand.

"Ma'am, do you know who it was that shot you?"

STATIC

She coughed and spat, though he saw no blood in it, which was a good sign.

"Hank," she whispered, her throat dry and voice raspy.

Coolidge nodded. "Okay, then."

Her eyes, which had been lazy and half-closed, suddenly opened wide and she endeavored to sit up again, though he held her down and not without considerable effort.

"My baby," she groaned, "Hank...he killed Jacob?"

She was staring up at Coolidge with bloodshot eyes, wide black pupils set against deep brown.

"I haven't seen any sign of the child, ma'am," he replied, as slow and clear as he could manage, hoping it would be a glimmer of hope to her.

She nodded and seemed to drift for a moment, then returned. She crossed her arms at her chest, fingers splayed out and tapping slowly as if holding and comforting her babe, though there was nothing there at all.

Then she began to weep.

Unless the woman was delirious—and he didn't judge that she was—there *had* been a child present. And if that were true, Coolidge deduced, then there must have been a third party to this tragedy. Someone who had taken the child with them. It was a logical conclusion, though the trooper had seen no sign at all of anyone else having been there.

Coolidge felt his heart breaking and hated to leave the woman in such a state, but he needed to call for the EMS. He stood and leapt toward his cruiser with a speed that surprised even himself. The trooper spent the next few moments on the radio with dispatch while he briefly laid out the particulars. Ambulance needed right away. Attempted murder. Suicide. Apparent abduction of an infant. His stomach turned with every uttered word and when he released the call button and tossed the radio onto the seat of the cruiser, he turned and vomited into the dirt of the parking lot.

Bent over, spitting out the last bits of his supper from the night before, he set his mind to the next task. He would go to the woman and apply direct pressure to the wound. He would assure her that she would be all right and that the police would find her son.

He would do this, though he knew none of it for certain.

The only thing he did know was that right now she had a fighting chance to live, but as he listened to the wailing cries of the mother now bereft of her precious child, what he did not know and could not so much as guess at was whether or not she would even want to.

ACKNOWLEDGMENTS

Reaching back to thank the folks from the time when most of these stories first saw the light of day would require a feat of memory I do not possess. Instead, I'd like to offer thanks to Greg Chapman for working with me on the cover art and design as well as Todd Keisling for the interior book design. I'd also like to thank a few folks who had a hand in this in some way, great or small, even if they didn't realize it at the time—namely Bob Ford, Kevin Lucia, Suzi Madron, Shawn Cosby, Red Lagoe, Joe Maddrey, and Michael Rook.

ABOUT THE AUTHOR

D. ALEXANDER WARD is an author and anthologist.

His most recent novels are *Pound of Flesh* from Crystal Lake Publishing and *Beneath Ash & Bone* from Bleeding Edge Books. His forthcoming novel, *Nightjar*, will be released by Watertower Hill Publishing in 2026.

As an anthologist, he edited the Bram Stoker Award-nominated anthologies *Lost Highways: Dark Fictions From the Road* and co-edited the anthologies *Gutted: Beautiful Horror Stories* from Crystal Lake Publishing; *The Seven Deadliest*; *Shadows Over Main Street* Volumes 1-3; and the mini-anthology *Strange Echoes*.

He is an Active Member of the Horror Writers Association, current Chair of the Virginia Chapter of the HWA, and very involved in the small press publishing world of horror and dark fiction, where he runs Bleeding Edge Books.

Along with the haints in the woods, he lives near the farm where he grew up in rural Virginia, where his love for the people, passions, and folklore of the South was nurtured. There, he spends his nights writing, collecting, and publishing tales of the dark, strange, and fantastic.

COPYRIGHT ACKNOWLEDGMENTS

"The Red Delicious," *A Quick Bite of Flesh*, Hazardous Press, 2012

"Notches," *Dark Corners of the Old Dominion,* Death Knell Press, 2023

"Broken Things," *A Feast of Buzzards*, Hazardous Press, 2013

"After the Fire," Dark Hall Press, 2013

"The Blackest Rite," *Horrific History: An Anthology of Historical Horror,* Hazardous Press, 2013

"Night of the Nanobeasts," *ATTACK! of the B-Movie Monsters: Night of the Gigantis,* Grinning Skull Press, 2013

"Cruel Moon," *Shifters: A Charity Anthology,* Hazardous Press, 2013

"Dark Rosaleen," *The Midnight Diner IV*, 2013

"The Dying Place," Fantastic Horror Press, 2008

"Static," *A Feast of Buzzards,* Hazardous Press, 2013

Printed in the USA
CPSIA information can be obtained
at www.ICGtesting.com
LVHW042022101224
798765LV00007B/142